FALLEN ANGEL

KEITH TURNBULL
KEN HAMES

Published by

MELROSE BOOKS

An Imprint of Melrose Press Limited
St Thomas Place, Ely
Cambridgeshire
CB7 4GG, UK
www.melrosebooks.co.uk

FIRST EDITION

Cover by Graham Saville

ISBN   978-1-912026-85-2 paperback
        978-1-912026-86-9 epub
        978-1-912026-87-6 mobi

Printed and bound in Great Britain by:
Airdrie Print Services Ltd
24-26 Flowerhill Street
Airdrie, North Lanarkshire
Scotland, ML6 6BH

Author Bios

Ken Hames:

Ken has had a fascinating life. From humble beginnings as a boy working on his grandfather's hill farm, he eventually rose to the rank of major in the SAS, commanding Britain's Anti-Terrorist Unit. He is one of the very few British officers to have worn the red beret of the Parachute Brigade, the green beret of the Royal Marines and the sand beret of the Special Air Service.

More recently, he gained an honorary doctorate in business administration, from Bristol University for his work in developing outstanding leaders and high performing teams in diverse business environments. In Ken's words, he has been 'very lucky', but he had to work extremely hard in order to make the grade in the world's most highly selective military unit.

Having left the military to join, as he puts it, 'the more dangerous world of civilian life', he had to make a massive re-adjustment to working in the complex and often unforgiving world of television and business development.

Ken has made sixteen documentaries to date and was recently awarded the MBE for his charitable work with people with disability, and homeless and disadvantaged ex-service men and women.

Keith Turnbull:

Keith has enjoyed a diverse career to date. Graduating from Glasgow University with a Master's degree in Politics, he first went into the world of finance. From there, he moved into defence sales, quickly rising to senior managerial and director positions. At one stage, he commanded a European-wide defence sector sales team and would travel daily to one European country after another. This first 'spell' in the defence sector quickly pulled him in for good.

He speedily learned about the secretive side of commercial defence-related products and services and his next move into working as a security-cleared contractor for the Ministry of Defence in Whitehall was an obvious move. Within this role, Keith would spend much of his time in or around military establishments for all three arms of the Service, both in the UK and with European allies, working also with high-ranking officers and having his first hands-on experience of British special forces operations.

From the MoD, he moved to a classified position (Top Secret) within the British Foreign and Commonwealth Office in London. This secretive role brought him in touch with a huge array of other law enforcement and security intelligence service personnel. Today, he continues to work, periodically, in this environment.

Contents

Preface

Barents Sea, January 2012

Selkirk wished he could write a last note to his paternal grandmother. He could see that odds were heavily stacked against him and that he was probably going to meet his end in the Barents Sea if the sub failed to turn up. His grandmother would cry if she could see him and he knew there was nothing he could do about it.

He suddenly saw the paradox of being a spec ops operator – loving the sea for all its power and beauty, but now it was to be his grave and it would hide the details of his death and funeral well. It would be a secret that only he and the admiral would ever know. His friend of twenty years had definitely, even deliberately, sent him on 'operation certain death', as difficult and dangerous missions were affectionately known by the Counter Revolutionary Wing, a secret element of Special Boat Service operations.

Ice station Makarov was utterly destroyed. Chris, his best friend, was dead, and as blood dripped off his fingertip from the bullet wound in his right shoulder, he felt a sharp pang of utter helplessness in the icy desert. *How can a 9mm hurt so much?* he thought, as he started to realise the enormity of his situation with shock, cold and fear starting to take control.

What should he do with Chris's lifeless form lying just a few feet away, a wisp of his blond hair moving in the Arctic breeze as if he were still alive? Tom knew he had to cast him adrift and he thought about checking one last time to see if he was really dead. For a parachute malfunction to happen, something really serious had gone wrong and he found it unfathomable that this friend of so long would make such a fundamental mistake. After the mayhem of destroying the installation single-handed and taking one in the shoulder for the team, he had given himself what first aid he could. He extracted the bullet with a knife and stitched it quickly with sail thread and a vicious needle. But there was tissue and some bone damage, and he knew that hard labour with that arm was impossible.

Selkirk carefully wrapped his dead friend's body in his parachute. He held his hand one last time and kissed his forehead then pushed the body out to sea. He had strapped a charge to his chest to go off in one hour, to send him to Valhalla, and he smiled as he knew Chris would have laughed at the irony of it all. He tried not to cry as it was against his better nature, but the tears came and he felt very alone. *When the charge goes off, the leopard seals and other predators of the Arctic wastes will do the rest*, he mused.

The sub had been due at 0600 hours and Selkirk suddenly imagined the sinister grey shape bursting through the pack ice and arriving only to pick up one, not two. Strangely, he knew it wasn't coming. He had been sacrificed with Chris, probably to satisfy the needs of politicians eager to cover up cold missions outside of a cold war.

Selkirk suddenly felt anger, an alien emotion, as he knew it made him irrational. But it grew inside his chest and the pit of his stomach till it fired the most reptilian part of his brain.

"Fuckers," came from his lips as he spat at the Arctic horizon.

While he swore at his military and political masters, he pondered whether to start walking across the pack ice. He had little clothing to survive and even less food, even water was sparse in this icy desert and he estimated his chances of survival as close to zero. And even if he did make it to Russia or Alaska, it was unlikely there would be anybody friendly there to meet him. But something made him turn west as he was, in fact, closer to Russia and maybe the unexpected would work, he thought, and they would send a Spetsnaz team to investigate the attack and perhaps would take pity on him as a fellow operator. A life in a Russian jail, but alive. *No*, he thought a moment later, *they would just kill me*. He held on to what he knew was a complete fantasy because it was really all he had.

Six hours elapsed and what had happened early that morning seemed like a distant memory. As he gazed west toward the horizon he saw movement – a trick of the light or a polar bear? Whichever it was, it was moving quickly. He really hoped it was not the latter or he really was done for. He made sure his pistol was loaded but realised that a 9mm sub-calibre round was more likely to piss the bear off than kill it, and he would be better to take his life rather than be savaged by the world's most determined predator. All options seemed pretty hopeless.

He fixed his sharp eyes on the horizon and looked for cover. If it was an enemy force sent to kill him it could be his last stand, but he would put up a good fight. Then, something totally unexpected happened. About one hundred yards in front of him the ice seemed to erupt all around. This thing coming closer was moving left then right at speed, towards him and right at him. Could it be some sort of sledge out here in this frozen wilderness? Then he realised, not a sledge but a skidoo, as the noise of the engine came into his hearing range. *Hunters*, he thought, and suddenly, in what was a fit of stupidity for a trained soldier, he revealed himself.

Two minutes later he was staring down the barrel of a rifle held by a local hunter, aided by a friend, riding passenger on the biggest skidoo he had ever seen.

Chapter 1
Bouvet Island

The present day

The Bouvet Triple Junction is the meeting place of three tectonic plates located on the South Atlantic Ocean floor. Rarely does this happen, making it one of the most volatile places on the earth's surface. Named after a tiny uninhabited Norwegian-owned research island a few kilometres east of the junction, it is significant geographically, albeit remote. This day its tranquillity was interrupted by the sharp impact of a geologist's pick as it struck million-year-old pyroclastic rock.

Weeks before, Isabelle and her research companion, Jack Betters, travelled to Bouvet on the Antarctic explorer *Blue de Nimes II*. So far, 'taking on the world' had only taken them from dock in Southampton to rough and featureless seas many miles south in the Atlantic Ocean. Those miles were ideal for reading, sleeping, checking and rechecking the equipment and supplies, and sending the occasional email, although writing in rough seas gave Isabelle violent sea sickness. That, however, was manageable. What was much harder to cope with for Isabelle was the crew who shared her floating home. Jack didn't care, but for her, it was the equivalent of a scientific rugby team on tour in the South Atlantic. After years of study she was familiar with the testosterone-fuelled male academy. However, coping with them on the rough seas was proving to be a different matter.

Finding the crew increasingly tiresome, she tried to ignore

them during meal times, but it was difficult to examine maps and charts and dates from the triangle while pitching in a force ten gale. She just really wanted to be away from them and the claustrophobia of the ship. Suddenly, three months' gathering of rock samples on Bouvet became something to look forward to.

Their now-distant employers, Star Frontiers Global, had taken Isabelle and Jack straight out of research at the university and, after a speedy but expensive induction, had put them on the *Blue de Nimes II*, packing them off to solitude and no family for three months. *Perfect*, she thought. The Russian owners of SFG had a vested interest in the tiny island in the South Atlantic. They had paid for basic survival and medical training for the intrepid duo at La Rochelle in Paris, followed by emergency pod training, which Jack had taken little interest in.

Star Frontiers was primarily in business to develop technologies that could chase down meteorites and capture their trail debris, analyse this and send findings back to their HQ in Greater New York. Now they wanted Isabelle and Jack to establish the potential origins of water on earth, thought to have started from a meteorite strike millions of years ago on Bouvet Island.

It was Tuesday but it could well have been Wednesday, for everyday seemed to have the same view and the same horizon. Sometimes, as the boat ploughed methodically through the waves and ice, they could glimpse a colony of penguins terrorising the local mackerel stock, or the occasional albatross resting on the water gathering up energy to continue onward in search of land.

On this day, Jack and Isabelle decided to check their equipment. After all, they had not done so for at least three days and sophisticated measuring equipment has a tendency to break when left untouched in securely packaged travel cases. The reality of the constant checking was that it gave them a break from page after page of images, maps and the statistical data that needed to be absorbed before they started work on the project.

Day became night quickly on such journeys and sleep was another method to break from its boredom. Right now it was dawn and the sky was lightening. Nothing seemed to stir on the waters or on the ship.

Jack woke suddenly.

Startled by the lack of movement, his first thought was that the vessel had run aground. Then, within that very same moment, as he looked out the cabin window it dawned on him that he had been dreaming and that the boat was still on its methodical, rather boring, journey. What startled him, he believed, was nothing more than a larger than usual wave passing through and under the boat. A bang on the wall from a neighbouring cabin also told him he must have been making a noise and had woken Isabelle. Settling back down and gazing at his cabin ceiling, he wondered what he may have said to wake her.

When both rose and joined the living on the deck of the ship, the crew seemed more excitable than normal. They were certainly more active than usual. Leaving his bunk and breathing in the sea air he soon found out why. They had reached Bouvet Island.

The *Blue de Nimes II* moored about one hundred yards off the island and, for the next five hours, a flotilla of small boats shepherded the equipment and supplies over to the shore and into the research shelter that was to become home for three months. Everything accounted for and in its place, tested and tested again, the two original crew members left to return to their colleagues. Suddenly, Isabelle had a moment of realisation. No longer swaying back and forth, watching the boat sail away towards dock and its scheduled maintenance, they were alone, truly alone.

For a few moments, neither spoke or moved but watched the boat slowly disappear. In this silence their close-quarter lives with the crew became a little more appealing. It was too late now. With confirmation that the day was Wednesday, and the three-month date circled on the calendar, they went back inside and sat in silence before finally sleeping where they had rested.

Their camp, their temporary home, Nyroysa, meant 'new rubble' in Norwegian and was situated in the northwest corner of the island on the site of an unidentified whaler's lifeboat discovered in 1964. Their shelter was built to survive the freezing temperatures and fifty knot wind chill and would still complete most of the designer's aspirations of protection and warmth many years later. It was not wasted on the pair, that the last people to witness this desolate place were sailors struggling to stay alive but failing. This was spooky enough, but for Isabelle and Jack, volunteering to spend three months on what is known to be the most isolated place on the planet was becoming more frightening.

The journey had taken its toll on both and, despite the specialised training in Alaska provided by their employer, this was like nothing most would ever experience again, or ever had. The island could sap energy as easy as running consecu-tive marathons. The cold could do that. Wearing the cumber-some life-preserving clothing made movement many times more exhausting than without it, but without this, death would follow very quickly. Hypothermia's 'friends' don't last long.

Jack ended the first day with a promise to himself to power up and position the early-warning sea beacons tomorrow. After all, they had seen no out-of-character swells en route, so one more day wouldn't matter. For now it was time to heat up, sleep, and hope to get through the night and put energy back into their own power cells.

Jack woke early the next morning and was up long before Isabelle surfaced. He let her sleep, figuring he had acclimatised quicker. He then had a very constructive two hours converting the life pod into a vessel capable of being manually propelled over waves of up to eight feet and prepared to set off with the first beacon.

While he waited for her to awake, he sat in the long-since abandoned, rotting life boat and took in what little sun fell upon his face. What had happened those many years earlier? Were the sailors' remains here under the ice? Were they going to find life, or death, as they collected samples?

Isabelle wandered out towards him and the noise of her footsteps brought Jack back to the day and the start of the task at hand.

Together they pushed the makeshift life raft over the initial swell and Jack climbed in. A now wet Isabelle clambered back to the shore. The beacons were to be positioned and secured several hundred metres out to sea but reaching this distance, in the cold and the wind, over the swell, sapped energy and took a while. Large swells could appear quickly and make his return to land more fun than he would want, so he planned to position three, if able, and leave the last one until tomorrow. There was the extra logistical issue of moving the life raft over land and the energy-sapping effect this would have on them both. The fourth and last, with the carry, would be a good enough day.

He reached the first beacon location in under an hour and secured the raft to it. Filling up on an energy drink, Jack again faced skyward for a short while and took in what little vitamin D the sun decided to offer. He fired up the beacon, tethered it to a marker and dropped the weight into the water. It disappeared instantly and all he could do now was to hold position as best he could and wait a short while to determine if he had been successful, or if the beacon would drift off. When it seemed to move only upwards and downwards with the water, staying within a few yards of Jack, he decided it was in place. Now for the second beacon.

From shore, Isabelle had decided not to watch her colleague. He was sometimes visible as a small speck on the horizon, but, she thought, he could swim, he had a life jacket on and the sea was playing fair. Instead, she went inside and emptied the medicine and first aid supplies into an airtight container. Next, she set up the food rota. Boredom could become a big enough issue without the mundane addition of eating the same foods day after day.

As she did so, she thought back to her university days where she first met Jack and where, in a moment of madness, the two had spent the night together. They went on to date for several months and now, alone on the island, it didn't pass her by that Jack still seemed to have feelings for her.

As he positioned the second beacon, Jack pondered over what may lie beneath him on the sea floor. Could there be a larger wooden boat with sailors in a watery grave? Given the solitude of his current location, he pushed such thoughts aside.

With the second and third beacon successfully positioned and tested, now exhausted, he focused his remaining energy on getting safely back to dry land.

Securing the boat onshore, he promised himself he would

get the fourth beacon in position tomorrow and also that he would sleep tonight and not lie awake listening to the noises of the wind and of Isabelle breathing yards away in the room next to his.

He secured the boat to a large outcrop and sat for a few moments. He was exhausted. He glanced back towards the location of the third beacon, but it was too far out to be seen.

In their separate adjoining rooms neither had much sleep that night, despite the fatigue that filled their minds and bodies. Jack's promise to himself not to listen to Isabelle breathing and to sleep was again difficult as they both lay and wondered what they were doing so far away from friends and family.

The next day Jack rose early. He woke Isabelle and reminded her about the plan for the day. He would also tell HQ about their work so far when they called back for the scheduled update.

The last beacon switched on but, unlike the other three, showed a lower battery life. That said, it was good for more than three months, and when comms were up he would report this. The sun was reaching midday, but Jack's next task was reassembling the boat back into a secure waterproof, life-preserving pod. Going out on the water was not now necessary for at least their remaining three months.

Both had a requirement to call into their employers on a regular basis to update them on their progress. In order to reach SFG via the darkness of space and allow the signal to be bounced back through the pollution and interference of a typical New York day, they had been provided a turbo-charged version of the best-selling Rigon Aegaeon secure satellite unit. With its operating frequency in excess of 96 MHz maximum transmission, through 12 Watts, and an operating range of 45–146 degrees non-condensing features, it was ideal for Bouvet Island.

The next ninety minutes passed slowly as they were lectured to from many different invisible faces and mono- tone voices coming through the sat phone on how best to conduct the preliminary research and when to feedback.

Then, as Isabelle pressed the red button on the GPS, the island, with a temporary population of two, fell silent. Meanwhile, many thousands of kilometres away in England, in a university laboratory, something huge and life changing was being monitored on the screens positioned around the room.

Brianna stared in disbelief at her monitor. Instinctively, she tapped the screen as if to assure herself that it was working correctly. She looked over her shoulder in a manner that would summon a second opinion. The readings that moved across the monitor were literally off the scale and must be wrong. If not, she was witnessing the movement of a mass of water that was larger than any ever recorded in the southern hemisphere.

Brianna's training as a rational scientist suddenly kicked back in and she looked at the screen more closely, trying to make sense of it and assimilate the alarming data. She sprang out of her chair having given the screen a final glance before running to summon her professor. As she did, she saw the numbers still climbing – quickly.

"Professor Roberts!" Brianna almost shouted, as she reached the professor's door and caught hold of the door- frame to steady herself.

"You've got to come and have a look at what's going on

in the South Seas. I've never seen anything like it before and it's big! Really big!" she said, now calming her voice a little.

The professor looked up from his work and, without a word, nodded towards the door and got up. Brianna turned and hurried back out, confident the professor was following her down the corridor. Within seconds they were back in front of her monitor, watching the numbers that proved, beyond doubt, that a massive wave was powering across the Bouvet Triangle.

To Brianna's surprise, Professor Roberts actually showed little dismay or emotion as he followed Brianna back to the operations room and sat down, very calmly, in front of the monitor. Brianna quickly pulled another chair alongside his and they sat together, for what seemed like an age to her, in total silence. Brianna carefully tapped in small instructions on her keyboard in a futile attempt to gather more information.

Eventually, the professor broke the silence and calmly asked, "Who else knows about this?"

"Nobody," Brianna replied, feeling a slight sense of bewilderment that this should be his first question.

"Are you sure?" He looked at her questioningly and she noticed that his eyes strayed to the rest of the room as if he was searching for possible onlookers.

"Absolutely," she smiled nervously, "there's nobody here except us. Shall I transmit the data to Washington?" She found herself stuttering and wondering why she suddenly felt so self-conscious.

"No, don't do that," the professor replied calmly. "Go home and get some rest, I'll deal with it."

Brianna was perplexed and, despite her nervousness, pressed on, "Professor, surely this is a serious incident, should we not at least tell somebody?"

"No!" He cut her off in mid-sentence and snapped, "Please do as I say!"

Brianna recoiled, sensing that there was some other force at play. The professor's sudden change of tone, and the way he was looking at her, felt altogether sinister.

As the professor left the room, certain that this was between them only, she screen-grabbed the data and quickly sent it to her private secure cloud thinking she could analyse it later from her flat. Then she packed up her bag and, as she did so, glanced at the professor walking down the hall.

"Goodnight then, Professor?"

He did not reply and she left the room.

As the professor returned to his office, he fumbled in his pocket for his mobile phone. He dialled a number and waited a few seconds for the reply. There was no flicker of emotion on his face, despite knowing that he had just sentenced someone to death.

At her flat, Brianna put instant coffee in a cup and watched the kettle as it started to heat up. She was beside herself with anger, confusion and growing anxiety at what had just happened in the control room. She looked out of the window over her sink unit and noticed how the city streetlights created trails in all directions. They mirrored her thoughts: *Why hadn't he seemed as concerned as I was? Why didn't he want to escalate the situation? That was just not normal, surely? But, come on, he's Professor Roberts for Christ's sake; he knows what he's doing. Don't be so paranoid. You are just being over dramatic.*

As the kettle boiled in her flat, she took her mobile out of her bag and texted her flat mate, Elizabeth, that she was back early. In addition, she sent her the access codes to the private data cloud where much of her research was recorded.

It included the latest data from Bouvet.

As she pressed 'send', she suddenly stopped and realised that she was panicking and wouldn't normally have done that. She and Elizabeth weren't that close anyway, more like ships that passed in the night. No, it was a wave of unease in the pit of her stomach that something terrible had happened and she had witnessed it. She paced the kitchen, weighing up her options.

She lifted her head, already focused on the plan for coffee, but before she could even reach for the kettle, an unseen hand caught her by the chin from behind and twisted her head so sharply that it broke it instantly and severed her spinal cord. She was dead before she hit the floor.

The 'cleaners' would remove her body from the flat with comparative ease. No one saw her demise and no one would feel the sudden loss of her life on the campus – just one more insignificant person, probably moved on.

The professor would need a new assistant now, but then he already knew that.

———◆◆◆———

Meanwhile, on the other side of the world, Jack had encouraged Isabelle to walk with him and explore the island a little more. The last of the sun's rays provided some comfort as they eventually turned and headed back to their shelter.

Returning to the lower ground and towards the safe-house base for the night, Isabelle stumbled on the loose rocks and fell to the frozen ground.

"Wow, Izzy, steady on, we haven't had a drink and you're down," commented Jack.

"Fuck, I may have twisted an ankle, Jack. The ground just gave way."

"Izzy, my lovely Izzy, have you been tippling while I have been working?" he teased while still helping her slowly down the incline and crumbling rock.

Looking back to check where she had almost fallen, she saw something. "Jack, look, what's that? I think I stood on it," she exclaimed.

Protruding out of the dust and ice was a box, a black box that was clearly out of place on this remote island.

Jack reached down and picked it up. He looked at Isabelle in amazement. "Izzy, this is no ancient, washed-up sailor's thing. This is way too new," he said.

"Yeah, ok, so what are you saying?" she replied.

"Someone else could be with us on the island," his tone was full of trepidation. "Let's take it back to the shelter." Without waiting for her or helping her down the remaining part of the slope that had revealed the box, he walked off at pace.

Isabelle looked around as a chill came over her. This was not to do with the outside temperature on Bouvet Island. She looked at Jack moving off, and then turned to look out to sea, then down at her feet, watching where she trod while she gathered pace in an attempt to catch up with Jack.

Back inside the shelter the two looked at the black box on the table between them.

Jack reached for it while Isabelle leaned back into her chair trying to distance herself from the uncertainty of what might be inside.

Jack unlatched the four silver clips and opened the box towards him. Isabelle watched quietly.

"Hmmm, it's just some locator or signal thing, Izz," he commented in a somewhat disappointed voice.

Turning the box around, she too could see that securely cushioned inside was a shiny, new and very modern transmitting device. Other than that, the two had no further knowledge of what it could do.

"This proves it then," he said, "this is new so someone is, or has been, here very recently."

Instinctively, out of a slight feeling of fear and surprise, she spoke, "Will they be good people, Jack?" but she knew she would not get an answer, nor would she wish to have.

Jack toyed with the new find for a moment before noticing a small switch down where he presumed the battery was kept. He reached for his tool sack, pulled out a sharp, pointed instrument and flicked it up. At that exact moment he felt a power surge take over the instrument as it seemed to come to life.

"I think it's ready to go, whatever it is," he said out loud.

He showed her the power button, which was situated on the side.

"Do you think it's safe? Could it bring someone here to us?" she asked.

"It's just a transmitter, Izz, what harm could it do?"

He pushed the power button and put it down onto the table.

Again, both simply stared at it waiting for something to happen, but there was no instant genie from the lamp, nor were there extraordinary noises or lights. The transmitter remained motionless.

"Well, that's an anticlimax," she said, "how dull after all the buildup. Really, boys and toys, and as always – nothing …" She stood to put the kettle onto the gas burner to make coffee.

"Yup, oh well, nothing. Perhaps it doesn't actually have any power, or the elements have killed it," he replied as he moved his gaze away from it and towards the gas flame.

The two had no reason to suspect anything other than the obvious, but the transmitter had set off a series of actions. It would take several hours to initiate the sequence, but it was working and it was now transmitting.

————◆◆◆◆◆————

High up in a skyscraper in New York City a man would rush into a meeting of stern-faced, well-dressed men and inform them that this transmitter had been activated. On a ship now sailing away from Bouvet Island, which it had recently visited, two soldiers dressed all in black would look at each other in shock and start a search of their equipment for a black box, which should have returned with them back on board. And, in Cheltenham at GCHQ, an analyst would stare at his screen in amazement while also turning dials controlling his headset.

The very same analyst would also interrupt men around a meeting table. "Sir, I have found something. Well, something found me actually," he started. "I have been listening to an encrypted signal."

The man at the top of the table looked at him strangely and began to wonder why they had been interrupted.

"Sorry, yes, I should say, this signal, which has only just started, is from a while ago."

"OK, Rogers, settle down. It's just started but it's from a while ago? Explain please."

"Sir, a Cold War encrypted signal has just started to be transmitted and I have tracked the source to a tiny, uninhabited and inhospitable island half way around the world."

The people in the room sat in silence and contemplated the meaning of the words they had just heard.

"Cold War, encrypted and from an island where no one

lives?" he said, almost asking for clarification and confirmation.

"Yes, sir, that; that very exact thing."

The room went silent, but on the other side of the world and yet unheard by any living thing, a wave was thundering at speed towards a tiny remote island.

———◆◆✕◆◆———

At twice the height of any serious and understandable wave, the Draupner phenomenon was first confirmed on New Year's Day, 1995. Prior to that, it was considered a near mythical event. This freak wave is believed to be the result of a massing of many earlier and smaller events. It can cause damage and flooding in certain circumstances on an unimaginable scale. However, on this day, something much more significant than the freak phenomenon of the Draupner wave was making its way toward the island. A fearsome series of waves compounded sixty times the height, speed and density of any normal raised swell moved forward, in places led by steam, as the heated water rose from beneath the surface and mixed with the chilled atmosphere.

Close to Jack and Isabelle, but hidden from view under the icy waters, the superior heated material forced the colder and subservient mantle rock downward and further into the darkness. The overwhelming force would rise like a silent assassin who hides in the shadows, only then to show his evil face and utilise his surprise and power against his victims. The subduction zone upon which Bouvet Island lay would be a victim in due course.

Bouvet Island lay on the triple junction. Jack and Isabelle worked away on the surface, unaware that hundreds of metres below and away from where they sat, the earth was literally moving, and hot magma was forcing its way with unyielding momentum into the opening ridges of the sea floor.

They would not get to experience the warming water as it hit the cooler surface atmosphere, or hear the hiss of a million snakes as the sulphur dioxide gas reached up and out into the air. Neither did they see the unnatural rippling of the water's moments earlier as the sub ducted colder plate was triggered into action by a powerful explosion at the sea floor and forced downwards at greater than usual speed.

This massive man-made phenomenon was hundreds of metres under the cold waters a short way out from their home-base island, but would soon enough rise above them and the island in a catastrophic manner.

As the plate moved downward and the sea water was being forced upward at speed, the wave would be seen from miles around due to its magnitude and height, but on this occasion only two people would witness its destructive power. For now, Jack and Isabelle worked on, stopping only to look out over the cold and the quiet of Bouvet Island.

For Jack and Isabelle, interrupting the silent paradise with sharp crisp chips of their palaeopicks on rock and only occasionally pausing to glance out to sea, the third week of twelve on the island was nearing a conclusion.

When the easterly beacon went off, only to be followed, almost immediately, by the southern, the next few seconds lasted a lifetime for the small island's population of two. The noise of the sirens could only mean one thing, the imminent arrival of a large wave.

"Jack, check your pager, is it real, is there a mistake?" screamed Isabelle. Her face filled with fear and confusion.

He reached for his pocket and the specially adapted GPS pager. Pulling it out, he stared at it in disbelief, "Fuck, they're going off. They are fuckin' going off! Christ, something huge is close!" His voice was trembling and his mind racing.

"What do we do, Jack?"

He didn't hear his island colleague, for Jack was frozen, staring at the reading showing that two warning beacons had been triggered. Something massive was indeed coming their way from deep under the sea.

"Jack!" as she shook him back to consciousness, "Jack, what do we do? I'm scared."

The massive wave was close and was getting closer every minute.

The beacons were programmed to transmit a signal if they were moved more than forty-two degrees and for more than thirty seconds. Anyone who works close to troubled seas is well aware that a significant swell is a warning that something worse is imminent and only a fool would ignore it. That two beacons had gone off in rapid succession was dire, and Jack's mobile transmitter was letting him know a third beacon was also signalling danger, then the fourth. This was proof enough to him that he had made the right choice rebuilding the life pod. His handheld device vibrated as the beacons continued to shout out their warnings.

The island was the end of the world, forty-nine square kilometres of ice and rock, featureless and surrounded by freezing and life-numbing water, but somehow that site was far more appealing than the four by six-metre yellow life pod. Further reinforced with Kevlar and having the most basic of amenities, this was to be called home should they ever need to exit the island in a hurry. Then they had the prospect of floating aimlessly, waiting for someone, or something, to pick up on the pod's signal and rescue them, all within the ten-day period before water and food rations disappeared.

They had rehearsed a speedy exit many times, so as they

entered the life pod all of its safety features were prominent in the minds of Jack and Isabelle. For a moment, their eyes met. The fear and anxiety was evident to both. Jack had grasped the mysterious transmitter and threw it into the pod. He hoped that if it was, indeed, transmitting then it could get them found. He was not to know that it would indeed have that effect, but that he, himself, would not see freedom from the impinging danger.

Jack took the lead, instructing Isabelle to lie down on the secure bed. Then, as he had practiced many times, he started securing the straps around her body and head ensuring that the release mechanism was clearly in reach for her. She lay down and allowed the necessary bondage to be imposed. Jack then went through the real-life drill that had been done many times in Southampton on how to self-secure. Thankful he had mostly paid attention, he managed to get himself into the bed and secured. The pair clasped hands, but could do nothing more than wait.

The only noises they could hear were those of the closest beacon and Jack's transmitter reminding them both that death could be racing towards them, together with their own accelerated breathing.

Jack moved a little and, to his horror, realised that he had not fully secured himself into the bed. He had failed to secure his head correctly into the fixed helmet and was stuck between leaving it as it was or unstrapping himself to have a second attempt and risk being caught by the wave. So as not to panic Isabelle, he reassured himself he was secure enough and returned his gaze upward to the roof of the pod.

As they listened to each other's highly charged breathing they became aware of another noise. A rhythmical noise at first, but one that was definitely becoming louder as it got closer. It wasn't really possible for Isabelle to grasp Jack's hand any tighter, but she tried to do so all the same.

The tsunami waves would all follow the same pattern as they approached land. As the water depth decreases, they slow. Their energy flux, being dependent on both wave speed and height, remains constant, so as it reaches shallower water the height of the wave grows in a shoaling effect.

Outside, and approaching at great speed, the first wave did indeed rise up as the water shallowed, getting higher and more angry as it readied itself to take on this tiny piece of land that dared to be in its way.

The pod started to tremble and sway as it was hit by the preceding winds, themselves running away in vain from the first giant wave close behind. The pod was now moving along the beach, digging into the sand and ice, powered only by the retreating winds. Both inside knew that this was just the beginning. Isabelle began to sing quietly to herself. The song failed to calm her nerves but did give Jack something different to focus on rather than the fear of what was imminent.

The first giant wave was so huge that it engulfed the tiny island and all the sea around for many miles. As it struck the land it descended rapidly downward, capturing rock and debris as it moved, then it appeared to wait for the one behind to catch up and repower its onward momentum.

The pod was flung forward and upwards hundreds of feet, a momentary pause before it spun downward, seemingly rolling down the wave before the process was repeated again, and again. Like the worst ever imaginable fairground ride designed to be ridden just once.

Both appeared to be asleep yet still moving as if they were having the same horrific nightmare. Jack had screamed for his mother at the initial big impact, but the word had not been completed before his life had ended. No longer holding hands, the nightmare had already ceased for Jack.

Unable to properly secure the head straps, the very first impact had resulted in a catastrophic fracture of his neck, killing him instantly. His journey was over even though the life pod continued on its violent way.

Isabelle was spared the horror of experiencing her colleague and friend being smashed and broken, for she too lay as if asleep. The initial jerk and push and rapid acceleration of the pod high up into the water, together with the sudden, but temporary, lack of oxygen to her brain, had caused a syncope collapse and unconsciousness. It was in fact this willingness to move with, and not against, the water that saved her, or perhaps Jack securing her straps more securely from top to bottom. She would never get to determine which.

The pod travelled for many hours, sometimes on the wave but often inside it. It never really stopped moving. As the violence calmed the currents took over.

Nearly three days had passed since that moment of impact on the island and now the pod's movement had become more rhythmical, now more peaceful, taking the sleeping Isabelle somewhere unimagined and unrequested.

It was her stomach that first told her it was time to return to consciousness. Then, upon returning partly to the living world, it would be the ache from swollen wrists and ankles, and the cutting and burning feeling from a torso that had suffered near unimaginable gravitational pushing and pulling, that would suggest to her to sleep again.

At first she floated in and out of consciousness and sometimes, when able, she would peer through dazed and swollen eyes over to Jack who appeared at peace, resting and sleeping, she thought to herself. Reassured that they were both now safe and believing that the pod's transmitter would be merrily pinging their location, she allowed her brain to win the battle over her hunger and sleep more than wake.

The life pod's location transmitter was indeed continually telling anyone who would listen exactly where Jack and Isabelle lay, but more dominant was the signal being pushed out to the listening world from the shiny new find Isabelle had stood on three days earlier. And the world was listening.

Jack was still motionless when Isabelle finally started the release procedure. *He must have suffered really badly to still be sleeping*, she thought. She groaned as she tried to raise her body upwards. Then, rolling over onto her front, she found the strength to lift her battered frame into the upright but sitting position.

"Jack, wake up. It's stopped, Jack, we're alive, we've survived," were her first recognisable words.

She crawled over to him to release his strapping.

"Jack, wake up now," her heart had started pounding faster.

"Jack, please wake up, please speak to me. Don't leave me here alone." An instant realisation hit Isabelle full in the face. Jack hadn't survived and he would not be waking up.

The slow rise and fall of the water outside the pod did nothing to relax her. As the pain and hunger took control of her body and mind once more, she fell back down onto the makeshift bed and her eyes closed. It was easy for her to sleep. Fatigue and pain were currently stronger emotions and drivers of state than the sorrow she felt for her long-standing friend.

When she did finally wake she did not dare look over to Jack. She started to sing to herself, but, as before, this didn't have the desired effect.

---●→)●(←●—

Many strangers watched as two tiny, red body-shapes had been violently buffeted, disappeared, reappeared and slowly changed colour. When it finally came to rest, the predominant colour was now blue, although, alarmingly for some, traces of red still remained strong in one. They were watching a survivor whose heat signature was very low but, all the same, still evident. Many thousands of miles away they were looking at a survivor and this was not supposed to have happened.

---●→)●(←●—

Three days earlier the body of a young woman was found in woodlands close to an English university campus. The same campus which had first discovered the massive wave in the Southern Sea. Her neck had been broken.

---●→)●(←●—

As the local news channel reported on the apparent murder of a student from the city's prestigious university, a few hundred miles north in a remote part of the Scottish Highlands, a helicopter was landing near a stone-built cottage.

It had taken the admiral almost two years to find him, but he had been determined to do so for reasons other than pure guilt. Tom Selkirk had become a solitary and lonely figure compared to the man who had taken that Arctic mission years earlier. With an appetite for too much alcohol and distaste for health and exercise, Selkirk had fallen into a simple survival existence where solace was occasionally found out in the hills hunting and eating the deer and stags he once safeguarded from poachers. Now, he was the fallen, and outside his former brotherhood, *persona non grata*, and a man without portfolio. His body and mind hurt and he would wonder, as he viewed the glens, if he could ever be that soldier once more. However, what remained was his native cunning and dogged determination. In this, he remained strong, the result of generations of Scottish genes, the living essence of the ultimate warrior.

As the noise of the rotor blades changed and strengthened, he knew a helicopter was descending nearby.

Selkirk also knew instinctively who it was, for he had been expecting his former friend, the admiral, to return to his life when things got tough and his country needed him once again. He just didn't know when it would happen.

He also knew the two other suited men who exited the helicopter. One was a tall, strongly built American whom he had been on operations with him many times before, and the other was his former controller with the British Secret Service on that ill-fated mission in the Arctic. Selkirk also knew that they were going to ask him difficult questions in their bid to persuade him to return with them.

Selkirk opened the front door and faced them down. He was determined to control this encounter and he would decide in the next twenty seconds if they were to be allowed into his home.

"Tom, you look like shit, mate," said the American, his former friend and past colleague.

"Dekker, they got you involved? So they sent their best errand boy then," replied Selkirk with a wry smile as their hands clasped tight in a handshake.

The two men's long-awaited reunion was cut short by the senior ranking official from the party.

"Good to see you again, Tom, alive. It has been a while

and you were hard to track down," said the admiral.

He continued as he gestured towards the front door. "Let's go inside and chat, Tom. Perkins has brought you your favourite whisky, Bowmore I believe from memory. Perkins, you better have bloody brought it ..." he said, as he firmly pushed his way past Selkirk and went inside towards where he assumed the living room was.

The four men spoke for nearly an hour. Selkirk kept drinking steadily throughout the conversation topping up Dekker's glass as often as he could, while ignoring the admiral's need for acceptance and council.

Selkirk listened to the admiral's attempt at apology, but instead held back the emotions in him to extract revenge, there and then, for his past betrayal and crimes. Dekker could see his friend's rage and, suspecting the outcome, tried to make good of an escalating situation fed now by strong malt whiskey.

Occasionally, his former controller would interrupt the flow, but Selkirk would never address him.

Eventually, Selkirk could hold his silence and his patience no longer.

"Listen, you can all fuck right off, right now, if you expect me to drop things here and simply just brush the past under the carpet and join you on that bloody helicopter holding hands. I paid with more than my life that time, Admiral. I lost everything, my soul buried in the ice, my country killed me, my wife gone, my family split, and, then there was Chris. Dead on the snow and forgotten."

"Tom, it was hard ..." started the admiral, but he was interrupted by a now standing, more sinister-looking Selkirk, practically barking in his firm Scottish brogue.

"Hard, what the fuck do you know about hard? You are

a Whitehall warrior with clean fingernails and no doubt membership of some Piccadilly club. You don't know hard. You abandoned me. I was picked up by hunters, spent time in some fuckin' hell hole only to escape and return here without your help. Oh, and yes, Julie left me because she couldn't wait any longer! Probably told, by you, that I was dead! Hard? You don't get to talk to me about hard," then, strangely, through his anger came respect, "sir."

The admiral stood, hearing the bitterness in Selkirk's voice, he gestured to the others to do the same.

As the admiral left the room he placed a card on the table, but not before turning back to his former friend. "Tom, I am sorry," he said in a quiet, private voice.

Perkins signalled to the pilot to up start the engines and prepare to go.

Dekker stopped and turned to his friend, now just inside the front door. The whine of the helicopter engines now filling the air.

"Come back, Tom. We need you, brother. This time you have me on your shoulder and I don't leave anyone behind," he said.

———————————

As the noise of the helicopter softened and it drifted out of sight, Selkirk walked out towards the mountains wrestling with his anger and his conscious. Thousands of miles away, the ebb and flow of gentle waves could be heard from inside the small rescue craft. Somewhere far away, resting on the cold waters of the Antarctic was a yellow life capsule with two occupants. Inside it, a left-behind transmitter was pushing out an encrypted signal. The men in tailored suits would advance their plan targeting the coordinates of the signal.

Chapter 2

Atlantis

Light from the surface faded quickly as the specially designed steel and titanium minisub slipped below the waves. Named *Discovery II*, she began her lonely descent into the depths of the Ionian Sea off Santorini. The three occupants inside studied their controls, carefully looking for the slightest deviation in the cabin's environmental readings. Even the smallest fluctuation could mean a loss of consciousness and certain death.

Captain Amalfi, on the support ship *Albi,* peered anxiously over the side, his face locked in a grimace as the sub disappeared. In his impatience he barked too many instructions to the crew, who looked harassed while trying their best to carefully lower the vessel to a point where it would jettison its umbilical support lines and continue down unassisted.

Amalfi knew all the risks involved, not least what it might do to his reputation if it all went wrong. The year before, the first test vessel had failed to reach the target depth in the deepest part of the trench. Not only that, but the vessel failed its structural integrity tests and Amalfi did not want three fatalities on his hands. The scientists had reassured him that the sub had been re-engineered and strengthened and was fully ready and able to withstand the intense pressure at immense depths. Despite all the setbacks and arguments, he had reluctantly agreed to continue with the dive, for a price.

"How we doing, Spencer?" said Peter as he looked across

at his colleague who was the sub's expert engineer.

"All good," Spencer replied, his hands a flurry of activity as he adjusted the delicate controls of the sub.

"How deep are we?" the gruff voice of Phillip echoed in the chamber as he peered out of a portal into a world of black.

"One thousand feet and closing on the release point," replied Spencer, visibly excited at the prospect of steering the sub to the entry location.

A few years earlier, two of them had stood proudly on the stage in Santorini's main conference centre addressing the world's most eminent volcanologists and archeologists. They were rhetorically laughed off the stage when they presented their findings. Standing by the side of one was a young and emotional Isabelle Braving who idolised her father and became tearful when the audience moved him off and away from his personal dream and quest.

Now, however, they were closing in on a lifetime's research work, descending slowly and steadily downwards towards the last known location of both the massive earthquake and tsunami that destroyed the Minoan world thousands of years earlier. The myth behind the magical city of Atlantis sprang up from the disaster.

Joining Spencer Braving were Peter Lassey and his research partner Philip Beaconsfield, now preparing to break free from the surface cables and steer their vessel down to the point where three tectonic plates had met. They believed, and hoped, there was a massive tunnel of trapped air drawn down by the gravitational pull of the seabed's movement and the separation of the waters many hundreds of years earlier as the huge eruption brought the destructive wave to life. For the next few moments, the three men held hands in the dark and remained silent.

"Gents, as we go down to a new world my lovely Isabelle is half way around the planet on a different one," said Spencer. "She is searching for the origins of life while we search for evidence of a past one," he added before the others could reply.

"She is a fine young lady, Spence, and she will do you proud one day. You know this, don't you?" was the first response, but before the conversation could continue further it was interrupted by the sparking voice coming through the radio.

Three hearts started to beat faster. It was time.

Routinely, each man awoke from their anxious private thoughts and started the preprogrammed and focused actions and checks. Powering up the mini submarine meant they were past half way down and reaching the limit of the surface ship's winch.

The light was so bright inside the submarine against the pitch black and space-like environment just inches outside that all three shielded their eyes for a moment and then returned to their duties and instruments. Now *Discovery II* could be seen for miles around under the waters, if, in fact, anything existed to see it.

"*Discovery II*, bring us back Atlantis, and God be with you all the way to its discovery," came across the radio as they separated from the binding security of the surface vessel.

Then, when Jones readjusted his controls against the swaying movement of the energy burst from the release, the three men moved slowly forward into their seat belts as the sub pointed downward and towards its date with destiny.

"Phillip, what's our depth and how is the outside pressure

holding up?" said Spencer.

"Good, all very good, thank Christ. We are reading everything normal," he answered in a relieved and calmer voice now.

"Batteries at full power so there's no bloody excuse now, let's find this thing. I can't wait to get back and see their faces when we prove them wrong," came sharply back from Peter.

As *Discovery II* fell further down into the darkness, forgotten creatures of the deep ocean eerily drifted by, oblivious to the dangerous pressure being exerted on the sub. Gravity and time took the explorers so deep they passed out of our normal world into a death zone, where survival depended on technology and the skill of the explorers. As they passed the four thousand foot mark they continued to talk systematically, without emotion, containing their anxiety by concentrating on data and the job in hand. Like all explorers, they knew only too well that success and failure were separated by narrow margins; by making the right decisions at the right time. Each of them dreamed of completing the greatest feat of human endeavour since the first moon landing by discovering the origins of Atlantis.

The hours passed slowly in the featureless darkness. Downward they travelled.

Science had dictated, with geomorphology and data, the existence of a massive tunnel deep in the Ionian Sea. This tunnel, devoid of water, crafted by huge gravitational forces and a chaotic mix of fire and molten rock, was the rationale for the construction of a super sub capable of going to enormous depths to find the entry point.

"Spencer, it's time. Put the search lights on. The readings are showing the seabed is close."

"Yup, going bright, team," came the reply, and it did instantly.

With a flick of a switch the seabed exploded into light. They could have easily been on the moon's surface. Their first view was of nothing but mud, silt and seabed rocks. Nothing stood out and nothing was worth a second detailed look.

It would take the crew a further two hours of manoeuvring around the sea floor before they found what they had waited so long for. Their target was called 'the entry point', a seemingly narrow gap in the seabed rocks with no discernible depth or reference. They took a couple of runs around the area to confirm its exact location and take photographs and then carefully manoeuvred the mini submarine to be in position to make a run into the mysterious ingress. What they would find on the other side was at the back of their minds – it was the run in that was critical, calculated by precision mathematics, taking all variables into consideration. Get it wrong and they would smash into the rocks, fracture the sub and implode to fish bait. Despite the computer-driven thrusters, Peter hung onto the controls like Captain Ahab driving his ship toward the white whale.

With the opening of the ballast tank the minisub could move easier on the seabed. With this action its inhabitants were now totally dependent on the one last oxygen tank for their planned triumphant rise back to the surface and sunlight.

"Are we doing this, gentlemen?" came from Spencer, his voice being firm and determined. He knew the answer to his question.

"Fine with me, Spence," from one.

"Atlantis is waiting," from the other.

An agreement had been reached. It was always going to be reached, but it was good to hear the noise and the confidence in the voices, they all thought to themselves.

"Release the GPS beacon, Peter," said Spencer. "Let them know we're going in."

The beacon would take forty minutes to get to the surface and let the dive ship know that the men were still alive and progressing according to plan. However, by the time the surface vessel had found the beacon and repositioned itself, the three men and their tiny craft would have passed out of knowledge and time to a place no man had been before.

"Look at that," commented Philip. "It's breathing, it's alive," following on in a calm and fascinated tone.

"How can the water move like that, it's not natural," was Spencer's retort. "Are we getting this?" he asked straight after.

"Yup, all being recorded, Spence," was the response from behind him.

The water appeared to oscillate. Waves of light and colour exploded around the entry point. A show of force, but with allure. A Venus flytrap with a will of its own, trying to lure the craft into the swirling, turbulent world the like of which the explorers had not seen before. They all suddenly forgot the crushing force of pressure around them, mesmerised by nature's ability to distract.

"Our future awaits us, gents. Shall we grab it?"

"Lead the way in, Spencer, the world's waiting," replied Peter.

With that, Spencer lifted the minisub up off the seabed and out of the dust cloud that had risen up around them, using the spinning of the eight directional motors that would be so crucial to the steady decline into the breathing and bubbling entrance that waited for them a few dozen yards ahead.

Discovery II moved ever closer towards the fate to which it was designed and destined to meet. The three men inside strained their eyes, looking straight ahead and into the moving water.

Within thirty yards … within twenty yards … and then they became aware of a power outside moving the sub slightly left then right. Spencer sat upright in his seat, aware that he would now have a more difficult task on his hands than he had originally assumed. Controlling the sub into the mass of living water would likely be trickier than anticipated.

Within ten yards now, and they could feel their vessel actually being drawn into the vortex. It seemed to be calling them in, showing them the way and offering a helping hand. *Discovery* accepted the offer and within seconds was surrounded by a hot mass of bubbles and steam. As the entire sub was engulfed, the lights flickered and the external cameras failed leaving the monitors to go fuzzy, and then to the disbelief of the other two passengers, Spencer took his hands off the controls.

"Spence, what you doing?" shouted Philip, "we could hit rocks or something," he exclaimed.

"She's in control now, my friends, look, she is taking us in and I trust her," he replied.

Strangely, this calmed the nerves of the other two. They too could now see that a current of water was gently moving them along and inside, and they felt safe in its grasp. It was difficult for the three inhabitants to know exactly how long they had been in the grasp of the current, but *Discovery* started to rise clearly upward, and, when she reached the surface and floated, it took them a further few seconds to realise what had happened and where they were.

"Gentlemen, feast your eyes upon the new world, the oldest of all the worlds, but for this life, the newest world on earth," prophesied Spencer.

The three men sat staring out of the closest portal to them.

"We've found it. All those years and we have found it. This must be Atlantis!" Peter shouted when his heart stopped pounding enough to let him engage his brain.

A second disbelieving silence fell upon them only to be broken by Spencer, "Shall we, gents? We know there's air, as we're floating. Shall we?" and without waiting for a response, he was up and out of his seat, moving towards the sealed inner-chamber door that would lead out to the exit.

The other two looked at each other and, as if not wanting to be left behind, sprang up and followed Spencer through the inner seal. All hands on the exit, they turned the wheel.

Whether it was the vacuum or the anticipation no one cared, but as the hairs on the back of their necks moved and rose as they stepped out into the shallow water, they knew they had, indeed, found something very special.

The three believers, after years of research and many more of hope, had found the fabled tunnels under the sea. Filled with air and clearly worked on by many men thousands of years earlier, the three scientists walked the main tunnel, shining torch light onto the walls and down the adjoining darkened network of routes. They may have found their 'Atlantis' but they were not the first to do so – they just didn't realise it yet.

Two hours had passed with the three men exploring the main cave, yet keeping close to their landing site, when they decided it was time to return to *Discovery* and begin the off-loading of equipment and supplies. Now, more appreciative of the task ahead, they retrieved their sampling and photographic equipment that would show the non-believers back in Santorini and elsewhere that they had been right all along and the outside world was wrong. They would start the process of collecting evidence that they required.

The drone was set up and ready to fly ahead. The thermal-imaging camera and tiny spotlights would allow it to be manoeuvred by Spencer along the major tunnel that spawned in front of them. Occasionally they would catch a glimpse of the secondary offshoot tunnels that could lead to the discovery they dreamed of, but for now, Spencer and the others were content to fly the drone down and along what appeared to be the main passage. They had time, and the three men were in no hurry to return to the surface just yet.

"This place goes on forever. The drone images stretch for well over four hundred yards in front of us and I can't see an end to this tunnel," Peter exclaimed. "It could actually be true; it could be as we believe. This could go all the way to the mainland in Southern Europe," and as the last word exited his mouth, he was duly interrupted.

"Peter, we're all very excited and none of us know what's ahead of us, but let's not get ahead of ourselves," replied Philip.

Like a teacher to an overly excited pupil, the words had the desired effect. They moved further and deeper into the tunnel network, and as their torches passed beams of light along the walls, darkness would fall in behind them. They could no longer see the series of markers left in a trail that would be used to guide them back to *Discovery* and back up to the surface.

"OK, stop here, let's get some better light," said Peter. "Phillip, let's use one of the lamps."

They were deliberately economical with the use of these, as they could only be charged from the precious and limited battery power in the sub. As Phillip switched on the lamp, he filled the chamber with light. What they saw next left them dumbstruck. Stretching way into the distance was a road similar to an ancient pavement with what appeared to be markers at intervals left and right. These markers were man-made and, more crucially, they were new and recently placed, not having yet been covered with a layer of dust.

"My God, oh my God," whispered Spencer to himself. "What in the name of Christ have we found?"

They walked slowly forward and picked up the closest marker. He could feel a slight vibration from inside originating from its battery power-source. Looking back at his thermal monitor, what he saw shocked him – there were faint red images of people moving quickly towards them. With a sharp intake of breath, Phillip stopped and turned to the others, and with a look of certainty and also fear in his eyes, he spoke.

The words were hard to say and even harder to understand, but as he said them the other two turned and looked down the dark tunnel.

"We are not alone in here."

Chapter 3

Discovery

Nathen had not heard from his sister in over a week now, and that was very unusual. Despite her being so far away on a small uninhabited island with her friend Jack, it was unusual for her not to contact him, even if only to put their parents' minds at rest. He decided the silence and news of the recent murder of the research assistant from Isabelle's old university department warranted his searching her emails for clues.

Isabelle was never the most security conscious in her life in general, nor when it came to protecting her work or private data. Nathen was confident he could troll her favourite animals or places and using her lucky number, get the right password to get into her mails.

He sat in one corner of the library ITC suite and went to the sign-in page.

"OK, let's start with the obvious, our pet and lucky number. Can my sister be so apparent?" he said to himself a little out loud.

Typing her email address into the ID he then followed this with 'Brandy16' enter.

The screen changed just as he was thinking of his next brilliant hack attempt.

"Oh Izzy, how stupid, so easy," he said as her inbox came into view.

Feeling slightly disappointed and a little cheated that it

hadn't challenged him, he started scrolling down the emails. Within seconds one stood out. It was from the now dead Brianna Lightman and had only an attachment, no text or subject matter.

"Perhaps done in a hurry?" he again said to himself out loud, but this time, hearing his voice, he looked around him. No one close.

The attachment opened in a new page and was initially just a huge mass of numbers and coloured line graphs, way too dull for Nathen's imagination. He scrolled to the bottom of the last page and let out a sigh of disappointment. He didn't know if what he had opened was important or not, but being the only recent email from his sister's good friend, who had likewise not been seen or heard from for a while, he decided to print it out, and also send himself an electronic copy. Just as he was about to sign out, he went to her sent items and deleted his entry then emptied her trash. Not really knowing why, but suspecting it was the right thing to do. He signed out and left the library.

The next day, he tried to call his sister again. Still nothing, no signal and no option to leave a message. He decided to contact her employers and see if they knew that she was out of communication.

In the afternoon, Nathen planned to visit her alumni friends to try to find out what the numbers and lines meant. Isabelle had an email file of her alumni, so this would be easy.

His morning work was not constructive by any stretch of the imagination. Isabelle's employers knew nothing more than he did and suggested that bad weather would most likely be the reason that they could not contact either of the two on Bouvet Island. They tried to assure him they were doing everything possible to ensure they were both safe and that he should not worry, but they failed to do so. His visit to the police to record his concerns was met with disdain. Their jurisdiction did not reach the South Atlantic.

The morning had left Nathen with a feeling of growing anger and he spent the next hour firing emails off to everyone in his sister's alumni group.

Deciding not to raise concern with his parents, he entered a local pub and sat and waited, watching his mobile for signs of life.

Perhaps an hour had passed when his phone vibrated on the table in front of him. He took a moment to watch it slowly judder across the surface, than grabbed for it.

"Yup, hello, it's Nathen."

"Nathen, hi, this is Jennifer, and Helen's with me. Where are you now?" came back at him.

"Oh, good, yes," stumbling for understanding, "you are, em …" he said, now a little confused and desperate to determine who this was that had his number and knew his sister.

"We're your sister's friends; you sent us the data sheets."

Nathen sprang up in his seat and after a few more excited words, had arranged for the two respondents to join him in the pub. His heartbeat quickened at the thought that they knew what was happening and could help him get answers. After all, why would they agree to meet soon if what he had sent them wasn't of real interest?

"Nathen, do you know what you have sent us?" Helen said after they sat down either side of him.

"Of course I do, but best you tell me," was his anxious reply, made more so by Helen's very direct opening question.

"It's a wave, but no ordinary wave," Helen continued. "It's a huge wave – imagine a huge wave then add more to it. Nathen, where did you get this?"

They both looked at him waiting for an answer.

"I got it from Isabelle's emails. I hacked in; she really should have had a more secure password ..." but before he could continue, Jennifer interrupted him.

"Nathen, where did you get this, people need to know? Have you heard from Izzy today?"

Nathen was now a little more humble as a growing anxiety built up within him, "It was sent to her from her friend Brianna at the university."

"Brianna?"

"Yes, Brianna. Why, what's the problem?"

There was a short pause, but to Nathen it felt like minutes.

"Nathen, Brianna's gone. Her professor sent her home to rest and she hasn't been seen since ..." and before she could finish he interrupted.

"Yes I know. Wait, you said a wave, what's that got to do with my sister?"

"Fuck, this is wrong. Brianna has disappeared but sent the wave detail to Isabelle, who hasn't contacted anyone for over a week," claimed Helen. "And wait," as she saw Nathen about to reply, "the wave, the detail showed it as the biggest ever in that region," she got out before Nathen stood and forcibly spoke.

"That region?" but he already knew where.

"The wave destroyed the island where your sister was working and everything around it for miles!"

Jennifer reached out a sympathetic hand to him but he sat down, moving a little farther away and out of reach.

By the time Nathen, Helen and Jennifer parted company, he had received further calls and emails from Isabelle's alumni colleagues. He didn't feel the need to respond and get similar depressing news. More anxiety was to befall Nathen before the night's end.

———•◆×◉×◆•———

In London, in a secure location, men had intercepted his mobile and opened up the microphone app. It was usual and routine for this team, who, after working backwards from the Cold War transmission to Isabelle's movements, family and friends, had found her brother speaking with others in public about a wave that they, too, had seen move at a ruthless pace across a cold and barren Atlantic Ocean.

The eavesdropping was enough for the team in their dark place in London, and *she* was activated to go get him.

It would be a couple of hours later that Anniken made her way into his flat, uninvited, and walked into the living room, where people were talking.

"Nathen," and looking for a response from the three male students that now faced her in shock, she took two steps over to him and spoke again, "Come with me now please, Nathen – it's about your sister."

Nathen, like his two flat mates, just sat and looked at her. She was an imposing presence with her long, brunette hair and muscular body, but for most, it was Anniken's body-length tattoos that caught the attention. They started on her neck line, covering her left arm and, when visible, running all the way down and across her torso, showing again on her right ankle.

Anniken came from mixed stock; she had a Jewish mother and Norwegian father, and this left her with a tanned complexion and sharp, crisp facial features. Her teenage years were spent with her mother in Israel after her parents divorced, and this family breakdown contributed to her joining the army and excelling at national service.

She would never leave the harsh environment of a military life, rising up the ranks, quickly moving into the dark world of the Mossad, the intelligence agency of Israel, where she became its first ever female unit commander.

Now, standing in front of three students, their gaze was transfixed upon her natural beauty and captivated further by the glances of her body art, occasionally visible as her long hair moved. While very imposing, she did not come across as threatening to the flat mates, who rarely had females in their accommodation. They had totally forgotten that she had in fact broken into their residence.

Anniken spoke his name again. "Nathen, we are going now, let's go," was the reinforced statement.

"Isabelle? The wave? You know?" was all he could get out before a firm hand landed on his shoulder.

"Last chance, let's go," and with that he felt obliged to stand and walk with her. His two flat mates rushed to retrieve their mobiles as soon as they heard the front door close.

"Please don't talk, Nathen, it will just complicate things," said Anniken, as they exited onto the street towards the black Ford waiting close by. Its engine started up as they got close.

"So, you know my sister?" he said again, instinctively.

"Nathen, do not talk," came back in a firm and authoritative tone. "I have to deliver you to friends," she explained. "They will look after you. You will be safe, but for now let me do my job and sit quiet like a good boy."

He stayed quiet for the duration of the car journey.

Back in the apartment his two flat mates excitedly called their friends to tell them of the imposing woman, and something about a wave, and that Nathen was taken. They did not hear the two men walk up the concrete stairs and to the front door. Anniken had noticed the car pull up as they had left, but focused on the task at hand and the retrieval of her target.

The doorbell rang, and believing it to be Nathen's return with the imposing woman, the two students ran in unison to answer.

Before either could reach the door, it was forced open and two men walked in without invitation, their faces masked, dressed all in black.

One of the men spoke in an accent they didn't at first recognise; the two students were now visibly trembling in fear.

"Nathen, which one is Nathen?" The two men looked down at both students, who had stumbled and fallen down after the door had opened so fiercely.

The two intruders looked at each other, realising that they were too late and Nathen had gone.

With one last look around, the two men in black turned and left at speed.

Anniken did not yet know who had pulled up at Nathen's flat, but had suspected that her team may not be the only ones after answers and those who could provide them. She sat in the front of the car and allowed the driver to take them to their destination. Nathen sat in silence, occasionally lifting his head to look out the window.

Chapter 4
Race to Capture

When the huge waves did eventually subside and the sea became relatively calmer, the pod stopped spinning violently and came to rest. A tiny dot in the middle of the Southern Ocean. Despite the pounding it had taken it remained in surprisingly good shape, but it had been driven many hundreds of kilometres from the initial impact zone. The same, however, could not have been said about Isabelle, one of the two occupants and sole survivor, unconscious inside the pod and mercifully oblivious to the carnage around her and her precarious situation.

Having had nothing to eat or drink for days, her body had shut down, and while to some it would look like she was conserving energy, to others who knew about survival this was a dangerous state where infection could set in quickly – organs could malfunction with such aggression that there would be no way back. She drifted in and out of consciousness, unable to get a grasp on reality, as the ocean currents carried her farther and farther through the ice-cold wilderness.

———•◦•✕•◦•———

A great distance away, and equally trying to get a grasp on reality, was Admiral Phillip Standard, commander of Britain's naval Special Forces. He had been bombarded with new information and spent hours with his most trusted staff attempting to put together some sort of coherent response to the uncertainty unfolding before him. Despite the gravity of events there was something missing, something maybe obvious that would pinpoint a specific threat. But as things stood, he only had the encrypted Cold War codes, older than the Berlin Wall itself.

Well, truth is stranger than fiction, he thought to himself. With a growing sense of unease, he began to accept that some of his most feared enemies were most likely on the move again, and whatever he decided to do, he had to do it fast and probably without authorisation, whose laborious and bureaucratic path he knew only too well.

It had only been a few hours earlier that Standard had been woken in the middle of the night with a message from Santiago in Chile. The news was alarming and concerned a radio intercept from a UK listening station that did not altogether make sense. He ascertained from his friends in GCHQ that it had been an encrypted code and that it had been sent to some kind of receiver in the South Atlantic Ocean. To what end, was a mystery so far.

The admiral knew how difficult it was going to be to get the suits in Whitehall to listen to his speculation, so he had to deal in half-truths. Combined with his customary belligerence, he had managed to get the COBRA to acknowledge some of the facts. They would then piece them together and feel enough anxiety to order a nuclear sub to the location of the Cold War transmissions and the emergency pod containing two unfortunate scientists caught in what could only be described as a catastrophic event.

Tom Selkirk stood in front of the admiral, having left

Anniken and the team to prepare for operations. It was a private meeting, as Standard did not want Selkirk's team's deployment to be common knowledge. The sub's redeployment was probably hitting rumour control, but the deployment of Selkirk's A team was another matter altogether, and some would see it as extravagant in the least. Keeping ahead of the suits was Standard's speciality, even if it would probably spell his early retirement.

For Selkirk, having to return to London for a private meeting with his former boss and former friend was history repeating itself. Tom wondered, as he stepped out of the tube station into the cool London air, how the history between them might affect their ability to work together. He dismissed his thoughts, choosing to focus on the immediate action required to rescue something strategically important in the Southern Ocean. He had long since mastered his emotions out in the field, because if he did not he knew it could seriously affect his judgment and, perhaps also, his chances of survival.

He and the admiral had conducted operations together many times, and it was Philip Standard's meteoric rise to the senior naval ranks that had turned their relationship into long-term dependence for Selkirk. The admiral had a subtle ability to get the right assets together quickly. A former captain on hunter-killer class sub HMS *Tireless*, Standard had often surfaced the vessel to allow return entry by Selkirk's special forces team.

As Selkirk entered the admiral's office, he noticed how old school it was. Pictures of warships and forgotten naval heroes decorated the walls, and there was the familiar leather-topped desk covered with maps and papers, a testimony to his colourful past. He had put on a suit for the day, the only evidence of his Scottish roots being the hint of tartan in his tie.

"Morning, Tom," said the admiral as he stretched out his hand, looking Selkirk straight in the eye.

Selkirk took his hand, acknowledging the friendship that existed between the two men despite the drama and despair of the past.

"Are you good, Tom, are you strong?" he mused, reaching for two glasses and a whisky bottle.

"I am good, sir," replied Selkirk, "despite the globetrotting air miles and sleep deprivation."

"Well, I have a small problem in the South Atlantic," continued the admiral. "We need to get an identified, sealed vessel, a pod, and whatever or whoever is inside it, before someone else does."

Challenging Selkirk directly, he added, "You have been fully briefed, haven't you, the pod and all?"

Selkirk simply nodded his acknowledgement.

"Fine, right, the sea air will do you good," and with that his brief encounter with his old friend was ending.

"It's overrated," replied Selkirk, "especially if you have to walk home ..."

"Tom, look, let's clear the air a bit," he replied sternly. "You know I had no choice – I was locked down, you know, direct orders from the PM, with pressure from the US," he continued in a more reconciliatory tone.

"Yup, don't worry, sir, I won't leave anybody behind. That's my bottom-line promise to you, even if I have to hijack the sub itself," replied Selkirk.

Now smiling and facing the admiral, Selkirk continued, "You know, sir, this has a bad vibe about it. I'm not sure why, but the indications are that we're dealing with something far more sinister than just some old KGB operators getting together to make trouble," he said. "If all this crap is true then we may have to look within as well as outside. As you know, some bears hibernate for a long time, Admiral."

"I know," said the admiral with a furrowed brow, "I will keep you updated the best I can, but the chiefs are watching me like a hawk and if they knew about this, we would all be in the shit."

"Understood, is *Parthian* ready?"

"Yes she is. She'll RV with you at the drop zone. Oh, and one more thing, I don't need to remind you how horribly vulnerable she is on the surface."

I know, sir, unfortunately so are we," and with that, Selkirk turned and walked out of the admiral's office and out into the corridor leading back into the cold London air.

<hr />

Some six thousand miles to the south, diverted from patrolling the Falkland Islands, under orders from the admiral, the hunter-killer submarine, *Parthian*, set a direct course for DZ Sierra Foxtrot, with Isabelle and the pod floating some six hours southwest of the rendezvous. With a displacement of over sixteen thousand tons and two Rolls Royce nuclear reactors, the sub made best speed at forty knots beneath the waves. Armed with torpedoes and cruise missiles there was no other vessel in the world to match her for stealth and sheer power, but even with all her military prowess, the sub would still take forty-eight hours just to reach the RV. And that was just the last confirmed satellite location of Isabelle and her floating coffin. The engines were at full tilt and the crew utterly focused, knowing they were heading for the danger zone.

Captain Phil Harrell was deep in conversation with his second in command, Lieutenant Commander John Nichol. Both the naval officers had hundreds of days experience in subs, but their latest mission was making them slightly uneasy because the enemy was more likely to be on the surface. To make matters worse they had the complex and difficult task of picking up Selkirk's SF team from the freezing-cold Southern Ocean, with a host of equipment and weapons. Then, all being well, the search and rescue phase would commence, which meant going to the surface for protracted periods, making them visible both to shipping and spy satellites and, of course, vulnerable to attack.

"Have we got the co-ordinates from London, John?" asked Harrell.

"Yes, sir, we are about eighteen hours away," was the instant reply.

"Good, do we know their take on time and flight plan?"

"Yes, sir," followed.

"You know as well as I do that they cannot survive long in the water, despite the dry suits."

"Yes, sir, we have cleared a space in the cruise-missile storage-centre to process the team as they come aboard."

"You know, they are the best, but with that comes a degree of demanding behaviour that we have not seen the like of for a while." Without waiting for any acknowledgement, Harrell continued, "We need to warn the whole crew to give them every assistance."

"One of them is a female, sir," said Nichol, "I'll put her in JCO quarters."

"OK, and better warn the crew; if she is anything like the others best they don't give her too much traditional naval cheek, if they want to keep all their bits," Harrell responded with a slight smile across his face.

"I will Tannoy the crew now, sir," said Nichol, reaching for the communication system.

Both officers knew that to find the pod before anybody else did was a task fraught with difficulty. That said, looking for the veritable needle in a haystack would at least be made easier by utilising the small minisub attached to the top side, aft of the conning tower. Manned by the special forces team, the minisub would give a far greater range and concealment for the small pod, recover survivors and retrieve the transmitter and any evidence that could further support the disturbing facts being uncovered by London. Although the minisub was small it was quick and well-armed, could carry a team of four and could also operate on the surface.

Nichol was proud of the crew. While he was not the boss, he still operationally controlled the sub and all its weapon systems. It had firepower that could give even the most hardened attacker a bloody nose, yet at a displacement of over sixteen thousand tons, they were big, black and highly vulncrable to anything that could shoot at them on the surface. *Parthian* had a head start on any potential adversary and she was going to need it if she were to be successful.

The MV-22 Osprey remained motionless in a rather drab looking hanger on the edge of Islas Malvinas airport on the southernmost point of Argentina. Once a base for numerous sorties into Britain's Falklands airspace in the early 1980s, this private airfield was shared between an array of drug enforcement agencies, corrupt politicians and anyone with enough money to make onlookers turn away.

Men in dark work overalls moved around the modified

MV-22 Osprey, which looked remarkably different to those grey and rather benign transport aircraft used by the United States military. This was to all intents and purposes a long-range gunship, faster than an attack helicopter and armed with a three-barrelled Gatling gun that could traverse on a belly mount through 180 degrees linked to the pilot's heads-up display. It was capable of delivering two thousand rounds of armour-piercing bullets a minute from a distance of two kilometres away. Technicians worked hard getting all the weapons operationally ready, confident that the aircraft was more than a match for most adversaries.

The loadmasters checked the long-range fuel tanks and ammunition supplies for what was to be a potential fight to the death with only one outcome, total victory. They had modified it to have a huge but obvious advantage: able to work with the attack speed of an aircraft and the agility and hover capability of a helicopter gunship. It was both manoeuvrable and powerful, able to fly below the radar and at night in all weathers. There was nothing to match it.

As the captain of *Parthian,* a hunter-killer submarine, Harrell thought through his options and tactics. As did the two pilots and the four-man assault team on the Osprey, led by somebody who knew Selkirk almost better than he knew himself. There was a different mindset, however, brainwashed and indoctrinated by the promises of men in suits, the six Osprey passengers dreamt of enormous wealth and power. They would stop at nothing to win, having lost their moral compass long ago. At their head was a man who had definitely turned to the dark side. Unbeknown to Tom Selkirk, Julius Falco, former UK Special Boat Service, prepared the nameless, faceless team for action.

Neither he nor Selkirk yet knew they were on a collision

course. If they had, they would have thought very differently about the operation. As it stood, both were working in isolation, concentrating all their efforts to get to the pod and retrieve the contents. But both also realised they would not be the only ones who knew about the pod and its precious cargo. If they got in and out with no fight that would be a surprise. Both minds were ready for whatever was to come, but neither really knew what was in the pod or its deep significance.

Like any well-drilled team, the MV-22 engineers and loadmasters operated largely in silence, each knowing his role intimately, seeking no acknowledgement or social contact from colleagues. The armed guards looked on bemused as they witnessed the preparation of a lethal attack-aircraft with an equally belligerent crew heading for confrontation. As dusk fell and the countdown began, the crew dwindled until only four remained, tasked with the final checks and helping to secure the small but heavily armed patrol boat onto the ramp of the plane.

As Falco's four-man team emerged from the shadows, the two Argentinian pilots stood up. They all shook hands and climbed aboard. Falco lit one of his favourite Havana cigars. It would take him a few hours to smoke. He had a second one for the way back.

As the MV-22 started her engines, ready to fly to the first refuel point, a sinister shadow made its way steadily, submerged at five hundred feet under the Southern Ocean. For those inside the hunter-killer sub, *Parthian*, the watch rota had been broken and the whole crew was at battle stations preparing for the RV and the arrival of Selkirk and his team.

It had been around five in the morning when the last night watchman rose from his restless slumber and made ready for action. Space-utilisation was crucial to the smooth operational working of a submarine. Generating oxygen from sea water and producing clean drinking water from the same source was easy. Moving around inside the sub, finding a bunk to sleep and a space to think was a more difficult task than anticipated, but it was an accepted part of life in the noise and confined spaces of the underwater boat. On this occasion, however, places had to be found for the new crew members and their equipment as their arrival was imminent.

If Selkirk's team managed to get any sleep it would be found on top of the cruise missiles, where cots could be stowed. The irony of sleeping on a bomb that could obliterate them, the boat and three square kilometres, while built to kill the nation's enemies, was not wasted on the crew.

Although built for speed and stealth, *Parthian* had a few other tricks up her sleeve. Hidden from general view were machine guns that could be rapidly mounted on the deck. Although their range was limited, and they had no real target-acquisition equipment other than the naked eye, they still could spread their cone of fire and provide a lethal wave of lead. The real prize was stored well away from the eyes of the submarine crew and was only known to the captain and the four Royal Marine commandos on board. Four Stinger missiles were kept in two sealed lockers just aft of the operations room. The captain wished that he did not have to surface to attempt to use them, but he warned the Royal Marine commando lieutenant to make sure they were primed and ready. The sub would make the right RV but the question was, would the special forces team get dropped in the right place? If not, they would be surfacing for nothing and become vulnerable.

———◆▸※◂◆———

As he boarded the special ops C130 in Cape Town, Tom Selkirk felt sick. He had sworn that he would never smoke again, but Dekker offered him a Marlboro Lite on the tarmac and he had taken it, hoping for some magical effect. The opposite was the case and he cursed the attraction of nicotine. The team had been flown to the South African Air Force base, Bloemspruit, to pick up the Hercules for the drop. This they knew was a one-way flight, and a long flight at that, before they took the plunge and parachuted into the cold waters below.

The team had been issued with immersion suits, specially designed to combat the intense cold, and all knew the high risks involved. What worried Selkirk more than anything was that, by the time they strapped on all their equipment and loaded the equipment pods that would go with them, they would all be overweight for the parachutes.

"This is ridiculous," exclaimed Dekker, who was hardly visible with all his new possessions piled around him in no semblance of order, "we are going to sink like bricks, my friend," he went on.

"Good job it's a soft entry then," Neeman said from behind him.

"That tin fish better show up!"

"Well it's the navy, you know," replied Neeman, "senior service and all that. I just hope their map reading's up to scratch." He carried on shouting above the noise of the four powerful engines, "Last time I did a water jump the RAF fucked up and dropped us five miles short of the RV, claiming after that it was a test."

Anniken raised her head, "Typical boys," she declared, "winging it … can't take the pressure."

Selkirk smiled. He knew what Anniken meant. Sometimes the team could whistle up a storm when things got tense.

"Let's hope for the best, shall we?" he said while he visually checked all the equipment over and over again, hoping that everything was there.

Parachute drops had the potential to go horribly wrong, especially when dropping heavy pods. Everything had to be tied down and all rigging checked. All it took was something to get loose, or parachute lines to get snagged, and they would face a literal bow wave of problems while coping with the Atlantic Ocean at its worst.

"What we going to be jumping into, Hog," asked Selkirk, as De Boer was responsible for the climatic brief.

"Well, boss, it could be worse," declared De Boer with his customary forthrightness. "Winds gusting to the limit at thirteen knots. Sea state is four high, air temperature five degrees, so with the chill it's below freezing, and that's out of the water. In the water it's bloody cold."

Suddenly out of the corner of his eye, Selkirk noticed a large commando knife strapped to De Boer's leg. "Expecting trouble, my friend?" asked Selkirk looking at the dagger. De Boer shook his head but his face gave it away. They were nervous and the jump was real. Training or no training, the best of the best they may be, but they were human and about to conduct a leap of faith from which they could all die. That worried Selkirk. He had learnt to trust the team's gut feelings.

Selkirk tried to make contingencies in his mind. Plans that could, if something went wrong, save their lives. They had a small inflatable raft, but this would be a last resort and render them extremely vulnerable to any passing threat. Selkirk knew only too well how the cold could very quickly make them inoperative despite their backgrounds. The next few hours were going to be critical. They had opted for a daylight jump, simply to give themselves a chance to regroup and make ready for the RV with the sub.

As the team made their final checks and the loadmasters on the plane secured the hold for take-off, Selkirk looked at each of his team in turn with more love than mere admiration. They trusted him explicitly, not just to make the right decisions, but to keep them alive as long as possible in the most exacting of environments.

He would give his life for each of them, as he knew each of them would do the same for him. That level of selflessness came at a cost. All understood that they may, at any time, have to pay the ultimate price.

As the tailgate closed, Selkirk made his way to the cockpit to talk to the pilots, both of whom were seasoned veterans of many wars in Angola and Mozambique. He knew that they were high grade and would get them to the right place at the right time. Selkirk asked the obvious question, "How long to the drop?"

"About seven hours till you need to go to action stations," replied the pilot, Wing Commander Dani de Klerk, his South African accent piercing the air, "we will then be about an hour out." He continued, "Pods will go first, Tom, and then you guys immediately afterwards. It's low level so you shouldn't have any trouble locating them, depending on the sea state. Weather looks good for a low level at eight hundred feet, OK?"

"Any word from London?" asked Selkirk, hoping for more information other than an order to retrieve a small life pod floating in the vastness of the Southern Ocean.

"Only that the sub is hours away," replied De Klerk. "That's good at least, but I hope they don't get delayed under the water for any reason. Tricky things nuclear engines," he laughed. But Selkirk could not see the funny side to any delayed RV and time in the cold water.

"Let me know if you hear any more," said Selkirk insistently.

"Of course," replied the pilot, for the first time sensing the anxiety in Selkirk's voice.

As darkness fell over the airfield so it did in the hold of the plane, with only the dim green of the operational lights giving off an eerie glow. The team sat in a huddle discussing their options and plans for what lay ahead as the C130, in its jet black livery, rumbled forward to the end of the runway. It turned abruptly, pausing for a few seconds for clearance from the tower for take-off.

As was customary with the C130, the pilots pushed the throttles to near full power with the brakes still on to test the engines on line. Once happy, they released the brakes and the C130 lurched forward, and in a little more than five hundred feet it was airborne, the light of the airfield and the town disappearing quickly below as the plane gained altitude. Selkirk knew it was going to be a long seven hours before they could kit up and he decided to call a meeting on the cargo netting to discuss operational matters and to gauge their state of mind.

"Look, guys," he started earnestly, which surprised the team, "we know we are not the only people interested in the pod and its contents, and we have all been here before, operating in a cold sea. But my fear is that while we try to get the sub back under the water and get the pod, something or someone, will turn up with hostile intentions." The others remained silent. Selkirk went on, "If it happens, it's going to happen quickly and we need all the firepower we have to come to bear. If it's in the water, we have a better chance as the sub can take it on, but if it's airborne then that's an altogether different scenario.

"I know for certain that the sub has two Stingers and I intend to take one with us in the fast-mover rib. Although I feel we may need to leave one with the sub to defend itself if it's on the surface, as it's only got GPMGs and side arms." Selkirk stopped and looked at each of his team in turn.

"What about the cruise missiles?" asked Dekker. "Can't they take out an aircraft or something airborne?"

"Well, they are the new tactical Tomahawk, so in principle, yes," replied Selkirk. "They have an immediate arming distance, but are not specifically for anti-air. The Stinger is the best option, but an aircraft could have countermeasures that defeat them."

"Oh, for my trusted Giat 20 mil," shouted De Boer, "it can make a mess of most things."

"Well, we don't have one, do we?" said Anniken somewhat sarcastically, "so we'll just have to make do."

"What we must be able to do is to concentrate all our firepower at once if we face contact," Selkirk continued, "but let's hope this boat's speed and stealth win the day. Once we find the pod we have to retrieve it quickly and get out as soon as possible."

"Do you know something we don't, boss?" asked Neeman.

This surprised Selkirk, who prided himself on giving every piece of information or intelligence to his team he possibly could.

"No, I don't," he replied, "but I have a gut feeling that we are up against something that has our every move covered, despite the security and need-to-know basis. The admiral seems to trust nobody in London, but there are those in the MoD who don't like him, remember? The jealousy of others, as ever, is hard to deal with for a man who has saved UK Ltd's bacon on more than one occasion.

"Last thing," said Selkirk, "if you find yourself alone in the sea for whatever reason, don't panic, conserve your energy and we will find you. Remember the drill and head toward the last canopy drop, and if you are last, move quickly as best you can to the group."

"Careful, Annie," said Dekker, "remember the last time under canopy you steered one eighty in the wrong direction."

The comment broke the ice and Dekker got the finger from a smiling Anniken.

"Get some rest, NOW," said Selkirk, "when we rig up let's be snappy."

Back in London, somewhere near Whitehall, two things were happening simultaneously. The admiral paced the room, waiting for word from both the sub and C130, while a few doors down someone else picked up a mobile phone and dialled an international number.

"Hello," the man said, "please assure me the package has left."

"Yes," came the reply, "first class."

On hearing the reassuring reply, he put the phone down before the call could be traced and continued drinking his expensive malt.

The admiral's mind worked overtime on the idea forming in his head that someone in the corridors of power was working against him. Intent on what, he could not yet be sure. What he did work out, though, was that his operation was not one hundred per cent watertight, and he hoped that the assets and their rescue attempt had moved quickly enough to avoid too much interest.

Then, in the depths of GCHQ, the two-man listening-watch had picked up a strange conversation between a caller originating from central government in London and an apparent disused airfield in Argentina. They rang the admiral immediately and told him the news.

The admiral listened to the operator. "It could be nothing, sir, but 'first class' is not an Argentinian term as far as I am aware," explained the nameless and faceless operator.

"Thanks," replied the admiral. His heart skipped a beat as he realised they could have been compromised. *Could this be related to his operation?* he thought. He was not aware of any other British or American operations going down at this time in that location. He leant on the edge of his desk and considered his options.

Were they heading for a trap, or just an inconvenient rendezvous with something unknown? Should he alert them, or should he leave it to them to assess the situation as they saw it?

He gave himself a limit of ten minute's deliberation and, as he had done so many times before, he rang his wife to say he would be back late.

Her calming voice always got him to the right place in his head, and having put the phone down he grabbed a signal pad and started to write a 'flash message'.

'For HMS *Parthian* and SAAF C130 SF01'.

'Message from Zero Alpha Intelligence suggests possible interest in pod from unknown source STOP Intention unclear, suggest treat as hostile STOP will continue to seek more info STOP'.

Standard took the signal personally to the comms room and told the operator to send it immediately.

———◆◆◆◆———

In the cockpit of the C130, Selkirk's worst fears were coming to light as he read the signal. But he suppressed the feelings of anxiety, and thought at least they now knew to prepare for the worst.

In the control room of *Parthian*, Captain Harrell was having a similar experience to Selkirk and he knew that the whole operation had suddenly become much more serious. He turned quickly to his number one.

"John, something is not quite right. What other shipping or submarine activity have we in the area that could reach our RV point?"

Searching his screens, then looking up at Harrell, "Nothing, sir," he replied, "the nearest warship is the Falklands guard ship; the nearest sub we know of is the USS *Pennsylvania* and she's a bomber, sir, on patrol."

Nichol knew how subs could hide for weeks, waiting for their opportunity to strike, and he also knew that stealth technology had made detection of naval assets that much more difficult.

"Look," said the captain, "when we get to the RV with Selkirk I want full action stations and all weapons deployed for defensive action. We need to get them on board as quickly as we can."

"Right, sir," replied Nichol, "we will be ready."

As Nichol called the commando unit to close up and conduct final preparations, the MV-22 Osprey made its refuelling point on time, all but a few hours short of the pod.

An hour out of the drop zone, Selkirk's team started the long process of getting rigged up for the jump. As the pieces on the maritime chessboard moved ever close together, Isabelle suddenly woke inside the dark pod in a panic, breathlessly surveying her surroundings.

She was in pain and she screamed, but in doing so she wasted some of what little energy she had left. Weak with hunger, her body starting to attack its own fat reserves, she could feel intense cold and a growing sense that the end was near. She checked the beacon out of the corner of her eye. Even though it seemed to be operating normally, there was little comfort. Holding herself upright against the side of the pod, she gazed in bewilderment at her surroundings. She coughed violently and blood accompanied the exhalation.

She knew her lungs had begun to slowly fill with blood from an internal wound and they were trying to remedy this with coughing spasms. She thought about a chest drain, but the thought of the effort to find the first aid kit in the chaos of the pod left her inert. Tears followed, the only warmth she had felt on her face for a long time, and she started to pray.

As the pod rocked in the swell of the sea, she felt overwhelming fatigue and gently pulled herself into a better upright position to minimise the effect of the internal bleeding, but then fell back into unconsciousness and down to horizontal again with a bump. Inches away under a pile of detritus lay a small device that had been retrieved by Jack days before. It looked harmless enough, more like a cell phone than anything else. It continued to transmit its merry signal to anyone that could listen.

At 0730 hours, the submarine *Parthian* surfaced in to the cold environment of the Southern Ocean.

The whole sub was at action stations, and within seconds, the commando team was out on the deck deploying the general purpose machine guns and situating another container which housed the precious Stinger missiles.

The crew was well rehearsed in this emergency procedure and in less than five minutes was ready to defend the sub and pick up Selkirk's team. The commodore asked for the readiness of the tactical Tomahawk system.

"All on line, sir," came the reply from the weapons console.

Minutes away, Selkirk's team stood and hooked up their square, static-line chutes. They were at about one hundred feet above the waves and Dekker shouted, "What do we need the chutes for at this height?"

Nobody laughed as the plane put in a tight left turn, its wing almost touching the water, and all of a sudden the whole team caught sight of the black and menacing outline of a British hunter-killer submarine sitting directly below them just under the waves. It was time for the pilot to attempt to drop the team as close as possible.

Assessing the wind and current direction would prove critical. The whole cockpit was alive with staccato conversations aimed to get the aircraft in exactly the right position to make the drop. The pilot made a long run downwind for two miles and then turned again on the drop run. Too early and the wind would push the parachutists away from the sub, making their retrieval far more difficult. Too late and he risked putting them and the pods on a collision course with the black monster. He steadied the plane and then abruptly pushed it up to eight hundred feet then throttled back almost to stalling speed.

At the tailgate the wind roared in and the engines groaned with effort of flying as slow as possible. Selkirk's team smelled the sea salt and felt the cold for the first time. Each member sounded off as 'OK,' ready to exit, weapons loaded and cocked, but secured tight to the parachute harness.

"Red on!" shouted the loadmaster thirty seconds from the drop and Selkirk, who was always first out, positioned his boot firmly on the edge of the tailgate, with the loadmaster gripping him tightly in the turbulence. Within seconds, the green light came on and out went the two containers. Then the loadmaster shouted, "Good luck and GO!' and Selkirk launched himself out into the freezing cold air of the South Atlantic.

One thousand, two thousand, three thousand, release, check canopy; canopy's good, steer away.

After several hundred jumps, the drill remained the same and despite the familiar tug there was still the sigh of relief when a good canopy appeared. Selkirk grabbed the risers and turned into the wind. The pilot had done well and Selkirk silently saluted him as the C130 disappeared into the horizon, his job done. He looked for his comrades and immediately saw trouble.

Somehow, two of the team had become entangled in the severe backwash of the aeroplane's engines, which was a common risk with the C130 – they were spiralling together and heading straight for the sub's deck. Best case, severe bruising; worse case, broken limbs or death – something the mission could not afford.

Selkirk was seconds from impact, about fifty feet from the sub, and screamed over his left shoulder, "Cut away, cut away!" A drill that released the main chute so that the reserve could be operated, but at only eighty feet, he knew there was no time. But at least if they were untangled and not above the ship's hull they could take a fifty-foot drop into the sea.

Neeman and Anniken fought hard to control their descent.

Anniken shouted above the roar of the sea, "Cut away, forget trying to steer!" She could see if she got this wrong both would pile into the hull at high speed. At less than two hundred feet and falling fast, the sub loomed large and both could see it. They struggled to control the chutes in any way and were at the mercy of the gusting wind.

"I'm going to cut," Anniken shouted, straining to make herself heard. "We are still over one hundred feet. It's going to be like hitting concrete."

Neeman smiled at her reassuringly.

"Three, two, one, cut!"

With both the chutes away and blowing on their own in the wind, Anniken and Neeman dropped like bricks into the ocean from around fifty feet, missing the sub, and broken bones, by just a few metres.

The captain and his first officer barked orders at the crew and ladders were thrown over the side of the sub for the team to climb on board. With all their equipment this was a supreme effort and all but the super fit Anniken struggled onto the slippery deck. As quickly as they had deployed, the sub crew started to dismantle the guns and equipment in preparation to dive quickly. In less than three minutes everything was below deck, including the new additional crew from above who had had a miraculous escape.

"Nice one, Annie," said Neeman, putting his arm around her broad shoulders.

"You're welcome," she pouted, "good job the girls are here, that's all I can say."

Selkirk was less impressed. "What happened up there?" he barked.

"Just the wash from the props, boss," replied Neeman, hands on hips.

"Really," said Selkirk, "or did you jump too early, Steve?" Selkirk would always call them by their Christian names when he was not happy with them. It was his way to show his displeasure.

Neeman had no time to reply, nor did he really want to, as the captain interrupted the premature debrief.

"Good to see you all in one piece," said the captain. "I hadn't expected any theatre from you boys, but nevertheless, I'm glad you're OK."

"We will continue this later, Neems," said Selkirk with a frown, but now starting to relax a little.

"Permission to come aboard, sir," said Selkirk.

"Yes, of course," replied the captain.

"Thank you, sir, sorry about the extra exposure time we caused."

"No worries, we are going under now, and all's well that ends well, and all that," he replied, moving along the narrow submarine corridor.

As they walked one behind the other towards the control room, Selkirk spoke. "Did you get the signal?" he asked. "The one about the possibility of hostile craft?"

"Yes, I got it and worried about it for a while, but now we are just going to have to see what happens. There is nothing on the radar at all and no aircraft tend to fly this far south," the captain responded.

"Well, whatever it is, or whoever they are, they are after the same thing as us," replied Selkirk, "and that makes us prey, sir."

"I get that, but don't underestimate this sub, Tom, she's got a few surprises up her sleeve. For now, I'll give you some time to get orientated and then I guess we should make a plan."

"Yes," replied Selkirk, "that would be good."

<hr />

The MV-22 Osprey had been specially adapted by Kharkov's technology arm of Space Frontiers Group and, as such, it was now a long-range maritime flying fortress capable of immense damage. What really made it special was its ability to fly almost unseen, with the latest stealth technology reducing its radar signature to nothing much more than the size of a seagull. Perhaps more significantly, she could loiter for considerable time out of missile range before pouncing on her unsuspecting prey. But at the end of the day, as far as any counter-measure ship was concerned, the Osprey was still just an airplane that could also hover and therefore, theoretically, could be shot down.

Falco had no intention of failing and no fear of whatever lay in wait four hours ahead. He had long given up being the good guy, preferring to accept the indoctrination that taught him anarchy and subversion were a better way than the democracy and freedom he had once fought for.

Six minutes had elapsed and the MV-22 was already cruising at four hundred and eighty kilometres per hour and, at only fifty feet above the water, was attempting to evade radar for as long as possible. Falco sat near the pilots, waiting for any news that would improve his chances of success, He knew this was a race to capture the life pod and he intended to win. The previous night's preparation would give him the edge. Most of the crew sat in silence. Some tried to sleep while others meticulously checked and rechecked their equipment. For those inside the Osprey there was no arrogance, Falco had beaten that out of them all. But there was confidence, and that would have worried Selkirk if he knew what was coming.

Falco was suddenly woken from a daze, induced by the steady beat of the rotors. Over his headset he heard an insistent pilot calling his name.

"Señor Falco, we have a message from control. There is possibly a ship in the area, but suddenly it disappeared off the radar."

The pilot continued, "If it moves towards the pod it will get there too late. We would have been and gone, sir."

Not if it's a submarine, thought Falco, suddenly realising that if it was a sub it had surfaced for a reason, and that was more than likely to pick something up from the surface.

He shouted down his microphone at the pilot, "Get a move on, guys, we have no time to waste! If that vessel is a sub then it can do up to forty knots under the water and some of those new designs have missiles that could take us out!" The rest of Falco's team looked around at him, slightly startled by their leader's anxious bellow.

"No subs come this far south," replied a visibly shocked chief pilot.

"Exactly my point," said Falco, "they know we are coming." Then he bowed his head and thought intensely who it could be.

Unable to sleep, Selkirk was especially agitated with the inactivity and decided to take a walk around the submarine. The others barely noticed him leave as he climbed the ladder from his missile bed and into the reactor compartment. He immediately ran into members of the crew who acknowledged him with a smile, but asked no questions. Selkirk was worried that they would struggle in the intensity of a firefight, especially being exposed on the surface of the sea. He suddenly felt vulnerable, aligned and somehow attached to an asset that, although fit for a role in a subsea sense, was no match for fast-attack boats or aggressive aircraft. He knew he had to think on his feet, outside of a shrinking box, and to do it quickly.

Reaching the captain's quarters, he suddenly had an idea. It was both risky and belied common sense.

Could he have a standoff long enough to lure whatever was coming towards him and spring a trap?

The only lure he had was the pod itself, or the sub on the surface to draw any threat away from the objective. The only place to hide was either behind the submarine or under the water.

The pod was small and offered no cover unless he got there first and got in it. Could he ask the others to do this? He knew about the Stingers available on the sub; but was the pod stable enough from which to operate the missiles? Questions raced around his brain and no immediate answer came forward.

Seeing a light on inside, he knocked on the door.

"Come in, Tom," said the captain rising from his chair

and reaching an outstretched hand towards him.

"I have some questions, sir," said Selkirk, frowning as he spoke.

"And so have I," came the reply, "lots of them," he continued, "and before you bombard me with all your imperative, you of all people know I have to think about this sub and its crew as well as the mission. I won't let you make Her Majesty's vessel a sitting duck to any aggressor above the water, despite the missiles we have."

Selkirk nodded, trying to hold his ground while saying nothing. He was trying to keep as many options open in his head as he could, while taking in what the captain had said.

"Sir, we have only a few options, considering the limited information we have and that we have no idea what or who we will be up against. Our mission is to recover the pod, and Whitehall has given an urgent priority to this, as you know," argued Selkirk.

"Tom, talk to me. No subtle games," the captain interrupted. "What can we do to help you without any unnecessary risk to vessel and crew?"

"We have the minisub, we can be underneath the pod – if and when anybody arrives," he responded, his voice sounding more hopeful than certain.

"We can launch the minisub submerged and take two of the Stingers with us," came Selkirk's first gambit. "On my signal, you surface and help with the firefight, or just pick us all up," was his second.

"Sounds simple," the captain replied, in a slightly unimpressed manner.

"The best plans usually are," the now confident Selkirk said back.

"I need time to deliberate," said the captain. With this,

the men shook hands and parted. Now, just three hours away from the last known GPS readout from the pod, both men knew there were so many questions to answer, so many uncertainties. However, best to stick with the basics or paralysis could set in and a successful mission would prove much more difficult.

In the missile bay, Anniken prepared her sniper rifle. It was state-of-the-art and she had used it many times before, taking out helicopters behind enemy lines by shooting the pilot from six hundred metres. As she made sure that every working part was clean and lightly oiled, she felt emotion for her fellow comrades. She herself felt invincible but feared for her colleagues, her friends. This thought and its subsequent action made her lethal and unstoppable, even in the icy waters of the Southern Ocean.

Dekker, however, thought of nothing but the plan that was in Selkirk's mind. He had been with him on so many operations that he had grown to trust his judgment. So now, this time, how was his mind shaping up, and what would he pull out the bag?

De Boer, like Neeman, was older and wiser and had seen things go horribly wrong without the clarity and vision of a well-worded mission and the right plan to back it up. He was a veteran of African bush warfare, where wits and aggression meant the real difference between life and death. He needed the assets to be in the right place with no room for second guessing and empty magazines. This was the man who knew the difference between success and failure, the awful tipping point where, in his words, you knew you had fucked up.

This was Selkirk's brood, a team who were perfectly balanced, *his* special force, no matter what the top brass said about ownership of UK's precious assets. He watched as they readied themselves.

Like all commanders, Selkirk's personal kit came last, and he found himself struggling to get it in the right state while his mind was so distracted.

He made sure his M5 Armalite was good to go with six magazines. He hoped he wouldn't use any. He made sure that he had his favourite grenades to hand for surface water dispersion, together with two SIG sidearms for close combat.

While he understood the art of war, he also understood that close combat relied on speed, agility and surprise; something not lost on special forces black-operations, but perhaps the difficult part to master. To keep skilled – especially as he had spent a few months isolated in his Highland retreat, after that operation in the Bearing Straits went bad – was a real challenge.

Two hours out from target, Selkirk turned to the team, "Right, the plan," he said nonchalantly.

"Yup, Tom, that would help," said De Boer, who needed to know his role so he could rehearse it time and again.

"Operation Certain Death, I suppose," said Dekker with a smile.

"Hmm, something like that, but aren't they all?" replied Selkirk.

"Well, there's a surprise," added Anniken, "scared boys? You should be, cos I reckon there are some bad-assed fuckers heading this way for the boss's bitch, or whoever it is in the pod."

"Well, for a start, we need this minisub in action ASAP," said Selkirk, "and we need to brief the crew – we have little time." They sat and listened to the rest of his operational plan in silence.

Falco leant over the pilot's shoulder, scanning the feature-less waters ahead, then glancing down at the radar.

"How far?" he asked.

"About one hour to the beacon's last signal," replied the pilot. "We have about one hour of loiter, but that's not in the hover, sir. We can afford no more than fifteen minutes of that."

Falco turned and gestured to the team he had trained and readied for this moment. Each one of them was totally loyal; each one would give his life if needed. Falco loved that – blind, loyal stupidity. Mind you, that reminded him of many of his former colleagues in the British special forces. "Nothing changes," he said to himself, "same shit, different day."

Isabelle was not happy with her predicament. While she had never faced death before, she knew its smell and it was all around her, having now invaded her very soul. She wanted out one way or another. He friend was dead and she knew she was close to it too, with no obvious escape from her purgatory. She stank. She knew that, and she could feel infection rampant within her body. She thought of the peacefulness of Bouvet Island and the waves lapping on the lonely shoreline. With the recent memory of Jack and her on the peaceful island came some sort of unexpected energy. It started to flow through her, and she thought of dressing her wounds, stitching up the holes and waiting for home again.

Isabelle, like her forbears, was a fighter and she had just

stepped into the ring. She held the Browning pistol in her hand and declared in a loud voice to whoever might listen, "If any of you fuckers come near me, I will blow your balls off!" Her words spurned her into new determination and a desire to get the questions answered that were boiling in her head. Then, as soon as she felt strong, her injuries reminded her she was not and, in pain, she lay back down and thought again of Jack and her on the island of ice.

Parthian's operations room was buzzing.

At the centre of it was the sonar operator whose earphones listened for the slightest blip on the horizon. These well-trained ears could pick up a sea lion turning through the waves and determine if it was friend or foe.

Then – "I have something, sir," he said to his number one, close by, "bearing 172 – 515 yards east-southeast."

"Radar, what do we have? Identify please," came the order back.

The response was immediate. "Nothing on the surface, sir, too many waves, but wait ..." And for a long few seconds the control room faces all looked directly at the main radar operator.

"I seem to have an aircraft, sir, at about two hundred miles. It's flying low, very low and at about two hundred and fifty knots. I repeat, very low, this is no commercial aircraft, sir."

"Bridge, sound battle stations," instantly echoed around the room. At almost the same second the alarm rang out in every compartment of the submarine.

"How long until it's upon us?" came the next demanding question. All eyes remained temporarily upon the radar station.

"At this speed and heading, sir, perhaps thirty-five minutes."

"And how far are we from the pod, if indeed that's it on the screen?"

"About three thousand metres, sir," anticipating the next question he continued, "I would estimate ten minutes from current position to pod, sir."

"Number One, take us down to minisub launch depth."

"Roger that, diving to one hundred metres, now."

Selkirk had been on the edge of the control room, but had seen and heard everything that had just happened.

Looking over to where he stood, the captain gave his final order for the time being, "Go, Tom, quickly, it's an aircraft. No idea what yet, and no ID, but I would say it's not going to be a friendly one. Get in that sub and be prepared to go." He carried on as Selkirk turned to leave. "Communications could be difficult at times, but keep trying. If I have to fire the missile, remember, it has well over a kilometre-wide blast area."

Heading out of the control room and walking as fast as he could towards the others, he gave a soldier's customary retort, "Thanks for that, I will stick my head under the water and kiss my ass goodbye."

Selkirk and the team struggled into the hatch, barely big enough for the four spaces it was designed for, never mind five fully loaded with equipment. They waited nervously for the lock to fill, which would then give them direct access down what was little more than a garage to the small secondary sub, anchored in position with neat hydraulic locks that could be released once it had been activated. It resembled a fish in shape, with a sharpened nose to cut through the water and small wings either side for stability.

Selkirk suddenly worried about Dekker's ability to drive it, a pointless mental exercise under the circumstances. The airlock released and they found themselves in the cramped hanger with the clock ticking on their efforts to get into position. They mounted quickly as Dekker fired up the motor, connected to the main sub by an umbilical cable to keep the batteries topped up. He then flicked the hydraulic release switch, but nothing happened. Panic set in. Selkirk suddenly remembered the manual release location and started pointing frantically at it in the murky water. It was taking Dekker too long to realise. Selkirk spun round on the minisub's hull and pulled it free.

The minisub shot backwards and leapt in the turbulence created by the wash from the sub's tower. As they sped backwards, Dekker gave full right rudder, but even so, they just barely missed the sub's colossal fin, which would have cut them in two. Control returned to Dekker's hands and off they went at speed towards the life pod.

Falco looked ahead, his eyes straining through the haze created by the spray off the choppy sea.

"There, over there," he said pointing towards what appeared to be a large orange buoy, "left, eleven o'clock."

The pilot responded and said, "Yes, Señor Falco, I see it, what are your instructions?"

"Give it a close once round so we can determine if we are alone, arm all weapons and open the tailgate for the rear gunner."

"Captain!" Then the next instruction came, "Drop to one hundred feet and hover," shouted Falco.

"We could lose comms, Señor."

"Do it!" and with that, Falco entered the aircraft's hold. His team was already up and armed and waiting their own orders.

The small sub moved steadily towards the pod, which, without any on-board radar, could have been only feet away. Selkirk touched Dekker's shoulder as a signal to hold position. As instructed, Dekker calmed the controls and the engine, and the sub adopted negative buoyancy. There they sat, ten feet under, the pod motionless and hopefully out of sight, assisted by the white horses dancing across the Southern Ocean's surface.

Isabelle suddenly awoke and sat upright, even though she was in great pain. Her conscious self was alerted at the sound of the rotors close by. *They have found me*, she thought as an attempted smile came across her face. Slowly and in more pain she got to her feet and held the side of the life pod for support. She would release the escape hatch, letting in the clean, fresh air and signal to her rescuers.

The Osprey continued its slow observation, three-sixty manoeuvre. "OK, let's get in close and low and drop the divers," Falco instructed the pilot.

Selkirk and his team remained below the water, blind and oblivious to the Osprey's tactics. Not happy that he had to second guess the actions of the enemy aircraft presumably above them, Selkirk signalled to the others to stay put on top of the small, submerged sub and to prime all weapons. He especially signalled towards the harpoon guns each of them carried, with three harpoons loaded on each.

In the relatively calm swell below the pod, the rest of the team took up all-round defence just above the motionless minisub, its motors occasionally whirring into action to keep it in position.

Selkirk slowly headed up toward the black shape of the pod above his rebreather. Three feet from the surface he spotted the outline of the aircraft and shuddered as he suddenly realised what they were up against.

A fucking Osprey gunship, he swore to himself. *Is that possible? How in God's name did that beast get here and whose is it?* He knew he had to think quickly about how to get the Stinger in a position to fire. The only logical place was on top of the pod, and the steps to the roof were on the side where the Osprey hovered.

In those golden seconds, watching the aircraft from inches under the surface, three divers entered the water with a rhythmical thud around forty feet northwest of the life pod. Returning to the surface, they started to head straight towards Selkirk's position. The sharp eyes of Anniken spotted their entry; the others heard the thumps into the water. She gave the others a tap and they formed their familiar attack line, harpoons at the ready. Selkirk saw what was happening from his position under the pod and took a course of action that could prove suicidal but necessary. He quickly dived under the pod with weapon at the ready and, as he surfaced, he tore off his mask and released a full magazine of armour piercing 5.56 lead into the cockpit of the Osprey.

The co-pilot screamed as a number of bullets literally tore off his leg, and blood sprayed the roof of the cockpit as his femur erupted. The pilot reared the nose of the Osprey and confusion set in inside the plane. Before the aircraft could turn away or properly recover position, Selkirk caught sight of a man in the door peering at him. In a state of disbelief he recognised an old friend. An old friend who he knew had turned his back on all he loved a long time ago. Falco. He almost screamed the name out loud as he pulled out his sidearm and aimed straight at the man that he once admired and loved.

Falco fell back as the Osprey turned away and banked sharply to the right, away from the developing threat. The sudden move had almost certainly saved his life from the sharp aim of Selkirk, metres below on the surface.

Isabelle screamed from within the pod and Selkirk shouted above the noise of the rotors.

"Get down, stay, we are British forces; we've come for you," was what she heard in her panic above the loud noises. He knew in a split second he needed to get Anniken and the Stinger onto the pod and into action. They were all lost if the Osprey returned and lay down fire. He put his mask back on and as he dived back down, he was met with six inches of shining, pointed steel heading straight for his body.

Below the water, chaos reigned.

As the divers came into range, the harpoons fired and, to the team's dismay, merely bounced off the enemy.

"Bloody Kevlar suits," swore Neeman, pulling his knife, which he had sharpened especially for occasions like this. The two sets of divers clashed blades drawn on both sides, and a struggle began that they all knew would end in death or victory, perhaps both. The water soon started to change colour to a dark, blood red.

Anniken's adversary managed to wrestle free from her grasp and made for the surface, knife in hand. The huge frame that was Selkirk slammed into him, right next to the pod's entry ladder. This diver had made his last dive. Selkirk thrust his knife into his foe's neck and ripped off his face mask as he did so, further disorientating the now dying enemy.

Now recovered and damaged assessed, Falco stood in the Osprey, holding on to the side as he looked out over the fight below. He was unaware of the exact situation with the divers below, but like the others, he could see a body floating on the water. The pilot looked like he had had enough. "Bring her round so I can use the canon," Falco cried, but the pilot didn't respond. Shock had crept in as he looked at his friend, now cut in half, in the seat next to him.

"Bring her fucking round, you moron, or you join your friend," he screamed, pushing the muzzle of his pistol into the pilot's temple.

As he shouted at the pilot, something broke the surface of the water and suddenly the mighty bow of the hunter-killer sub *Parthian* rose up out of the sea, like a marauding blue whale ready to do combat. Before the pilot could even manage the gun controls, now wet with blood, he saw the hatches blow open and several marine commandos burst onto the deck, firing their machine guns from the hip at the ailing Osprey.

As the seconds ticked by, Dekker and Neeman's struggle with their adversaries became easier, as Anniken and then Selkirk made the remaining fight a grossly outnumbered affair. Blood filled the water as the last diver assassin fell limp and to his pending watery grave.

"Get on the pod and arm the Stinger. This isn't over," yelled Selkirk to anyone of the three that could hear his instruction.

As Anniken turned and started to climb onto the pod, the Osprey backed off again as best it could, signs of grey smoke from one engine started to blow in the light breeze. As they backed off, the tail gunner on the Osprey let rip with all he had. Bullets splattered everywhere and two marines caught in the crossfire fell motionless onto the hull of *Parthian*.

All this was background noise to Anniken, who climbed the ladder to the top of the pod, Stinger slung on her shoulder and armed. As she passed the hatch, she could not resist a word in Isabelle's ear.

"Morning, sweetheart, you better be fucking worth it," came from her mouth while her eyes remained focused on taking aim at the Osprey, now around one hundred and twenty metres away, hovering a similar distance above the waves.

"We must abort," said the pilot, now panicking inside the aircraft, "we will not have enough fuel to reach land if we stay any longer, and one engine's struggling, Señor."

"Shut up and just do as I say," said Falco, "or we all die. Use the canon and blow those bastards to hell."

As he said it, he knew he didn't fully mean it. He had seen him. The last person in the world he expected to see. Tom Selkirk, a former colleague and friend, lost in the Barents Sea, retired, forgotten, disregarded. And now here messing up the party.

"I can't get the canon on line and we must be leaking fuel," the pilot yelled back, now clearly distressed with his enforced position.

Suddenly, one of the side gunners in the Osprey shouted, "On top of the pod, a Stinger missile – Stinger."

Before Falco could even move, Anniken had pressed the trigger and the missile left its launcher, accelerating to one thousand miles per hour in less than a blink of an eye.

It found a target, but not the Osprey as the pilot fired his countermeasures and chaff, momentarily distracting the missile homing device, pulling it away to the left of the ailing gunship to explode harmlessly.

Anniken looked over the top of the launcher in disbelief, "Christ!" she said.

Inside the sub, Harrell shouted orders, "Confirm missile launch."

"Forty seconds, sir."

"Not sure we have that long, Number One," replied the captain.

Falco saw his moment. "Turn her round, use the tail gunner, and go backwards – do it!"

As the aircraft in a hover turned quickly, the tail gunner started to spray the area with anti-aircraft tracer down onto the water around *Parthian* and then more accurately onto the top frame of the sub. Everybody on the sub's deck got down and only Selkirk's team was in the water, unable to find any sort of cover from the lead hornets that filled the air.

Bullets ricocheted off the water, around the pod and inside it; Isabelle wished she was back on Bouvet Island looking for fossils. As all hell broke loose, she cowered in the bottom of the pod, unable to move and running out of the will to live.

Dekker and Neeman had returned to the sub's deck to help bring firepower to bear, while De Boer and Selkirk tried their best to fire back from behind the pod, the sitting target they reluctantly now hid behind.

"This isn't working," shouted De Boer, "why doesn't that fucking sub fire its main armament?"

Then, from on top of the pod and ignoring her own safety, Anniken produced her favourite weapon, which had been secured across her back – the small but deadly sniper carbine. She quickly brought it to her shoulder, aiming into the rear end of the Osprey. Within a couple of seconds, the tail gunner was dead.

For a moment the battlefront seemed to go quiet. Falco searched for Selkirk, who had already laid eyes on him. Too far for any handgun, and with no second Stinger option imminent, Selkirk simply stared at the tailgate of the Osprey and the man standing just inside, now transfixed on him.

Selkirk nodded towards his former friend. As the Osprey throttled up and away from the submarine, leaving the spoils to be recovered by Selkirk, Falco returned the gesture. Both men knew they would surely meet again.

Then, just as Neeman and Anniken were about to rope-in the life pod, they witnessed a marine on the sub waving frantically at them. They also saw other sailors lying flat on the deck, hands covering their ears, face down.

The life pod and Isabelle could wait a moment longer – they knew what was coming.

Launch.

As they swam to a more protective position behind the pod, a massive burst of gas and air flew upwards from *Parthian.* The water around the submarine rippled and the sailors on deck held on to whatever they could.

Slowly at first, then, after what sailors call the 'wave goodbye', the cruise missile left the launch tube and its secondary thrusters burst into fiery life. Gaining speed, it was out and up and heading round towards a now helpless, departing Osprey.

Fucker! Take that, mate, thought Selkirk as he watched the aircraft burst into a million pieces, now being blown in all directions. The sky lit up in bright colours at first, followed by dark grey smoke and a fuselage falling into its watery grave, never to see the light of day again at the bottom of the cold and inhospitable sea. The crew on the deck of *Parthian* shouted and cheered as they stood and watched the firework display.

Dekker and the others turned back to the life pod and started the operation to recover it and complete their mission. Selkirk stared longer at the falling aircraft, or what remained of it. He wondered about Falco. This was not how he imagined his relationship with him would end. Climbing out of the ice-cold waters onto the deck of *Parthian*, Selkirk had no clue that his former friend did not join the aircraft as it started its last journey downwards under the dark water.

Neeman entered the sea and swam, powerfully, the short distance to Isabelle's floating coffin. With rope in hand, he struggled in the heaving cold to secure the pod so that it could be tethered to the minisub. It was the only way of getting Isabelle out as the sea was too rough to try it while unsecured. The cold and wind were intense, and Dekker and De Boer felt their strength ebbing: whatever warmth was left was being sucked out of them by the bitter Antarctic weather. After a long five minutes, the pod was eventually secured and Neeman shouted above the wind.

"Come on, let's get her out quickly."

As De Boer and Dekker secured the pod to the sub, Neeman made straight for the main hatch and found it opened easily. He was surprised by this, considering the battering the pod had taken in the Southern Ocean. What he was not prepared for, though, was the carnage inside, and he felt himself wretch at the smell of rotting flesh, faeces and stagnant sea water.

"Oh my God," Neeman muttered to himself, feeling sickened as the stench of several days of minimal ventilation and decay from Jack spilled out of the hatchway. He let his head clear for a brief moment then, with a determined grimace, he disappeared into the pod.

Inside, it was chaos, and Neeman struggled to find his way through the clutter of the interior, evidence of the pod's heroic struggle against the unforgiving ocean. He found the remains of Jack literally torn to pieces, and wondered how he would get Isabelle out without her having to touch or stand on the scraps of her departed friend.

"Harrison, get in here, please!" Neeman shouted back towards his colleague. Harrison duly entered the pod without a second thought.

Dekker kept a watch out for company, clasping his amphibious rifle tightly while De Boer maintained the sub's position trying to protect the others in the pod from the swell of the sea. Once Harrison was inside, Neeman quickly took a shell dressing out of its plastic sheath and blindfolded Isabelle so if she did wake, she would see nothing.

Harrison looked at Neeman, "There's not much else to salvage," he said. "Let's get her out."

Neeman nodded and they both quickly wrapped her in as many blankets they could find and then released her seat from the floor of the pod. Getting her through the hatch was tricky in the pitching sea, and as she went up and out the cold wind and clean air hit her sensory circuits, activating her brain. All she could hear and feel was a sense of freedom; and who the voices belonged to mattered not, just to be out of the pod was liberation enough.

"Get Jack, get the bag," came from her lips, and then pain, sorrow and sheer exhaustion kicked back in and she passed out.

Neeman looked at Harrison, then back into the pod. Perhaps they had missed something. He went back inside to search for anything that might offer clues or information. He could stand the stench no longer by the time he found the waterproof duffel Isabelle had mentioned, and he left the pod for the last time and signalled for it to be cast adrift. Jack would remain in the pod, forever drifting in the vastness of the Southern Ocean until it naturally filled with water and started its slow descent to the seabed.

Selkirk climbed down the hatch and into the submarine, leaving his trusted colleagues to finish the job up top. A part of him felt relief that Falco had left his life, but a second part worried that, without visual confirmation, this once friend now hated enemy, might reappear. Fighting his anger and emotions, Selkirk settled in for a long return journey under the waves with his colleagues.

It would be a few minutes later, but several hundred metres away, a man entered the cold water with a splash, followed closely by a flapping parachute.

Chapter 5

Waking the Bear

Kharkov moved like a man confident of staying above the water, should he decide to attempt walking on it. As Russian president, and one of the old guard, he still harboured dreams from the days of the Soviet Union and was a driving influence for Soviet domination during the Cold War, but for now, Kharkov simply lived in the past and forced those around him to do the same.

The Kremlin sparkled in the sun. The golden domes of the many churches inside its walls reflected sunlight across the city as if to say, 'we are here, we are everywhere, and we are watching you'.

Today, he was to meet with his closest ally, Barishnikov, and together they would move their plan forward at speed. The New York groups had been informed and were on board with his timescale, and now it would simply be a case of pushing the button to start the process.

Barishnikov sat as instructed. He and Kharkov had known each other for so many years that neither could remember how many, and when Kharkov gave an instruction, subtle or otherwise, Barishnikov obeyed. He had seen what his friend had done to other such so-called friends who had dared to question policy and instruction. They always disappeared. So it was best just to do as one was told and without question.

When the door opened for a second time, a tall, silhouetted man stood in its frame. Alexander was the head of the

FSB now. He had gained the president's favour several years earlier when he headed up the Spetsnaz special forces, eliminating Kharkov's political enemies without question or conscience. Now, Alexander was the president's right-hand man, and like Barishnikov, had benefitted from the sale of private Siberian oilfields when they returned back into state control. Money, for both of these men, was not an issue, nor ever would be, such was their wealth. For both men, nothing was ever out of their reach or influence.

Alexander spoke first, at length, and without interruption.

He explained in detail of the emergence of the African continent's financial power base, which was built mainly on Western and Chinese money. He emphasised that relations depended on a significant return on investment to avoid upsetting the markets in London, New York and Hong Kong.

Kharkov stood and this was a clear signal for Alexander to stop speaking.

"Comrades, we must destroy their power base and then their dreams," he started. "We must bring the motherland back to her rightful place as the dominant super power with absolute financial and political domination."

Both men seemed almost to sit to attention at the sudden outburst from the Russian leader. At moments, he seemed to be speaking to himself, oblivious of his two allies in the room. President Kharkov continued, "We must destroy the Europeans as we have done before – their pathetic little countries with too much influence. When we do, Russia will once again become the primary source of wealth for their economic recovery, at whatever rate I dictate. Of course, they will not see it coming, nor will they suspect anything." He walked to the window and looked out over the grounds of the Kremlin, lost in his thoughts and immersed in his thirst for power.

He turned from the window and growled in a low voice, "We will then take back what is rightfully ours, redress the balance in the Ukraine and crush those other treacherous states that dared to think about joining that pathetic European Union.

"Barishnikov, you must push on to the next phase as soon as possible; the island experiment worked as we expected, now we must start the next and hit them where it really hurts – in their pockets. We will destroy their new friends," the president concluded, as he moved slowly away from the window to pick up a glass of vodka.

"You may leave now, and be busy, comrades," said Kharkov reassuringly, as he placed a hand on their shoulders, and then, applying pressure, he spoke once more. "Do not fail me, or Russia!"

"Never, Comrade President," was the reply from the inspired Barishnikov, who then rose and stood to attention.

Then, with a firm handshake for each man, Kharkov lifted his glass and spoke out loud, "To Mother Russia." He drained his glass and left the room.

Both men sat motionless, in silence, for what seemed an inappropriately long amount of time.

Then Barishnikov suddenly sprang into action, taking out his mobile phone and keying in an eight-letter code. "Alexander," he said in a hushed voice as if the very walls of the Kremlin were listening, "it is time."

Chapter 6

Crumbling the Pillars of Hercules

As Casemates Square began to fill up with tourists and locals all seeking the best vantage point, Commanding Officer, Lt Colonel Aiden Stevens performed one last review of his soldiers. The air was cold for the time of year and, as they stood to attention, visible droplets of exhalation could be seen rising up from the parade ground.

The Royal Gibraltar Regiment continued the proud annual tradition of the Ceremony of the Keys and the securing of the island fortress against foes that would take this little piece of Britain from them.

The bugle sounded and the slightly muffled tones could be heard a little way off in the square, where those in the know whispered to those around them that didn't, that the march-through was imminent. Camera phones to the ready. The first band member came into sight to the sound of the 'voice of the gun'. The locals stood and admired while some others in the crowd, who were watching for the very first time, felt obliged to politely clap.

For Harrison, Gibraltar was like a home from home. While born in Cumbria, he had, in an earlier life, been brought up on the Rock, and as a wild kid had been calmed and educated at Royal Hibernian Military School. When his father was subsequently posted to Korea and places unspoken of, he remained on the Rock with his mother, playing football on the parade ground with the other children and regularly being chased off this sacred piece of concrete by numerous staff sergeants who would come and go as postings determined.

Today, Harrison had a few hours to kill before meeting up for a briefing with Selkirk and the rest of his team, now in transit from RAF Northolt. He and Kirk had been dispatched early to the Rock to set up a command and control base, so for now, Harrison walked alone along the cobbled main streets and back into the Friar pub, where he had spent many hours as a teenager.

The skies were slowly darkening as the night drew close. With no activity on his mobile, Harrison left the pub a few beers later and, turning left, continued his walk through the original city walls and arriving at Trafalgar Cemetery. He excused himself to the elderly lady resting on the bench and jumped onto the remaining space, leaping upwards and over the wrought iron fence and into the overgrown grass of the graveyard.

Once a defensive ditch during the period of Spanish rule, and subsequently the burial ground for casualties of yellow fever in the nineteenth century, it had become his father's last resting place. He had been assassinated by the Irish Republican Army, who had been on the Rock plotting an attack on the Royal Gibraltar Regiment. Harrison had been a teenager at the time, and the memory of his father's coffin passing through the thousands who had turned out in commemoration stayed with him to this day.

It had been a while since Harrison had visited the site of his father's grave, and the overgrown trees and shrubs now made it more difficult to find the right headstone. When he did, he moved the grass, pulling up some and using it to attempt to clean the stone of moss, before taking out a small switchblade to cut away the remaining overgrown grass. He used the metal point to run along the wording of the stone. Satisfied that he had completed his duty, he exited the cemetery by the more conventional gate and headed up the steep Europa Road towards the Rock Hotel to wait for the others and the briefing.

<hr />

At thirty-two thousand feet over Northern Spain, the C17 Globemaster had over ninety minutes flying time remaining. On board, Selkirk and the rest of the team sat in silence with their thoughts. The briefing at Northolt had raised more questions amongst them than it had provided answers.

As the cockpit door opened and the junior pilot exited, the sunlight rushed to the back of the plane, illuminating the darkened hold and the human cargo it was transporting to Gibraltar.

"Coffee, anyone?" said the pilot.

"White, no sugar," came back from Anniken as she stood and went over to assist with the drinks order. The others also shouted out their preference.

"Where are we?" she asked.

"Forty-three degrees north, five degrees west, ma'am."

"Again, my friend, where are we?" as she gave him a firm, disapproving stare. "Last chance now," changing her look to a smile.

"Yes, ma'am, sorry, ma'am. We're over Gijon and on a direct path to swing over Lisbon before starting our descent east into Gib, sorry, ma'am," he replied, clearly intimidated by her direct and imposing presence.

"Now that wasn't too hard, was it?" she said, patting him on the shoulder and picking up the coffees to return to the more familiar faces. They'd enjoyed the confrontation while waiting for their drinks.

"Poor boy," shouted Dekker over the noise of the engines. "He may need to change his pants now."

Anniken smiled and sat down, coffee in hand.

They still had ninety minutes to go and, as calm and quiet returned to the back of the plane, over in New York, things were moving at pace.

High up on the ninety-eighth floor of One World Trade Center, they gathered around a large oak table and waited their turn to speak. A series of microphones was randomly scattered around the group, all switched on and all transmitting the conversation far and wide around the planet.

Kharkov had made his way to New York from Moscow by private jet, and he would stand and walk the room as the others spoke. Silhouetted against the glass, looking out over the Hudson River towards the symbol of liberty and land of the free, he gestured to the others.

"We will send it immediately, the boat, we will send it now," he said in a calm, commanding voice. "I want it up and ready and entering the Med within forty-eight hours."

The others nodded in approval.

"Oh, I don't want any excuses, gentlemen. Forty-eight hours and get the *Azov* in Gibraltar and unloaded quickly before the British suspect anything."

Turning to face them, he acknowledged their efforts with a nod and walked out. Around the table, the planning conversations burst into life.

Meanwhile, back in Gibraltar, Harrison called Kirk and asked him to come down to the harbour. "We're going to snoop that Russian cargo ship," he said. "No reason really; it's just I've never seen a Russian vessel allowed on the Rock before and I'm curious."

"Suspicious, you mean, Harry," came Kirk's retort.

"Well, call it what you like – meet me by security as soon as, mate."

"Roger that, chief," and with that the phones fell silent.

The two men walked down to the harbour together, past security and on to dock three on the southwest corner of the complex.

As they got close, several men momentarily stopped moving equipment and watched them walking straight towards their ship. As soon as they had stopped their activity, they carried on again. None spoke, but simply moved boxes and secured crates down and off the ship into a number of vehicles, parked up in a coordinated and precise order.

"Hey, how are you?" said Kirk to the closest sailor. Silence. Looking to initiate a response, he spoke again, "Mate, hot day to be lugging crap all over, no?" Still no reply.

Harrison took up the mantle.

"Passes, you lot, show me your passes," he barked at them.

The closest five sailors stopped what they were doing, putting down trollies or boxes and retrieved their passes, handing them over to Kirk, who had walked amongst them. Harrison glanced at the ramp and saw a sixth sailor, who had easily been in earshot of his command, continue on and into the vessel at speed. Not before looking over his shoulder and mouthing something aimed directly at him.

Then something else caught Harrison's attention. A reflected glint of what was most likely glass fell upon Harrison's face and then immediately disappeared.

"Kirk, we're going, now!"

"What about the others?" Kirk replied.

"Now!" Harrison shouted back.

The two men walked quickly back towards the exit and, once confident that they would not be heard, Kirk spoke.

"What did you see, mate?"

"That man, the one on the ramp, did you see him?"

"No, what man?" Kirk replied.

"The one on the ramp that didn't stop when I called the others. He was no sailor. He wasn't sweating like the others," he explained. "He wasn't helping with the unloading. He was no sailor, mate. He was a soldier."

"Soldier? How do you know?"

"I just do, and there's more. I think I came under the crosshairs of a sniper on board," said Harrison. "I saw the undeniable glint of scope glass. We need to get back to HQ and call in the team."

Kirk knew Harrison made sense.

"Cargo ship, my arse," he said as the two men sped on.

Everyone on the Rock knew when Selkirk and his team had arrived. The noise and vibration of the C17 landing and restraining on the short runway would turn heads everywhere on this British outcrop.

Selkirk had anticipated that the plane's arrival may be observed. He had learned a paranoid safety drill over his time in Northern Ireland during The Troubles, and, as in those days, he sent the decoy out first while his team sat and waited for over an hour inside the belly of the plane.

Supply crates were unloaded and taken away and then

Neeman and De Boer exited, dressed in Royal Gibraltar Regiment colours, and made their way to passport control, then onwards by taxi to the garrison. Selkirk, Dekker, Biddiss and Anniken sat and chatted about their next steps and who was best suited to what task.

An hour after landing, the remaining four occupants exited the plane and entered a waiting Land Rover. It moved off in the direction of the garrison, then on to the hotel to be reunited with the whole team once again.

Harrison sat back down after letting the others know about his and Kirk's meeting down at the cargo ship earlier that afternoon. There was a moment of silence as his news was digested. Then Selkirk spoke.

"Harry, I get it, I trust your instincts, but for now, unless we get concrete sightings, we're sticking to our own plan and not venturing off line. If it helps you focus, mate, I'll get the major to plant a man in the harbour staff to watch."

Selkirk glanced over to the major, who held rank on his base, and he duly acknowledged and agreed to find a watcher from his regiment.

Not wishing to know what Selkirk's team had planned operationally, the major excused himself with a second nod and went off to find the right candidate to become a harbour cargo handler in the morning.

Kirk and Biddiss were next to leave, having been assigned the task of finishing the equipment and setting up the shadow HQ. The C17 had brought more than just Selkirk's team in its belly. The two men had a late night ahead of them as they emptied the two large, secure crates of their contents – weaponry, explosives, protective gear, scuba kit and the latest body comms. They would be speedily briefed on who was doing what, and what the requirements were, in the morning. When they were finished, they headed off to the slightly run-down former accommodation block on site, which was to be their base for the duration of their stay on the Rock.

The garrison major had proven much more supportive of Selkirk and the others than Permanent Undersecretary Jones had been to him and the admiral back at Northolt.

Selkirk was highly appreciative and planned to join the major for drinks later that evening, once the operational planning was complete. For now, however, Selkirk joined his team in the accommodation block and helped with the set up.

"Listen up, team," said Selkirk.

"I was going to send you out solo tomorrow so we can cover more ground, but in light of Harrison's comments earlier, I have had second thoughts. We will double up and just work harder round the Rock."

"Neems, you and the Hog take the cable car to the top and spec the route down, checking on anything unusual or out of place. Get into the top tunnels and scope them. Remember, we don't know what we're looking for yet, so take nothing for granted."

"Yes, Tom," replied Neeman, while De Boer nodded his acceptance and his understanding.

"Annie, you and Harry are to be tourists. Take the charter heli up and around the island. Do it a few times tomorrow and check shipping movements. Take photos for analysis. Wear casual gear and look happy in each other's company. I know you two can manage that. You've done it before," he said with a smile.

"Also, get your hands on a motorbike for helping out in the tunnels after you've done the tourist bit. OK?" Selkirk looked at them both awaiting some response.

Anniken turned to Harrison, who simply looked ahead at Selkirk.

"Yup, chief, we can do that," said Harrison.

"Kirk, you and Biddiss walk the foot tunnels. Take your time. I think you may have the short straw here, so keep your heads up and eyes open. Tool up discreetly from the armoury, and for Christ sake, don't get caught carrying."

"Yes, Tom, best two for the hardest shit?" joked Biddiss.

"What else you expect, mate?" said Kirk in reply to him.

"What are you up to, Tom?" asked Biddiss.

Dekker interrupted, "We're planning margaritas and a bit of vitamin D, I hear the sun's going to be strong tomorrow," he quipped with a smile.

Taking back the conversation, Selkirk said, "We will be over at Europa Point, then taking shade back down towards the harbour and our Russian friends."

"Chief," as Biddiss nodded his understanding.

"For the remainder of the night, I want you to read up on the major's notes and prep your equipment for tomorrow. And yes, I'm allowing you beers. Get out of my sight now, I have a major to flirt with," Selkirk said, looking around the room and gauging their emotional state.

With that, the team all stood and departed towards their designated quarters.

When the sun rose over the northern most point of the two Pillars of Hercules, the Barbary monkeys were screaming their usual songs and climbing the impossible as they ran and jumped around the Rock's summit. They would see more than tourists this day.

Selkirk walked the short distance to the junior officer's quarters, where he was met by Collins, who had been assigned by the major to become a dock worker. He was briefed on the earlier sightings and sent on his way. The major had prepared the appropriate documents, ensuring his passage from Royal Gibraltar Regiment to harbour worker would be a smooth one.

The journey by cable car to the old Signal Hill Battery at the top would take only seven minutes. In that short time, both men would view the Strait of Gibraltar, the bay out towards Algeciras and the scenery towards Marbella. Also, in those short, seven minutes during the ascent four hundred and twelve metres above the water below, both men checked their weapons and checked them again, agreed movements and confirmed their secondary plan should the unexpected occur.

As the cable car made its weary way upwards, both men, hanging from a wire, felt vulnerable.

"Sitting fuckin' ducks here, Neems," griped De Boer.

"Yup, I know, mate. Tourist cameras all over the place," he replied sarcastically.

As the Land Rover pulled off the road and came to a halt, dust flew into the air. The doors opened and Selkirk and Dekker exited the vehicle. With a final word to the driver, the doors were closed and the two men walked away in the direction of Harding's Battery on the southernmost tip of the Rock. Dekker looked back as the Land Rover disappeared back into Dudley Ward Tunnel, and for a few moments there was complete silence, broken only by the noise of his boots on the dust and rubble. The search at Europa Point was on.

With the passing of a couple of hours, most buildings had been cleared, as had the lighthouse and the Nun's Well, with Dekker abseiling down into its depth. With nothing to report and nothing standing out, they walked Europa Road and then marched down to the harbour and the Russian cargo ship.

Biddiss and Kirk smiled at each other as they entered the main tunnels and, walking deeper into them, looked forward to the moment they would exit Admiralty Tunnel and head back into the sunshine.

When the helicopter landed at the airport to refuel, Harrison went off to the tower to gain authority to fly within the restricted five hundred feet of the British listening station on the east peak of the Rock, while Anniken called in.

"Hearing you, Annie, anything to report?" came back to her.

"No, Tom, not yet. We're back up in ten and we're over the substation on east peak this time. Harry's after authority," she replied.

"Good. Keep going. Report anything, and I mean anything, that raises your curiosity. OK?"

"Will do, chief. We are getting a few good selfies from up here for the wall back at main HQ."

"If I thought you was serious, Annie, I would bollock you. Good work. Report anything!" Selkirk shut down the communication and Anniken walked back over to the pilot to ask for an estimated time for departure.

———◆◆◇◆◆———

Harrison buckled up in the rear of the helicopter next to Anniken. He informed their pilot of the authority code for the low-level reconnaissance over the substation. He gestured to Anniken to remove her radio headset.

Leaning towards her, he spoke into her ear over the noise of the rotary engines above their heads.

"I will say this just once, Annie. I was an idiot back in Iraq. There isn't a day since that I haven't thought of you and regretted walking away," he said.

She tried to reply but he didn't let her, raising his hand towards her mouth.

"I was in a bad place. We were all mission fatigued, but I didn't handle it well. Not like you did."

The helicopter rose sharply into the air and swung left out over the water. Both rear passengers readjusted their position.

"I know shit happens on a mission and that she needed to die. I was doing my job, but I lost it when the kids ran over to her, screaming," he said as a tinge of emotion entered his voice. "Like I did with you, I wondered constantly if those innocent children are coping in that bad land."

He allowed her to smile a supportive look and as her hand landed gently on his thigh, he signed off the conversation once and for all.

"I still care, I'm in a good place now, and, should circumstance allow me, I want to fight to get you back. But first, we have to do this crap," he said with a hopeful smile on his face.

Harrison turned away and put his headset back on, signalling the end of the conversation.

For a glancing moment, Anniken froze. As her senses returned, she opened the mic and instructed the pilot to head over to the east peak and the military base.

The pilot, who was in on the conversation with air traffic control, duly acknowledged his new flight path and pulled on the cyclic and collective accordingly. The helicopter sped low over the rock shore on the south of the outcrop and within minutes swung back east having spotted nothing out of the ordinary around the British listening centre.

They flew low and along the northern coastline towards the harbour.

Both back-seat passengers scanned the ground on their respective sides. The harbour got close, very close. Then, strangely, it was the pilot who first spotted them. Before he could gesture to his passengers, Harrison was onto it. He recognised one of them from earlier.

"They saluted that man as he walked past. Why would they do that if they were ship crew?" said the pilot.

"Mate, land this thing now, there, on that ground in the harbour," shouted Harrison.

"We're not fuckin' landing here and being caught out, Harry," came straight back from Anniken.

"Land the fuckin' heli now. I was right; this is no fuckin' cargo ship."

The confusion over commands had caught the attention of their targets. They stared at the helicopter, wondering why it had seemed to stop and hover and jerk left then down, eventually out of their sight.

"Harry, they've seen us – it looks like they're leaving. Look, in two cars!" she shouted. Carrying on, she barked instruction at the pilot who was now very confused and simply keeping the helicopter stationary less than a hundred feet above the two moving cars. "Land at the airport where we have the bikes – do it now!"

The helicopter jerked left and upwards violently and flew on towards the airport helipad, while the two cars sped off in different directions.

Confusion surrounded the harbour employees. A tourist helicopter had never come this close and most thought it was going to crash. All ran for cover as far away from the immediate area as they could.

Headsets and seat belts already off, Harrison and Anniken jumped out as the helicopter touched down, leaving both doors swinging open. The pilot watched in puzzled amazement as his two back-seat passengers ran towards a covered area near the landing site.

"I'm going after the one heading towards the Rock and the tunnels, you go after the other heading for the border," barked Harrison.

"No fucking way, Harry, I'm coming with you. We only need to get one car and the other will follow," she argued.

"I'm doing this myself. It's too dangerous and I don't want to lose you a second time. Do what I say, please," he said as they reached both the motorbikes, slightly out of breath.

"No, I'm with you on this," and with her reply, Harrison pulled out his weapon and fired it into her designated bike engine, disabling it.

"You're staying put, inform Tom."

As he climbed onto the bike and fired it up, Anniken forced her way on behind him.

"Together, now go!"

The two team members rushed down and across the runway without a glance towards the sky and out onto the public highway leading upwards and inwards inside the Rock's structure.

Dekker and Selkirk had seen the helicopter veer strangely and had concluded that the occupants were in trouble, so, commandeering a local's car, much to his annoyance, they raced down towards the harbour as Harrison, unknown to them, raced away from it.

Harrison brought the bike to a sudden stop, an action that led Anniken to fall further forward into his back, and their heads bumped.

"Fuck, warn me next time," she said.

"Which way, Annie? What's your gut saying?" he asked

as the two looked over the junction in front of them.

"Straight on is upwards and a dead end, so I say right and out to Europa Point. The others are there, so we have a better chance to take them alive," she reasoned.

Harrison spun the bike sharp right and, without a care for other traffic, headed into Dudley Ward tunnel.

———————

Dekker had called Kirk and let him know that something was happening. Both Kirk and Biddiss made their way quickly down the Rock towards the harbour, where, Selkirk had been informed, the helicopter had not landed but moved on towards the airport. The four men then followed its path, and a short while later were approaching the airport.

When Harrison drove the bike out into the daylight, both riders were partly dazzled and blinded. Slowing the bike to maintain control, both looked around for signs of the car.

It was another hot day and moving the bike off-road brought dust up into the air. Without time to put helmets on when they started up, the riders inhaled the taste of dirt and dust.

Anniken's mobile rang, it was Selkirk.

"Harry, stop, it's Tom," she requested.

Harrison stopped the bike and she stepped off to answer the call.

"Tom, we think we have them trapped in Europa Point, are you still here?" she asked.

The reply came back immediately with a tone of frustration, "No, we've left and are now at the airport. Are you sure, Annie? Don't push it, we will join you."

"Yes, we'll stay put until you get here, hurry." But as she uttered the words, Harrison geared the bike and powered off alone.

Anniken started running after the bike, gun now in hand, shouting in vain.

Harrison had got his way. He had his chance for personal retribution, which he believed would allow him his closure on the Rock after his father's murder many years earlier. He would do this himself and not lose another one he loved in the process.

When he saw the car, the same one he had spotted from above a short while earlier, Harrison stopped the bike and looked around. While his head remained focused on the search for the enemy, his heart was pounding with emotion. He climbed off the bike and let it drop, engine still running.

His training told him to take defensive action, but his heart overpowered it, and he walked in the open towards the car, gun in hand, pointing to where a driver should be sitting. However, this time, the car was empty.

Forty metres, thirty metres, gun barrel aimed directly into the car, he saw no movement. His head told him it was a trap, but he carried on. Twenty metres away and the first bullet struck, hitting him in the lower back and cutting into his left kidney, obliterating the flesh and organ in an instant.

He groaned and stumbled, only to steady himself again and turn towards the direction of the shot.

He saw the shooter, who stood watching, motionless, his gun at his side.

The second shooter shot him through the right shoulder, forcing him to the ground instantly.

In immense pain, Harrison dropped his gun and, kneeling in the dust, he searched, but when he found it, his arm could not respond to instruction. He could no longer pick up the weapon.

His vision blurred as his brain started to close down non-essential functions in a bid to maintain life, but Harrison still managed to make out the silhouette of a man dressed all in black, arm outstretched, gun in hand. It was the last thing he saw.

The car with Selkirk and the others drove at speed towards Europa Point. Anniken ran along the only road out to the tip of the Point while three men dressed all in black walked slowly down the slope towards the waiting boat and escape. All life had left Harrison's body.

She saw the third and last bullet hit him as she ran, still a distance away. She also saw them look at her before walking away down the slope. Their objective had been achieved, the signal had been sent. No need for a further confrontation with Anniken.

"Harry, you fuck, I said together! You never listen to me, do you?" Panic spilled out of her mouth and into her emotion-filled voice as she reached his motionless body.

She didn't know how long she held him, his blood soaking into her clothing. Neither did she notice the hand on her shoulder when it first appeared. She came back to the present when the recognisable tones and face of Selkirk came into her eye line.

"He didn't listen to me, Tom. He never fuckin' listened to me, not here, not Iraq."

"Dek, take him," said Selkirk. "Deal with this quickly, get him back, we will manage here."

"Yes, Tom," and Dekker knelt to loosen Anniken's grasp of the dead Harrison.

"Annie, walk with me, talk to me. Who were they and how many?" he asked. Selkirk held his emotion and thought professionally. He, too, had lost a colleague and a trusted friend. However, for now, assassins were on the Rock and no one knew why.

"There was something not right about how they did it. It was like they all wanted to have a go at him. As if they all wanted to send me a message."

"What do you mean?"

"The first guy hit Harry low and then he stepped down to allow the second then third to, well, like, have a turn." She went on further, "I've seen this type of thing before, you know, many times, it is the ultimate execution." Then, after a moment's reflection, "Tom, it's how I was trained, it was Mossad."

"How can you be sure? Why would they be here, and why Harry? It doesn't make any sense." Selkirk couldn't figure it out. "Where did they go, tell me?" he said as he placed his hands on her shoulders.

As she focused and came back to the operation at hand, Neeman and De Boer arrived. Neeman went over to help Dekker, while De Boer followed Anniken, who was now standing and back emotionally with the team.

"Annie, who were they and how many?" came from De Boer's mouth.

"I have this, Hog," Selkirk replied. Despite using a friendlier nickname for his colleague, De Boer knew he had to step down.

Dekker would call in the specialist team from the garrison. They would take care of Harrison and the site, looking for clues.

As Selkirk's team looked to determine what had just happened out on the water, a small boat with an outboard motor at full power made its way along the coastline and away from Europa Point.

That night, the Hercules would be granted special permission to land, and with a quick turnaround would be in and out again a few hours from now with Anniken and Harrison on board.

Selkirk had ordered her to attend a hurriedly organised funeral in Harrison's home town, but until she had to walk into the belly of the transport plane, she had insisted in staying by Selkirk's side to assist in any way she could.

Unable to follow Anniken to Northern England and say the last goodbye to their teammate and friend, they did so on the runway.

"My friend, I have a gift for your journey home," said Dekker as he put his hand in his pocket and pulled out a small bottle of bourbon.

"I know you hate the stuff, but now it's my choice," he said, twisting the top off and taking a mouthful before pouring some onto the coffin.

The others said their pieces, and together walked down the plane ramp and back to the garrison to plan their next move without Harrison.

Selkirk turned back to look up at her, "Annie, we need you here. When it's done, straight back," he said.

Anniken nodded and turned away to meet the pilots.

The funeral would be short and poorly attended. Anniken watched her former lover enter his last resting point from a distance and smoked a cigarette.

When Selkirk received the call early next morning from the admiral, the search team had already spent three hours on board the docked Russian cargo ship. Selkirk was expecting to inform the admiral that the vessel had given up clues.

"Sir, how are you?" opened Selkirk.

"Better than you and your team it seems, Tom. I'm sorry to hear about Harry. He was a fine fellow and a good soldier."

"Yes, sir, Annie's seeing him home. The boys are expecting more than dispatches, Admiral," he went on.

"Yes, Tom, yes I know. I will see what I can get through. Anyway, where are you now?"

"Rock's in lockdown; we've so far avoided press, locals are accepting, and our man at the dock came up with nothing. They seem to have just vanished," Selkirk replied.

"It gets worse, Tom. The permanent undersecretary has refused my request for more resources. We did what we could, but I can't push directly to the PM. It's just us now."

Selkirk could hear the disappointment in the admiral's voice.

"Career civil servants – the true enemy of the soldier, sir."

"I can't possibly comment, but know that what I can do I will. I am off to yet another pen-pushing get-together, so I will call you later, and let's hope we both have more positive news."

"Yes, sir, let's. Thank you, sir." Selkirk returned his thoughts to the three Russians and their possible whereabouts.

<hr />

Selkirk called the team together, and over a late breakfast they chatted openly.

Anniken was on speaker, the major was present and they all agreed their next steps. The temperature was rising, as was the overall anxiety.

The team call ended and a second call started. Selkirk gestured to the others to make no noise.

"Tom, I'm here with the permanent undersecretary," said the admiral. "We're ready to help you any way we can," he went on.

Selkirk looked at his phone, wondering why he had been introduced, having asked not to be.

Selkirk gestured to the others in the room not to make any noise. His team had been briefed on the admiral's failed attempt to get additional resources and as to exactly where Selkirk believed the blame lay.

After the introductions and situation update, Selkirk took command.

"Admiral, Permanent Undersecretary, as you know, we have a situation here that needs escalating. We possibly have three unidentified assassins on British soil for reasons unknown, one dead operative, and worse still, they have vanished out into the straits."

"We have no leads, but only one possibility. Something picked them up that was missed on our radar," Selkirk said.

"Are you suggesting there's an enemy sub in the Med, Tom?" asked the admiral.

"What else can it be, sir," he replied. "If you can get satellites to review the thermals in the area for the past six hours, we may know for sure."

"Steady on, Selkirk. Are you telling me we have an enemy submarine patrolling the waters of our allies and we don't know anything?" came from the speaker. The undersecretary couldn't help himself.

"Sir, thank you for your attendance. It is reassuring to know that you also take this situation as seriously as we do," commented Selkirk. Dekker smiled at Selkirk – he knew his friend's style.

Selkirk stood. "Sir, if you authorise the sat and our friends at GCHQ to check, we will know for sure. Is there a reason why you would not wish to do this?"

This most direct of questions was followed by a long pause.

"Very well, Selkirk. You better be correct about this blatant use of public funds."

Over on the Rock, those present heard the admiral thank his civil servant superior and then confirm he would action Selkirk's request.

The conference call ended, but the meeting went on for much longer. Selkirk and the major assigned new roles to start within the hour. Their primary objective was now to focus on why a Russian-registered cargo ship appeared to have Russian special forces soldiers on board, in British territory, and to find out what was unloaded.

———◆◆◆◆◆———

When the admiral came back to Selkirk a few hours later, the team was well into its new tasking.

A new search team on the Russian cargo ship was systematically ripping up each storage location on board, looking for the evidence that would justify their actions, while a second group analysed the maps and electronic data that the ship's control room would give up.

"The ship's clean, Admiral, but I will find something," Selkirk said.

"No, not the ship, Tom." Not waiting for Selkirk to reply, the admiral carried on, "The heat signatures picked up by the satellite were not under the water – they seem to come from the surface."

"Sorry, Admiral, I don't understand."

"Our three assassins were picked up, but not by a sub. They were collected by some fast ship." He paused. "Some ship that no one saw, no one heard and no maritime radar detected. They were collected by a stealth vessel. This could be bigger than we know."

"Fuck, I mean stealth, really, and it's not the Americans?" said Selkirk, the surprise making him leap up out of his seat.

"It was our NSA friends that confirmed the tiny heat trace. They've tried to track it but it's gone, and I mean vanished."

"Do we have *anything*, Admiral?" Selkirk pleaded.

"Nothing other than they believe it was probably travelling east and into the Med. Tom, it's not much to go on, I know, but if you can find something on that boat, or what it was that came off it, we may be able to figure this out. I know you'll do whatever you can, and know I will try to keep my side of the bargain here. Call me anytime with anything."

"Yes, Admiral, thank you." Tom ended the call, and for a moment he stood and tried to contemplate what he had just been told.

———————

Selkirk took a taxi to the Rock Hotel and called the team ordering them to do the same. It was time to figure this out together. The search teams would continue, but for now he wanted his closest and most trusted to be at his side.

The Rock Hotel was a flashback to the British Empire days. Selkirk felt at home in the large lounge bar, whose walls were enshrouded with memories of an earlier time, a time when Britain still ruled the waves.

He felt especially comfortable reminiscing over a signed

photo of a submarine he once knew, HMS *Tireless*, his first ever venture onto a hunter-killer class submarine. He thought about the time it had broken through the ice around the Arctic Circle during his first operation there. It was an impressive feat of seamanship and bravery on the part of the crew. Now his team needed the same.

"Shall I get the sandwiches now, sir," came from behind the bar.

"Yes, David, thank you," Selkirk replied.

The team was together. All together – apart from Anniken, whose return had been delayed due to the bad weather. Selkirk had her on speakerphone.

They chatted while they ate.

"Fucking stealth ship, Tom, you're messing aren't you?" said Dekker as he pushed more food into his already full mouth. "I mean, not even we've got that shit, so the Russians can't possibly."

"Yeah, yeah, look, we are here to figure out what was on that bloody boat in the harbour and where the others we saw on board could be," was the reply from Selkirk.

"We have a hold that can store twenty thousand tons of crap and a crew, including the Spetz, most likely. Where can something that big hide? The tunnels; where else is there?" he asked, expecting some form of reply and help. Selkirk was getting frustrated and feeling under pressure to supply the admiral with something.

"Twenty thousand tons, Tom, and the crew used trollies, not forklifts," offered Neeman.

"Good, Neems. What, if anything, does that tell us?"

"Lots of small items, weapons or munitions?"

"Logical, but nope, doesn't fit. Why would they store that shit without anyone to use it? Waiting for the Spanish to invade and take back the Rock? I mean come on, that can't be it," said De Boer.

"Explosives then. Perhaps to set up some fake terrorist plots so we're distracted from the political scene in the Ukraine with NATO?" said Kirk.

"Again, no, they would stay on the Rock, not leave it; and on trollies? A little risky, mate; and twenty thousand tons? They taking the whole flipping Rock with them?" said Neeman before Kirk had completely finished his suggestion.

"Why does the hold have to have been filled?" Anniken said through the speakerphone.

"What do you mean, Annie?" replied Selkirk, perking up at the first original thought. "Expand," he said.

"What if it's something small and easy to transport, with a huge impact. What if it's nuclear, like Bouvet?"

For just a second they all stared at the phone, contemplating what they had just heard.

"Annie, are you flying back soon?"

"Flying, yes, soon, Tom," she replied rather hesitantly and reluctantly.

"Get Isabelle and the brother and bring them here, and do it quick," he snapped, "I'll get a bomb specialist. Try to travel together and see what they come up with."

"Neems, get a radiation detector onto that ship and crew, pronto," said Selkirk, taking his phone out to make a call, signalling an end to the current discussion.

The others started conjuring up a plan for the eventuality that Anniken was right.

"Admiral, it's a bomb," said Selkirk as soon as the call was answered. "It's a nuke like the Bouvet one; I just don't know where yet. Can you get us a bomb guy quickly?"

"Christ, Tom, you don't do ordinary. Yes, let me see

what I can do. Tell the major, but no one else. Good work." The call ended.

———◆◆◇◆◆———

Darkness was drawing in and shadows fell across the bay as the sun dropped behind the British outcrop known as the Pillars of Hercules. As it did so, another darkness moved, but this one was boat shaped and remained undetected to the spy in space that continued to search the waters for linear traces of heat and displacement.

The three new crew members on the stealth ship, having escaped British Gibraltar, were reunited with their other colleagues. They would no doubt raise a glass and smile as they thought of their puzzled pursuers miles behind them still on the Rock.

The stealth boat sailed steadily on towards the Eastern Mediterranean and the Cyclades islands for the next phase of its lethal assignment.

———◆◆◇◆◆———

Anniken and her two reluctant guests were fast-tracked through airport security and made their way to a private area near the gate and their flight to Gibraltar. Isabelle and Nathen sat together talking quietly while Anniken left the room and spoke with the handler who had moved them through passport control moments earlier. With a nod and a handshake, he went off to fulfil her private request. Anniken returned to join the two, who were now sitting and watching the door.

When she entered the private room, both stood in anticipation.

"Are we flying now?" said Nathen.

"Sit, Nathen, sit down, I have something to tell you both," she replied in a firm and forceful tone.

Sensing something was not right, the siblings clasped each other's hand.

"It's your father. You haven't heard from him since you got back, have you?" Anniken went on without waiting for a reply, "We have reason to believe he has disappeared, presumed dead, on a deep dive in the Ionian Sea."

Isabelle turned to her brother and then back to Anniken, "The Hellenic Trench?" her voice now trembling in shock.

Anniken nodded. "There has been no contact with the support vessel in over twenty-four hours, and their oxygen supply will be spent." She moved close to them, "They are presumed gone. I'm sorry to break this to you, but you should both know before you fly."

"I'm passing you over to aircraft crew to deliver you to my team in Gib," she concluded.

With her eyes noticeably welling up, Isabelle spoke as Anniken headed for the door, "Are you not coming with us, Anniken?"

"I will eventually meet up with you in Santorini, but for now, you go to Gib together. I have business elsewhere to attend to." She opened the door and disappeared just as a tall woman in uniform walked in.

"Let's go, I will take you to the plane."

The flight to Gibraltar would last ninety minutes, but the two would not find the time to chat. Instead, they remained in shock and denial of the news recently delivered to them.

The plane would land in due course, and both Isabelle and Nathen would be escorted off and shepherded into a waiting car to be taken to Selkirk and the others, who, at this time, did not know that Anniken was not with them.

Neither Isabelle nor Nathen could shed any light as to where Anniken was, but Selkirk knew. He knew what she was like and that she would probably go after Harrison's killers in some manner. He knew this because he was the same, and he would have done the same thing.

———————

"Isabelle, we will do proper intros later, but for now, please grab some coffee and tell us what links Bouvet, Gib and the Med Sea," Selkirk said.

Isabelle spoke for over an hour, interrupted by the team only when clarification was requested, and supported by her brother when he felt confident enough to speak up in what was an intimidating environment.

Something resonated with Selkirk when she started talking about how the Bouvet wave could have been triggered by a strong enough device down under the water and along the island's fault line.

"I've heard this before, haven't I? This is the Professor Leech thing?" Selkirk quizzed.

"Well, yes, it could be similar, I guess, but with that experiment it took more than one device to trigger the seabed movement." She went on, and with a smile said, "Why, you got a bomb on the Rock then?"

No one answered or flinched.

"Go on, please, Isabelle," he said as her eyes wandered and fixed onto Selkirk's.

She spoke for a while longer, with the welcome addition of more coffee. As Nathen chipped in with his support, he became less anxious of the menacing collection of soldiers around him.

When the questions ran dry, it was an obvious time for

them to be excused.

"Nathen, Isabelle, thank you for your time. Please go get something from the restaurant and charge it to your room. We will need you again in the morning," said Kirk. "And please do not leave the hotel."

Selkirk was busy in a secondary conversation with Neeman and didn't look up as they left the room.

Adams had been brought over from the UK mainland as the expert. A bomb-disposal specialist for over a decade, he had served three tours in Iraq, but what he was to hear next would scare him.

"We got some bombs on the Rock then?" said Adams with a smile on his face.

"Neeman, can you widen your findings and help out our friends from disposal?" Selkirk asked.

"Chief."

"You will know that we checked the crew for traces of radiation on their clothing and person. Well, we found nothing. I don't think they were in on it – they were unaware of exactly what their cargo was. We did, however, find high readings on the boat and specifically in the hold. Annie's hunch was right: we have nuclear material somewhere on the Rock," said Selkirk as he sat down.

"You're shitting me, aren't you?" exclaimed Adams. "I mean, sir, sorry, sir."

Selkirk looked first at Adams and then over to his bomb-disposal colleague. "Too big a task for the 11th Division?" he asked.

"Nothing's too big, sir. But nukes, really? North Koreans, I fuckin' hate them!" he exclaimed and then quietly apologised again for his emotional outburst.

"Gents, now you know what we're up against, can I ask

you to leave us and get on with whatever planning you do in situations like this?" instructed Selkirk as he walked to the door and opened it for them before walking back to his seat.

The two new additions to Selkirk's team, now bewildered, shuffled out.

The final phase of the night's meeting began.

"OK, so we have a nuclear device somewhere on the Rock and possibly under the water. How hard can it be?" said Neeman as he reached for the coffee pot.

"I'm fucking hungry, Tom. If I'm to go swimming tomorrow to look for a nuclear device, the operating manual says I need steak. And a huge one at that," came from Dekker.

The mood had lifted, but no one took the task at hand lightly.

"Right, Hog, order for all of us; Deks is having a whole horse. We will carry on here until it arrives," he acquiesced. The team did indeed carry on late into the night, planning and assigning roles and tasks for the next day's operation.

———————

By the time the sun smiled on the Spanish coastline and made its way towards the Rock, the team was up and readying themselves. It would likely be a long day.

Selkirk had conversations with the admiral, the major and a short briefing with his two bomb-disposal colleagues and then set off for a little breakfast. He didn't eat well at times when his head was full of operational matters, but he did know that today could prove pivotal and tried to force as much as he could down to fuel him for as long as possible.

Later in the day he would be instructed to attend a meeting at the Governor's House, together with the major. In attendance would be the Russian ambassador, having arrived from

Madrid, who would no doubt want a full explanation for the unauthorised actions conducted on Russian-owned property. For now, he sipped his tea and thought hard about how the day would ideally pan out.

The previous night's threat assessment had raised two likely targets but no rationale behind an attack. Selkirk had stressed the powerful motivation of their adversaries to the wider team, for he knew more than most about the skills of the Russian soldiers they were up against. He had suffered at their hands many times, seeing colleagues and friends fall, and was now more determined than ever to avoid it happening again. He owed it to his most recently fallen friend, Harrison.

The airport was to be given primary focus while the garrison would intensify its own security. Extra armed guards were to be stationed around the base, while all aircraft would be more intensely scrutinised. Selkirk's team would spearhead the search for the bomb in the less obvious places, as this was his 'expect the best, but plan for the worst' approach to soldiering. It was this same approach that had kept him alive over the years and through the many disadvantaged skirmishes all over the world.

Each team member was designated responsibilities, together with an evac plan, while a separate and new control and command centre was established.

Kirk would spearhead the communication between the groups as they searched the Rock for the bomb, while also liaising with their American colleagues searching for the stealth boat. Kirk had requested additional black operators be assigned to Selkirk's team and sent to the Greek islands, especially the Cyclades, in anticipation of the stealth boat's discovery. But this was refused as Selkirk and the admiral wanted to minimise exposure and contact with the undersecretary back at Whitehall.

While the residents on the Rock carried on with their day to day activities, they would be evacuated if need be – the major had spoken with his Spanish counterpart and together a plan had been agreed and resourced. The covert search began.

<hr />

When Isabelle joined her brother in the hotel gym, she was a little surprised to see Neeman and Dekker already exercising. They had clearly been doing so for a while. She didn't really know why she was surprised to see them there, out of their military clothing and instead in shorts and casual wear, but she was, all the same. Neeman looked at her, while Dekker nodded in acknowledgement. Then, as quickly as the chat between the two had stopped, it started up again. Isabelle and Nathen had been accepted into the fold, and while they would never get to know the intricate details of what was actually going on, no one felt they had to avoid any conversation while in the company of their two reluctant civilian team members.

"I hope Tom and the admiral are holding back on us, Neems. I would hate to think that they are as in the dark as we are about this bomb shit," said Dekker.

Starting up her treadmill, she grunted a kind of agreement towards the bench where Dekker was lifting weights.

"I mean, we have a nuke on the Rock, the fuckin' Spetz involved and no one knows why. It's just bad shit and I don't like it," he went on. "If the thing goes off it will take half the Rock and us with it, while the Russians are hiding somewhere in Greece."

"Deks, if the Rock falls into the Med, the wave will be the issue. It'll be some record surf all the way to Africa."

Both Nathen and Isabelle perked up at the conversation. They caught each other's puzzled glance and, for a moment, waited for the other to say something.

"We should be going after the Russians and forcing them to tell us what the hell is going on. Me, I would happily warm my bones on some Greek beach while I chat to them," Dekker said loudly. Then Isabelle spoke up, surprising even herself.

"What if it wasn't just tectonic slip but was also a bomb? What if it was on the seabed on the plates, then it would be a bomb that encouraged plate movement!" she said in an excited and rushed tone.

"And if it was big enough, or wedged somehow between the weakest points, it could force convergent activity, further weakening the lithosphere and boom, or more 'whoosh' – massive wave," followed Nathen, "like the readings suggested at Bouvet."

"That would explain why Jack felt warm air just before he closed up the pod," she explained to her brother.

"Wow, stop. Bouvet, plate tech, what?" demanded Dekker. "Stop, slow down and speak to me."

Both started up again in unison.

"Nathen, quiet!" barked Neeman.

Isabelle walked over to the two and expelled her developing imagination into the willing ears of the two soldiers.

"Jack felt warm air, real warm air, as he entered the pod and locked up. This could have been caused by a thermal explosion. The readings show that the waters were unusually warm and not caused solely by the release of magma."

"Go on, Isabelle, this is good," smiled Neeman.

Isabelle felt reassured and somewhat closer to the team now.

"Now, I don't know the nuclear stuff, that's your job, but I do know that carefully positioned bombs, probably drilled into the plate's weakest points, could cause a tsunami like I experienced in Bouvet. I also know that it's been tried before, for real," she boasted.

"Leech?" quizzed Nathen.

"Leech during the Second World War," she replied.

Neeman texted Selkirk and once he was sure it had been delivered, he returned to the conversation.

"So you're suggesting a nuclear bomb drilled into the seabed could result in a massive tsunami when detonated, and that this could be applied as a tactical weapon?"

"No, Neems, I am suggesting that when bombs are drilled into the seabed, *in strategic locations*, then, and likely only then, a massive man-made tsunami could result," she responded with an air of authority.

Dekker looked over to Nathen.

"Yup, I agree, sir," Isabelle's anxious brother said.

The conversation carried on with Nathen and Isabelle trying to simplify what was a hugely complex topic until the door opened and Selkirk and Biddiss walked in.

"What we got?"

"Tom, you need to listen to them – we have multiple bombs!" exclaimed Dekker as he stood up to leave. "And I'm off to find me one."

"Deks, sit," barked Selkirk.

Dekker stopped walking but refused to sit. He stood and looked at Isabelle in a 'let's get on with it then' stare. She duly told Selkirk everything.

Within the hour, the search plan had been revised and De Boer left the room, but for him and Biddiss, Greece would wait until the two civilian team members had narrowed down where the Russians were likely to be heading based upon Mediterranean tectonics. They would then take Isabelle and head off the Rock for the chase. Nathen would stay and support the rest of the team. They couldn't risk the discovery being made public so, for now, Selkirk's team was in the hands of sister and brother volcanologists.

Selkirk called the admiral to bring him up to speed, while the rest of the team made way to the stores and the wet gear. The search area had been greatly reduced; however, the uncontested discovery of a bomb was now made less likely.

The team readied the submersible and prepared for time under the water.

Selkirk had requisitioned both harbour-patrol boats and manned them with the major's most trusted crew. This would be Dekker's primary dive base. With over fifteen years in the Navy SEALs prior to joining Selkirk's black ops squad, he was the go-to man for this task and Selkirk knew it. For the continuance of the search, Dekker had operational control. He was to have an unsuccessful and dull day under the water looking for a ticking bomb.

The day drew to a close and darkness crept in, and with Dekker exhausted from fighting tides and currents for over six hours, the Gibraltar team headed back to the garrison for a debrief with the ordinance team and the major. They would then head up Europa Road and to the relative comfort of the Rock Hotel, only to start again at first light.

Selkirk stood on the balcony of his room with a whiskey in hand and watched as the Hercules veered firstly upward and then sharply west. Inside were his two colleagues en route to the Cyclades islands and Santorini, accompanying a woman almost fresh out of university who may prove crucial to the success of the whole mission.

Again, he thought how out of control the operation had become and how they would need lady luck if they were to be successful this time. He hated these moments. It was this lack of absolute control that had almost got him killed those many years earlier in the Arctic.

The plane disappeared into the night sky; its engine noise was replaced by the sounds of a wedding party in the large hall of the hotel only a few floors below him.

When the sun rose over the bay of Gibraltar the next morning, Dekker was already waiting for his crew at the harbour. The admiral had agreed to Selkirk's new request for two additional team members to join De Boer and the others on Santorini. Nathen slept. Not being of the same world as Selkirk's team, Nathen had never seen the sun rise and would be left to join the others in due course.

Chapter 7

Anniken's Revenge

Eyal Lavin watched from a secure area, out of sight and, as ever, his intentions hidden and unavailable for public scrutiny, as Anniken's plane made its final approach.

The bonds between Eyal, her former commander, and Anniken were strong and would remain so until, one by one, they made their final journey to heaven or hell. Whichever called upon them first.

He felt a little apprehensive. He knew Anniken so well, but there was always a part of her that was unpredictable, wild, not cruel, but utterly ruthless. He wanted her to find some resolution with this situation, some normality amidst the chaos. But she was coming and hell was with her.

Thousands of miles away in a darkened operation centre, Selkirk sat with Dekker and told him about Anniken's unauthorised change of plan. In Tel Aviv, in a quiet suburb, two captives sat in a darkened room. They were bound and tired, and, for now, did not know why they had been taken.

"I checked the flight plans and passenger lists," Selkirk said. "She used an alias and one of her many passports, but as I suspected, she's headed for Tel Aviv."

"Revenge, a dish best served cold," snarled Dekker, almost feeling sorry for whoever was going to be on the receiving end of Anniken's wrath.

"She'll be landing about now, against my orders and could, if things don't go well, fuck up the wider operation," Selkirk exclaimed. "That said, I can't blame her for doing this. Under similar circumstances, I think I might have done the same thing."

"You going to discipline her, boss?" smiled Dekker. He went on, "Sometimes that all seems a bit pointless. She saved your bacon in the Southern Ocean. Maybe you owe her this one." He looked straight at Selkirk. "We need her – she knows that, she'll be back soon."

Selkirk understood Anniken more than most. He understood honour and duty but had also felt the cold contempt that comes with betrayal. He knew she had to purge it from her consciousness if only to make their chances of success better. However it was to happen, it would be unpleasant for those she targeted, who had killed someone she loved and respected.

———◆▸◖◗◂●———

Anniken considered her plan for arriving home. Ironic, she thought, that she was happy to see friends and share some time with them, to feel some comfort for her loss. However, she was in Tel Aviv for revenge and would not deny herself those intense emotions that would drive her to inflict pain and commit murder.

Of course she would spend some time with her former mentor and close friend, and both would make time to catch up on matters other than Harrison's killers. She knew that Eyal had been surprised and suspicious when she had contacted him after so long. Her voice had been full of anger and sadness when she explained what had happened over the phone.

Eyal may not have been convinced at one time that she could love someone so deeply and that the passing of someone close to her would prompt him to find those involved. He was further surprised that it was to be on his own front doorstep. Anniken knew he would quickly track down the men she was searching for and would have them watched around the clock as she had requested.

She knew he would not ask questions. Their bond was too strong and would always be so. He had messaged her to say he snatched two men in broad daylight. Eyal's teams were masters of the unpredictable and she wanted her targets to be frightened and to know that their lives hung in a fine balance. The only questions that nagged her, however, were what would Tom Selkirk's reaction be and what of the consequences if she did not try to get information out of any of them? She knew this would be difficult as these operators never spoke when interrogated. But she was who she was, and she might be successful. Years of fighting had taught her to never say never.

She smiled to herself. They were still at war, with everybody, or so it seemed. Their little Jewish oasis hemmed in with Palestinian terrorists on one side and crazy Arabs on the other, hell bent on the destruction of their homeland. But these captives were different. Remnants of the old Cold War and numerous Arab-Israeli conflicts. Israel was a confusion of nationalities and ideals, she thought. The men Eyal had picked up were her route to finding out more about what Selkirk's team might face, but they were also confirmation of one man's direct involvement. The one she wanted to torture and kill at all cost. *At all cost*, she pondered. Those words echoed in her mind. Sometimes it proved hard to see reason above the wave of hate and emotion that filled her.

Eyal lit a cigarette and moved out onto a balcony over-looking where the plane would eventually disembark its passengers. He had cancelled the shuttle bus and ordered steps, forcing the passengers to walk the short distance towards the terminal. He wanted to see who was getting off, and had two of his team watching the arrivals to the airport. Anniken was one of the very best, but even she could be followed by those determined enough.

Ten years ago, he remembered the intense and deter-mined girl who had enrolled in Israel's most gruelling special forces training regime. She had been one of the very few female operatives to make it through, and also one of the most difficult to manage. He had watched her grow as an agent over the years and admired her bravery, almost fool-hardiness, in the face of danger. He admired Tom Selkirk, her new commander, but wondered if he really knew how lucky he was to have Anniken in his team.

But this time things would be different. Eyal felt a sense of unease that he had not felt for a long while. He felt a pain in his heart for her loss and a growing feeling that something big was brewing on the horizon. Eyal Lavin knew that he had to be on his guard when these feelings arose, and as he watched Anniken's plane touch down, he knew he had many questions for her. He also knew, if he was honest, he didn't want too many corpses on his patch.

<hr />

Meanwhile, Selkirk paced the room. He felt out of control of what was happening, but still had an ongoing operation and team to lead. He needed the best team, but it came at a cost. He was now engaged in battles on three fronts. As the Gibraltar operation continued with its search for some sort of nuclear device, that of Santorini was just warming up. Elements of his team on two tourist islands simultaneously searched both land and sea for the veritable needle in a haystack.

Then there was Anniken, who was making her own war. Not under his control or guidance and somehow this worried him the most. Selkirk didn't fear for her safety but instead for the possible loss of intelligence if she did find what she was looking for. She might just decide to pull the trigger rather than try and get information first. He had to hope that some of her more refined qualities would kick in and prevent the kind of mess that London might soon hear about. He had not told the admiral about her revenge mission; he would strike her off his team and have her disavowed.

◆◆※◆◆

At the same time, in a wealthy suburb of Tel Aviv, a sniper took up position for a long wait. The second then third were quick to follow.

Anniken and Eyal did not meet at arrivals. Instead, she found herself a taxi outside the airport and headed for Eyal's home suburb of Gush Dan. She knew he would follow, and after only few minutes she told the taxi driver to make a sharp right turn and pull over, leaving her there waiting on the side of the road. His surprise was replaced with humble thanks at the fifty dollar note she handed over. As the taxi sped away, a black van approached, its windows darkened, then, as it stopped next to her, a door slid back.

"Shalom, my dear Annie," spoke Eyal. "Welcome home," and as she entered the van he smiled and placed a kiss on her hand, as was his custom. She could not have had better support. Eyal Lavin had only recently retired as head of Mossad's assassinations arm, the Kidon, and he had many willing friends still on the inside. When Lavin requested resources, they were always quickly forthcoming.

Anniken suddenly felt incredibly homesick seeing Eyal's smiling face and the familiar sounds and smells of her homeland. "Shalom, Eyal, my friend. I am sorry we always seem to meet in such dark circumstances," said Anniken.

"It is our life, Annie," he replied. "We just have to do the best we can with the time we have. Our home must survive and that is all that matters. We are the hand of God," he said as he placed a supportive hand on her shoulder. Anniken entered the van and closed the door behind her signalling to the driver that he should move off.

"How much time do we have, my dear?" asked Eyal as the van sped into the night to meet their captives.

"We have no time," she replied. "I have to be out of here in twelve hours."

Eyal laughed. "That special dinner is off then. Perhaps it's breakfast?" he said.

The man in the front passenger seat turned, "Ten minutes to location, sir."

Eyal turned to face Anniken. "Annie, one of these suspects is a double agent. I need him alive and unscathed, well, you know. I honestly believe he does not know much. My team has been slowly working him already.

"The other is a different story. He arrived in Jerusalem only a month ago, and I have reason to believe he knows who the paymaster is and what the objectives could be," said Eyal. "My problem is that both could actually be well connected. One disappearance is possible here, but both, now that's a real marker in the sand, and one I don't need right now."

"They are all scum. You know that!" she snapped back as she put a hand through her long, black hair now shining in the dim light of the vehicle's interior.

"Anniken, that may be so. We know what we *should* do," replied Eyal, with care written all over his face. "A sniper's bullet is one thing, but blood and mutilation is another." Eyal had called in his ace card and she knew it. When her friend and mentor called her by her full name, she knew she had to take his request seriously.

Anniken turned her head away to stare through the window and considered her options. She needed Eyal's help, but she also wanted blood.

They arrived at Mossad's main interrogation centre a few minutes later. It was well guarded, but soon, after the usual security checks, Eyal and Anniken were looking at two men. They were sitting in chairs ten feet apart, in a room devoid of any other furniture. They were blindfolded and handcuffed. The room was filled with white noise. A hiss of radio psychobabble designed to disorientate those unlucky enough to have to listen.

Eyal looked at her and she could tell it was his serious face. He spoke into her ear above the noise of the radio. "Annie, please remember these men are not expendable and while I need control of their destinies, I also need them with two legs and two arms, and able to see straight when you're done."

She nodded, and with a wave of her hand had the noise turned off.

In the silence the anxious breathing of the two men could be heard. The deafening quiet was an environment ripe for the business of interrogation.

Anniken spoke, "You do not know me. You will never know me. You will never see me. But be sure of one thing

– you will tell me what I want to know, or you will die badly without a trace.

"You have an accomplice here in TA. Someone who sent you to Gibraltar. I know his name, but I want to know who you met there. Give me a name. What happened there? I will give you one minute to consider. If you answer well, you might not feel pain. If not, you will suffer," she said to both men, who were clearly recovering their senses from a sustained period of psychological hurt.

"Why are we here?" asked the first man. Eyal had identified him as likely knowing little. "I have diplomatic immunity," he went on. The second man shouted something in Russian to the first and he stopped communicating.

"It's been revoked," snarled Anniken as she took out a small pair of sharpened pliers from a bag and brought them to bear on the man's left earlobe and squeezed. He screamed in pain. His chest heaving for breath. She remarked, "It's incredible what pain can be delivered with such simple effectiveness and yet leave only a small mark. Although this may not be so for the testicles." She laughed in such a manner that even Eyal watching through the smoked glass shuddered.

Neither man uttered a word, but the atmosphere in the room had changed. As the pliers found the first man's other earlobe, she started again. The pressure, while not being excessive, was very effective. Anniken waited a few seconds for a reaction. Then, not happy with her result, she produced a hypodermic needle of some width and rammed it in the man's thigh.

More screams filled the room, but Anniken was unmoved. "Needles: they hurt, but they are hygienic – they will hurt like hell down the end of your pathetic cocks." Another stab or two. "I am getting bored … I am going to count to ten and then one of you loses a finger and then an eye. Choose swiftly!" she shouted at both men. Eyal shifted his position to intervene. A lost finger meant hospital and questions. He saw Anniken take out some garden secateurs from the bag.

She reached for the left hand of the man, who Eyal suspected of knowing nothing, and when cold metal touched his warm skin, he suddenly spoke out.

"I only met him once."

"Who?" she quickly replied.

"The controller."

"Shut up, you idiot," gasped the other man. "Shut up and take it!"

Anniken walked the short distance to the second bound man and struck him across the face, almost knocking him over on the chair.

Walking back towards the first man, she spoke, "But you do know him? You both know him because you were there, in Gibraltar. You may not have pulled the trigger, but you were there, so don't lie to me!"

"He never told me. I just drove the car," said the first man.

"I just need a name," she said as she removed the top two centimetres of his little finger. As he screamed in pain, blood poured out of the wound and down over his clothing onto the floor. Eyal was worried and thought about stopping the developing mayhem but waited, hoping she would respect his requests. He also knew that what he was watching was just Anniken.

"You will tell me, or I go again," she said. Then, releasing the first man's injured hand, she turned her attention to the second.

"What about you? You seem keen to keep your friend here quiet," she said as she walked back over to him, wiggling the pliers in cold amusement. She released his left hand from the restraints and held it up and tight so he could feel the uncomfortable bend of his arm. Then, tightening the tool on his finger, she could see his eyes bulge through the blindfold as froth started to come from his mouth.

"We cannot say, bitch. If we do we will be dead anyway," he groaned.

Anniken tightened the pliers and she felt the skin give way to the metal. With a flick of the wrist she cut off the top of the man's trigger finger about half way down. It took a little more effort as the bone proved thicker than the first man's. As he screamed in agony, she flicked the bleeding digit into the corner of the room.

"Well, you can talk now, or it's a finger from you both every minute, or perhaps I should get to work on a more tender area?" she responded above the agonised whimpering of the two men. They were in shock. She knew she had to work faster.

The second man murmured under his breath. "Afram Barak. It was Afram Barak," he said, almost in a whisper.

Anniken nodded towards the glass window and packed away her equipment. She now knew where to go and who the target was. "You are lucky that I am in a charitable mood," she said, moving to the door. Then, as Eyal was watching, he saw her stop, as if in thought, and return to the second man. He froze and watched on.

Leaning down close to his ear, she spoke directly at him, "No more killing my friends, you fuck," and with that, she turned and walked out the door.

As she slammed the door behind her, she found herself

looking straight at Eyal.

"Annie, just tell me when and I will give them the order. It's over for him now, you know that. I can have him ended. We can do this," he said to her, looking exasperated. She checked her watch. He knew, however, she would want the kill herself.

He thought for a minute then continued, "Look, I want to send Abarron in with you. He's a good man, perhaps the best. You should have someone go in with you, Annie," said Eyal, waiting for her reply.

"Ah, my lovely Eyal. You will not stop looking after me like a father, will you?" she replied, kissing his hand and smiling before walking to the door. Abarron looked on disappointed. He had heard of Anniken and her reputation. She did not need him with her.

Without turning around she followed up with, "Please don't give too many orders, my friend, for I go in alone, and for Harry. Just take out the sentries."

———◆◆◆◆◆———

Around an hour later, four sentries lay dead where they fell and a lone figure scaled the first perimeter wall and ran quietly forward towards the first outbuilding. She, too, came under the crosshairs of a sniper rifle, but there was no pressure on the trigger. This time, it was a colleague watching and wishing her a safe return.

———◆◆◆◆◆———

Thousands of miles away across the water, Selkirk sat alone. The hairs on his neck rose as his sixth sense went into overdrive. This bothered him, but he couldn't determine what was happening, why he felt the way he did. It was as if he was with her, guessing her next move, watching her in his mind's eye, bursting into a building and shooting the guard inside twice, before moving on to the target. But, of course, he wasn't there, but he was sure that she was in play and that meant danger for anybody who got in her way. He sat motionless, trying to read the game, trying to second guess. He wanted Anniken back, but he thought about the rest of his team and found comfort in their progress to date.

———————————

Afram Barak had amassed a small fortune after retiring from the PLO. A career civil servant with a massive network of contacts stretching into both Palestine and the Kremlin, he was known to have illegal financial dealings but had kept his head down and out of the business of the current power brokers. But like all men who long for power, he had been seduced by an offer of greater glory. All he had to do was guard a shipment in Gibraltar and kill and dispose of anybody who got in his way. He had been successful, and although things had turned sour for the Russians, this was not deemed his fault. They had killed a British operative – so what? He got his money.

When Afram Barak heard the door burst open and the noise of the first shots, he knew someone had come for him. What he didn't know was that it was just one woman, and, one out for revenge. He held his son, Yahal, close and hid his pistol behind his back.

When the door flew open, Anniken had guns in both hands and immediately discharged them, shattering most of Barak's left ear and right shoulder. Splinters of bone smashed into the boy's face and his cheek started to bleed profusely. Barak shuddered with the impact and was temporarily unable to focus on the gun he held.

"Better treat that quickly," she said, looking straight at Barak's eyes. "Allah may not be so merciful."

"Don't hurt my son. He is innocent of any crime," he pleaded. Then, almost immediately finding his resolve, he changed his tone. "I knew you would come for me one day, you Jewish bitch. I spit on you and all Yiddish scum."

"And Harrison, the man you casually killed in Gibraltar, he was someone's son, was he not?"

"This is about him? Is that all?" he said as he stood up, temporarily ignoring his bleeding and cowering son beneath him. "You came for me because of him? It could have been any one of you fools, any one. It was just a sign, and he was in the wrong place at the wrong fuckin' time, you stupid bitch." Barak became more and more agitated despite the odds stacked against him. "What would you have done in my place?" he questioned, not really expecting a reply.

"Who are you working for? Who are they and what are they doing? Tell me quickly and the boy will be treated in hospital." She gestured towards the son who was quickly showing signs of shock. "You're fuckin' dead, no matter, but he still has a chance. What's it to be, Afram?"

"They are nobody. They are everybody," he replied. "I was asked to send a message to Selkirk's commander, that's all. I never met them. I just know they are Russian. That's all, I swear."

"Not good enough," she turned one gun back towards the son.

"Leave him, I beg you," his voice now more conciliatory.

"Talk now," she shouted as her gun went back and forth between the pair. "Shall we go through this all over again?"

He remained silent.

"I guess negotiating with you is not an option," and as quick as she finished the sentence she pressed the gun into his chest, hard.

Something clicked in Anniken. An unfamiliar sense of insight came over her. Could they use him? Was he of more use alive? Would he just sell them out? Perhaps not while they had his son. Her instincts were contradicted. Then she imagined the reaction of her team when she dragged the baggage of Barak into the fray. Blood rushed to her head. Her anger returned.

Anniken forced him to turn around and get down onto his knees. His face was pressed hard against the wall and her gun was pushed against the back of his head.

"Do you want to see your son again?" she asked, looking back over towards the boy, who had collapsed, immobile.

"Yes, of course," he replied in a muffled manner; it was hard for him to breathe and speak, face hard against the cold wall.

"You will work for me now. If you refuse, you die here where you kneel, and the boy will disappear forever," she said in a demanding and instructive tone. "While you work for us, we will look after your son and you will feed us information."

The seconds clicked slowly by in silence. Anniken's finger twitched on the trigger of her pistol.

"OK, I agree," he said, unable to handle much more pain.

"Remember, wherever you go, you will be watched. You cannot hide – you will not even be able to go for a shit without us knowing. If you do what we say and get us the right information, you may keep your life."

"Get the boy to hospital, now I have agreed to your demands," he pleaded.

"I give the commands here!" she barked back. "One last thing, tell me quickly and he gets help sooner. What is their end game?"

"All I know is that they talked about the Adriatic water; that's it."

"You mean the Ionian Sea and Santorini, don't you?"

"Yes, both, well, perhaps the Ionian, now please, get him out of here."

Anniken released the pressure on Barak's face, and he immediately slumped down before crawling over to his injured son.

"My friends, the cleaners, will be in soon." This was an affectionate term for the teams that removed any trace of confrontation, blood or dead bodies. The dead guards outside were already gone, of course. Anniken left the room and walked out in the direction of her trusted friend Eyal.

———◆◆×◆◆———

Eyal and Anniken sat in a café near the monument to holocaust victims. The smell of coffee was more appealing than the stink of sweat and blood a short while back. Anniken was clearly keen to get back to the team to give them the news, but felt obliged to update Eyal on what she knew.

"I am deeply concerned, Annie," he began. "From what you have told me, this is potentially a catastrophic move by Kharkov and his mobsters," said Eyal.

"That said, there is much detail missing," Anniken pondered. "We now know that someone in the British establishment is pulling out all the stops to keep it under wraps and prevent any intervention that might stop it, and stop us, my friend."

"I know you have no time now, but can I help?" asked Eyal.

"Follow Barak for me. He works for you now. He knows we need information and I want you to push the buttons to make him get it. His son goes into isolation somewhere for summer school. It's the best lever we have because we need intelligence, which, at the moment, we don't have. I must catch my plane now. I will miss you, my friend," she said in an affectionate voice, and, with a hug, she turned and walked towards the waiting car. Then, just before closing the car door, Anniken looked back at Eyal. Her eyes gave away her pending words.

"If you get nothing of value from him in a week, you have my permission to do Barak. Harrison would likewise approve," she said as the car door closed.

Anniken arrived at the airport with minutes to spare before her flight. She felt liberated from the hate and anger she had bottled up. Instead, her emotions had been channeled into something meaningful.

When his mobile acknowledged receipt of a text, both Selkirk and Dekker looked down at it. He lifted the screen to allow Dekker to see the name of the sender.

The message read: 'Sorry, Tom, needed to be done. Am not staying here, Tel Aviv in the summer's an oven. Heading to Santorini now, love to the team ;-)', and was simply signed off 'A'.

Chapter 8

Return to Atlantis

The tailgate started to open, signalling to the two men on the runway to move forward towards the plane. Inside, Biddiss had already sorted the gear and radioed ahead to the base for transportation. De Boer slapped his colleague on the shoulder as he moved off and out.

"Who has Tom got us?" he said as the sun and heat hit his face, temporarily blinding him.

"I don't care, mate, as long as it's not the Italian. Can't stand that fuzz ball after the Afghan fiasco," Biddiss replied without looking, instead picking up the gear and acknowledging his thanks to the two pilots who were now out of the cockpit and standing watching.

De Boer was now out onto the runway, with Isabelle following quietly behind, and, as his two new colleagues walked closer to him, silhouetted against the sun, he couldn't help but recognise the tall, wiry frame of what could only be the Italian in question.

"Don't get angry, Bidd," De Boer shouted back, a smile appearing on his face.

"You're kidding me, Hog; you better be," but as he turned and walked down the ramp out into the sunlight, he, too, could see the walking frame of Lamberti. Biddiss didn't know the other man with Lamberti but De Boer seemed to, so that reassured him somewhat.

De Boer had greeted both men and was in conversation

with the unknown man when Biddiss reached them.

"Hey, Bidd, it's been a while, no?" were Lamberti's opening words.

"Lamberti," came the reply as he turned his attention to his unknown teammate.

"Who we got with us, Hog?" he asked, turning his back on Lamberti and offering his hand to his new colleague.

"Bidd, this is Peterson, Mike Peterson, formerly Boat Service, now one of us; Mike, this is Biddiss, he's an angry man but sometimes comes in handy."

With introductions done, De Boer gestured that they move towards the awaiting jeep.

Biddiss dropped a bag at the feet of Lamberti and walked off towards the vehicle. Picking it up with a smile, Lamberti shouted, "This how it's going to be, mate?"

"I'm not your mate, remember that. We have been assigned together, that's all," Biddiss barked back at him.

Lamberti smiled to himself and duly picked up the bag and followed on.

Putting an arm around Peterson, De Boer started to explain to his colleague about the Afghan incident that almost resulted in Biddiss being left at the evac point and the mercy of the advancing Taliban; and how Lamberti had failed to see in the dust storm that he was not actually on the heli. The downdraft from the rotors had blinded everyone as it lifted up and slowly away. Biddiss was forced to leave his gear and jump up and in to the ascending helicopter.

They got into the awaiting jeep and it moved off in the direction of the small Greek military base out on the clifftop vantage point of the 'sunset town' of Thira. All the time, Isabelle had stood with the others and had moved as they did, none of the four had spoken to her or acknowledged her presence. She had not been introduced. She felt very alone once again.

——•◦×◦•——

A few hundred miles further west, on Gibraltar, Selkirk received the call from De Boer, which he left unanswered, assuming it was a routine 'arrived and setting up' check-in. Instead, he concentrated on his task and the discovery of the suspected nuclear bomb somewhere under the water of this tiny piece of Britain. For now, this was all that mattered to him.

Nathen had been instructed to find the most likely locations based upon typical fault lines around the Rock, with the caveat that the Russians had no deep-water drilling equipment, so they must have found some point fairly close to the outcrop's shoreline. He was given a free hand to move around as he pleased, but was under no illusions that he must find dive-target locations. Still distracted and saddened by the news of his missing father, his imagination and focus wandered easily.

Neeman nodded to Selkirk and returned to the hotel where the cargo-ship crew were being held. He would retest them for traces of radioactive material. He would also interrogate them once more to ensure nothing had been missed. It was difficult to believe that none knew who the additional crew sailors were, or why they had been on board.

Already out on the water patrolling the Rock, Kirk had control of HMS *Sabre* while the harbour master's team worked the second boat, *Scimitar*. Their diving gear on board, they patrolled the waters searching for signs of recent activity, all the time waiting on Nathen to get back to them with specific dive locations.

The waters around the shoreline were shallow enough in parts, allowing them to see the sea floor, although they would rely much more on the boat's multibeam sonar to search for the likely uniform shape of the weapon. They would be distracted on occasions by the numerous shipwrecks that littered the outcrop.

Back at the barracks, the major was talking on the phone when Nathen rushed in to his office, uninvited, displaying civilian ignorance for military procedure or authority, and started to talk at him.

"I have two locations; not one, but two," came from his mouth before a self-gratifying smile appeared.

The major frowned at the interruption, spoke quietly to the recipient on the end of the line and put the phone down.

"Better if it was only one location, no?" he replied. "So we know exactly where it is. Now we have to split resources."

Upon hearing the major's obvious logic, Nathen immediately felt less triumphant.

"Yes, sir, I guess you're right. I hadn't thought of it that way."

"Right, boy, come here and show me what you have found." Standing up behind his desk, the major cleared the paperwork in anticipation of the map waving in Nathen's hand.

For the next thirty minutes the two men claimed and counter-claimed the findings until, unable to challenge any further, the major thanked Nathen and suggested he find something warm to wear. "You're going to spend a long time out on the water. So go to the stores and ask for wet-weather gear. Tell Davies I have sent you."

For a moment, Nathen looked surprised. He had not anticipated direct involvement after finding possible locations.

The major left his office at the same time and, locking the door behind him, pointed in the rough direction of the stores before heading in the opposite way towards where he expected to find Selkirk. The two men met briefly and then Selkirk went off to brief his team.

"Neems, get Deks and wrap up, we are likely going swimming," came Selkirk's first order after his short meeting with the major.

"Meet me by the dispatch vehicle in ten," was the second blunt instruction. "Call the others, will you, and get the boats back to shore, pronto, and briefed," was the final one.

Neeman nodded and headed off, reaching inside his coat for his mobile to make the two pending calls to the patrol boats.

Selkirk would also be busy on his phone. Firstly, an update to the admiral followed by a call to De Boer in Santorini, bringing him up to date with the Gibraltar operation and encouraging him to focus the search on depths along specific fault lines.

———◆◆◆◆———

Santorini would prove to be a more complex issue regarding tectonics. With the still-active volcano dominating the horizon and the crossing of numerous tension points on the sea floor, the team would need both Isabelle's expertise and a good dose of luck if they were to get their solid lead and discover what they believed to be a second nuclear device.

De Boer had called a briefing for later in the day, but until then the team on Santorini would check their gear and fuel up for a long first stint, and likely longer night dive, where they would not be harassed by the coming and going of day-trip tourist boats.

Isabelle was last to arrive at the briefing point, due to being escorted into the secure area, so when she did arrive, the others were already deep in conversation. She looked to De Boer for instruction but instead heard the passive and somewhat supportive tones of Biddiss first, "Isabelle, have you eaten well?"

"Em, yes, sir, thank you," she replied.

"Cool, but call me Bidd; you're part of this team now and don't let anyone here say otherwise. So anyway, sit next to me," he said as he pulled out the chair.

She sat and, now a little more relaxed, waited for her moment to talk.

They told her what she needed to know and followed this with what they expected from her.

"You will be provided with all the support you need, Isabelle. Maps, equipment, just tell us and you have it," Peterson claimed without confirming firstly with De Boer, who had been assigned temporary leadership of the Santorini island operation.

"Thank you, erm, what do I call you, sir?" she asked. "You can call me Izzy if you like," she said, now trying to act like part of the team.

"Isabelle, you can call me Petes, as the others do. And he's Bert," looking over to Lamberti, "I think you know the others." She was comforted, but also confused as to why he would bring her into their fold but continue to use her full name when a friendlier option had been offered.

—————◆◆✕◆◆—————

As this new team talked through the intelligence and data, which would assist them to assign actions, others were also planning, hiding in plain sight and moored up on the tiny uninhabited sub-island of Aspronisi, a short way from the volcano inside the Santorini caldera. This location had been chosen for its proximity and closeness to the fast-moving passenger shipping lane and the distraction it would cause.

The boat had been prepared for public view, with most of the upper-deck stealth-panels removed, exposing a more standard and less futuristic structure underneath. They were also much less worried about whose passing communications they blocked and whose were allowed to pick up on their presence. It was a calculated risk, but one that would attract the least attention.

The crew, recently enlarged by a second Spetsnaz unit from the Gibraltar incident, would soon challenge Selkirk's team to find them. For now, however, De Boer would concentrate his search on possible locations for a nuclear device and leave the enemy confrontation until later. All the time, he knew that the enemy would likely come and find them at some point.

———◆◆※◆◆———

Isabelle was excused and told she should grab some food and get some sleep – she was going to be crucial in the assignment-setting and location-finding in a matter of hours. Against everything that they were trained up for, the team knew they would rely heavily on this civilian, who stood, as instructed, and walked towards the door, not really knowing what else to do.

"Isabelle, I need some air, let me walk you to the canteen," Lamberti stood, looked over to De Boer and then moved out of the room. He wanted to ask her all about the Bouvet incident. Several minutes passed. The others remained deep in conversation. Lamberti returned and walked over to the table to pour himself a coffee.

He poured two before walking back to the others, who continued their conversation without looking up.

"White, no sugar, as I remember," he said as he placed the second coffee next to Biddiss and sat down. This didn't go unnoticed by the others around the table. They knew there was tension between them, but the task was more important at this time.

"I told her to come back here in four hours, Hog. So for now, what did I miss?" he said, looking at the other three.

For the next short while the four men familiarised themselves with the unique land mass that was Santorini, positively ignoring the structures under the water, waiting for Isabelle's return. They studied the towns and populations and considered non-commercial mooring sites for vessels.

They ran through several options for action and hypothetical planning responses, and drew up a provisional timeline. The atmosphere became much more relaxed as they swapped coffee for brandy, delivered from the bar, and enjoyed a moment of downtime together.

It came as a little surprise for the men when the door opened after only two hours and Isabelle returned with rolled-up maps in hand.

"Right, you lot, I wandered up to the Centre for Volcanic Studies and called in a favour from a retired professor who's now living on the island," Isabelle began. "I have reread his study for engineering cavities together with the current seabed mapping and dynamic thermal electrodynamics and may have this narrowed down to only a few places," she beamed as she spoke.

Silence. They stared blankly.

"Right, OK, as none of you even knew what language

I have just spoken, I will continue, unless there are objections?"

Smiling and moving coffee cups and cigarette papers away, together with a holstered pistol – her first ever encounter with a weapon – Isabelle made space for two maps of the island, knowing all the time there would be no objection to her actions.

De Boer leaned back in his chair and, crossing his hands behind his head, gave the appearance of a proud father on a school sports day as he watched her prep. Biddiss stood and walked round so the maps were the right way up for him, while Peterson and Lamberti adjusted their chairs for the same reason.

The first map, the larger of the two, was titled Marine Topographic Sediment Flow, while the smaller second one was introduced by Isabelle as a cartography contour resistance map.

"So, gentlemen, the big map's all about mud, and this one is where it goes and where the sea hills are, OK?" she began, dominating the conversation, not expecting interruption.

"In other words, sediment shift and direction, and where the flows come from through the seabed, together with what landscape they will encounter under the water," she said, now waiting for one of them to speak up.

De Boer rocked his chair back down onto all four legs, signalling to the others that he was indeed about to talk.

"So, I know you know why you're here, Isabelle, but can you tell me what the two maps together mean to us? I guess you need to combine the two somehow … for your findings?" he asked.

"Together they show where the weakest and shallowest areas of the Hellenic Trench are around the island and where it would be easiest to work."

"Brilliant," perked up the now refocused Biddiss, "and the penned circles, what do they represent?"

"That, gentlemen are the only places where you will find your bomb!" she replied emphatically.

For a moment, all five stared at the map on display and no one spoke.

The silence was finally broken by Isabelle again. "This time I am going to get some sleep if you don't mind," and gathering up her rucksack, leaving the maps for their deliberation, she walked to the door. Stopping, she turned a little. Expecting some further revelation, De Boer lifted his hand towards Lamberti, who was about to speak.

"Oh, and I recommend the local steak here." She left the room unchallenged.

The something the team had been waiting for had just happened. They had their first real break and could now focus on the task at hand. Allocating their time and actions was just made much easier.

———◆◆◆◆———

Back on Gibraltar, Selkirk heard of Isabelle's contribution to the Santorini planning and nodded to himself in admiration. Whether he meant to or not, he spoke out loud, "Knew she was worth the effort. Pretty girl, also." Kirk looked up at him and wondered to what the comment related, but then returned to his gear and his own business.

De Boer and Selkirk had spoken many times on the phone that day and had agreed that additional support would be needed by the team in the deeper and darker waters of the Santorini caldera, compared to the waters around Gibraltar, where Selkirk's dive team were operating.

"Mate, if we're under the water over here looking for this

bomb thing, our bollocks are out there and exposed to the Russians," came through Selkirk's phone.

"Can you get us some backup?" De Boer asked.

"What you need, Hog?"

"I would love a Greek patrol boat to watch over us as we're under. No, wait, two would be better. And so I get some sleep, can you get the admiral to fly a satellite over the island to look in detail for the stealth boat?"

"That's not going to happen, you know this. We have to be under the radar and not in the Greeks' face. And as for the sat, never going to happen, again. The Yanks have given up and sent it back to Syria and the undersecretary won't facilitate more spending by the admiral."

Carrying on, Selkirk knew he had to give De Boer something to hang on to.

"What if I get a Sentinel to spend its holidays over Santorini?" he asked.

"Can it find a Russian ship and bad mothers waiting to surprise us?"

"Well, it's more likely to do so than you with binoculars," said Selkirk.

"OK, Tom, I will let the others know we have eyes in the sky but not exactly what, cheers. How's your side in Gib?"

"Good, mate, all good. I need to go, let's chat later," and without waiting for De Boer's reply, Selkirk hung up on the call. He had missed a call from the admiral back in London and was keen to speak with him.

When the call was answered he dispensed with pleasantries. "We have two probable locations in Gib, Admiral, and to date, seven over in Santorini, sir."

"I need an RAF Sentinel out of Cyprus to cover the team in Greece as they are way too exposed and going into this blind. If we can also get the Spanish ambassador to agree an evac schedule here in Gib if things don't go to plan, then that would be Christmas all at once, Admiral." Selkirk waited for the disappointment.

"The secretary's playing hardball and still pissed off about the earlier sat rerouting. So there's no way he's going to allow me to divert a Sentinel from our specials entrenched behind the lines in Syria to cover your swim team," he replied.

Anticipating this, Selkirk was ready.

"Don't tell him, sir. You know he's got an agenda on us, or he's in someone's pocket. Just don't tell him. The lads in Cyprus and dug deep in Syria will understand."

There was an unusually long pause. The admiral always knew how Tom thought, but even he was silenced by this most demanding of requests.

"Do you really need 'eyes on' Tom?" he asked in a challenging voice.

"Yes, sir, we do."

A further few seconds passed, "Let me see what I can do." This was often the admiral's way of accepting the request.

<hr>

Over in Gibraltar it was dark when the motor launch made its final docking for the night. Nathen had spent many hours in the cold, on the water, and wished he was back in the hotel bar in the warmth. He felt confident that he would be allowed a visit to the bar followed by bed for real sleep. He had worked well with his dive colleagues and they clearly trusted his judgement. Together they had shared conversations, and even a few stories, during the rest periods on board *Sabre*.

Out on the water he had no signal on his phone and only when he reached the harbour did it come back to life with a number of missed calls from his mother. They could wait for now. He was starting to enjoy himself and live the exciting life that all men of his age longed for. He certainly didn't want to spoil that with home chat in front of his soldier colleagues.

The others thanked him for his help on board and waved him off to the hotel. They had work to do at the harbour and would not take up his offer of a drink at the bar. Nathen walked towards the taxi rank.

A short while later, and now suitably warmed, Nathen went up to the hotel bar and stood, awaiting service. Seconds later, a smartly uniformed man wearing white gloves walked up to him and, looking down at his jeans in a disapproving manner, encouraged him to sit in the corner table and wait for service. Nathen did as instructed and sat next to the wall covered with photographs, many of which seemed to be signed. He read some of the names, but they meant nothing to him.

He was a little surprised when he felt a hand on his shoulder. "Expecting someone special, or can I join you?"

Selkirk pulled out a chair and sat down at his table.

"Of course, erm, yes, please. What do I actually call you, Mr Selkirk, because I have only seen you and never really spoken to you?"

"Well, if you're unfriendly you can call me Mr Selkirk. Otherwise, Tom will do," Selkirk replied in a friendly tone.

Looking out over the balcony and across the water, he caught the eye of the waiter, and within seconds he was over to their table, his attitude more humble now he realised the jeaned youngster was with Selkirk.

"How are we tonight, sir? Do you want what you have ordered before sir, gin, Indian I believe, with a twist?" Selkirk nodded. "And sir?" looking at Nathen.

"May I have a beer, please?" but directed his glance at Selkirk as if to ask for permission.

"Yes, sir, of course, sir."

Selkirk turned to the picture wall.

He stared at one photograph. Nathen could see a group of soldiers in a pose around a Land Rover. They appeared to be worse for wear, but smiling all the same. "Do you know them, Tom?" The first 'Tom' was always going to be the hardest, but when he received a comfortable reply, he relaxed.

"I know them all, Nathen. I mean, I *knew* them all. Now, it's just me," he said.

Not really comprehending what he had just heard, Nathen asked, "Which one's you?"

"The only one left alive," was the surprising reply. "You know, Nathen, the life of a special operator is not all glam. Actually, there is very little glam at all. Even we get it wrong sometimes," Selkirk concluded. "I remember a time when my team of three were to breach a rear exit of the Grand hotel in Bogota and run the staff area and kitchens before ascending the fire exit steps to the top floor. We would then blow the door of the Presidential suit and do the business we were asked to against those inside."

Nathen listened. Engrossed and waiting for the verbal guns and smoke to kick off.

Instead, Selkirk relaxed his position and slumped more into his chair.

"We got to the stairwell door – Dek was with me on this op, as was Harrison – to a flat metal fire door. None of us could pick the lock and we didn't have anything to jimmy it open. We were stopped before the op even started."

"So what happened, did you leave it?" Nathen asked.

"Of course not, we simply went round to the front desk, covering our MP5s under our raincoats. It was the rainy season, but three men in long coats must still have looked strange.

"We persuaded the lady on reception to allow us an access key to the top floor by placing one gold coin in front of her; she pointed towards the lifts and in we went. Christ, I remember the three of us standing in the front of the lift with two old pensioner types behind us, guns hidden and trying to make polite small talk. The elevator music did not help. I still see the absurdity of it in my head," said Selkirk as he remembered the event. "Yes, Nathen, sometimes things go wrong for us as well," and with that, Nathen knew not to ask further.

Nathen looked at Selkirk and then back at the photograph wall. He didn't know what to say next. He decided saying nothing was best.

Selkirk broke the silence. "So, why study seabed shit at university and not do what boys do, chase the girls, my young colleague?"

The two then had a comfortable and open chat for the next hour. Only occasionally would Selkirk drift off into reflection. His face saddened with what memories he had brought back at that moment.

Nathen was left feeling more confident with his role in the team now, and the operation. Selkirk would sleep well that night after having a safe and normal conversation – his first in a very long time.

Nearly eighteen hundred miles away, as the sunset turned the Santorini water a glistering shade of red as if on fire, De Boer and his team were having a less successful first dive day.

They turned in for the night and got some much needed rest, having taken only one of Isabelle's seven locations out of the equation.

Biddiss had been asleep for only a couple of hours when he suddenly awoke.

He sat up, already knowing that he would struggle to sleep again but without knowing why.

Something was bothering him, but what that was escaped him. He dressed and headed off for a walk into the still-bustling Thira town centre. In minutes, he was walking the cobbled streets filled with tourists from the numerous liners that were moored in the harbour. Soon, the ships' horns would bellow and they would make their way back down the cliff-side walk and on board to their cabin, only to wake next morning at some new island location. For now, however, Biddiss walked amongst them and passed the restaurants that seemed to have all the same menus.

Not really knowing, or caring, where he was heading, he approached the Cathedral Church of John the Baptist. As was the way in Santorini; it was open and welcoming to all. He headed towards the open door, but as he approached it, he suddenly stopped and turned sharply around.

The street was full of people walking in all directions, but something felt wrong. The hairs on his neck rose and his hearing heightened.

His hand automatically went to his chest and the reassurance of metal usually holstered inside, but he had left his room so quickly he hadn't thought to pick his gun up this time. He scanned the immediate area for something that stood out. A bead of sweat ran down his hairline as he felt his heart beat much faster inside his chest.

Turning around and suddenly focusing on an image a little way off, there appeared to be a man standing, looking right back at him.

Everyone was moving and chatting except this man, who did neither. It was just wrong, he thought. The man, the standing still, the arms by his side, the clothing he wore … all seemed wrong.

At that very moment a group of people walked up and past him, making their way into the cathedral. His line of vision was temporarily blocked. He pushed the last man away as he refocused on the now-empty step from where, seconds earlier, someone had been watching him.

"Fuck, fuck, fuck. Come on, man," he said to himself, not caring if anyone heard him or who he forced his way past as he quickly made his way to the empty step.

Gone. Whoever he had seen had vanished.

He quickly scanned the environment and walked the only route this ghost could have taken.

Fearing he may still be under surveillance, he placed a hand on his chest where his gun should be, to say to the watcher 'I am armed', and at the first corner he stopped. A waiter approached him and interrupted his chain of thought, "You want to come in for good deal and good food, yes?"

"Quiet," Biddiss replied back tersely, with an expression that encouraged the man to go elsewhere for his trade.

Just then he heard a motorbike firing up. Nothing too unusual, but after Harrison he decided to make sure this was just coincidence. It could be his 'watcher'. Quickly running towards the direction of the sound, he saw a man ride off, quick at first, then stopping a hundred yards away. He had ridden the bike hard up the old donkey trail and quickly to a point where he felt safe enough to stop and taunt his foe.

Biddiss' vision was fixed, more so when the rider looked over his shoulder back at him. It was dark and he wore a helmet, but Biddiss was convinced he was the target of the rider's stare. Quickly as he turned to look at Biddiss, he turned back and rode off.

Biddiss had not been prepared for an encounter that night and he knew he had been lucky. He should not rely on luck again. He'd had his first sighting of the Spetsnaz from the Gibraltar ship and the others needed to know.

"No fucking sleep for me now," he muttered. This time, he noticed a woman standing nearby screw her face in clear disagreement with his choice of words.

◆◆◈◆◆

The next morning, Biddiss looked out over the sheltered waters of the Santorini caldera and sipped his coffee, wondering where his foe had slept that night. The waters were still, but he was yet more convinced than ever that the sea was hiding a stealth boat and an unknown number of Russian soldiers whom he had encountered before and who he knew were the most ruthless yet competent he had fought against.

It was not a motivating start to the day. This would become a continuing emotion for the whole team in the days ahead. He had decided not to wake the others the previous night to tell them of his encounter a few hours earlier, but would do so soon.

It was early, but Biddiss called Selkirk. Selkirk didn't seem alarmed when he heard the news of the previous night's encounter.

"Mate, it means we're in the right place," he said. "So they followed you. It's not as if they have to guess what hotel you're staying at. It's obvious that they would have a watcher around the base.

"Anyway, take it as a compliment, Bidd, that they identified you as their chaser and respected you enough not to pop you there and then," and while Biddiss couldn't see it, Selkirk was smiling down the phone at his comment.

"Yeah, right, compliment, right," Biddiss said back, unconvinced.

The conversation went back and forward for a while and Biddiss was left to update the team in Santorini on the progress on the western side of the Mediterranean and Gibraltar.

———●◆)◗◖◆●———

Selkirk's team was already at its next identified dive position, and tension rose on *Sabre* – they had eliminated the last of Nathen's identified locations, leaving only their current one. As the boat bobbed on the water, all those on board suspected that, some distance below them, there was a ticking bomb, a nuclear bomb. On this day, the game could change for good.

Selkirk had already brought the admiral up to date on events in the two locations as instructed. The admiral had been called to the office of the permanent undersecretary and was expecting a difficult hour as he tried to defend Selkirk's corner.

He entered the room and waited to be instructed to sit by his line manager, the undersecretary. "Philip, I want you to give me something good, better still, lots of it. The PM's starting to ask questions and I can't have any deniable shooting-up of sovereign territory," was the opening remark from Winchester.

"Permanent Undersecretary, I fully understand," said the admiral. "Please let me reassure you, sir. Tom Selkirk is heading up a team in Gibraltar and believes they have the location, sir – the location of the first bomb. They are diving now as we speak," pausing for breath and to gauge Winchester's reaction, he went on, interrupting the secretary exactly and deliberately as he was about to respond. "The Russian cargo ship threw up several clues and was, indeed, contaminated with radiation isotopes. We're up against a big one, sir."

Still not allowing Winchester to speak, the admiral continued to control the flow of the conversation.

"So we have one nuke identified and will aim to secure it over the next few days, while the second team has travelled to the small Greek island of Santorini, where ..."

"I know Santorini, Philip. For Christ's sake I have holidayed with my family on the bloody island! Atlantis and all that ..." barked Winchester, trying to regain control of the discussion.

Not allowing Winchester to scupper the flow, the admiral hit back.

"Very good, sir, lovely, sir, but holidays aside, can I get back to business?" Without waiting for agreement, the admiral continued.

"The second team is chipping away at the likely locations for any second bomb, and having arrived on the island recently, they are making real progress. They may have troublesome tails lurking on the island, however."

Now, in a more controlled manner and slightly inquisitive tone, Winchester asked the question both Selkirk and the admiral had been waiting for. This very same question would subtly confirm to both that the permanent undersecretary was indeed working for two paymasters at the same time.

"So, Phillip, what of these Russians? Where are we with them? You said something about there being two units, six Spetsnaz on board the stealth ship, I believe?"

"Russians, sir? Spetsnaz? What do you mean 'six operators', Secretary? We don't yet know exactly who or how many we are facing," the admiral said quickly, while trying not to give away his glee at watching Winchester fall into the trap.

"Perhaps you know something we don't that can help my teams, sir?"

"Oh, sorry, Philip, but didn't you brief me earlier about six Russian soldiers, or am I getting confused with the cargo ship on Gibraltar or something else?" was his ruffled response.

"Of course you are, Secretary, you must be thinking of some other operation." The admiral stared directly at Winchester.

Both men sat in silence for a few seconds until Winchester stood up abruptly. "Right, good work, Philip. Pass my support on to Selkirk. Carry on," were the last words said as he directed the admiral out.

The difficult meeting had, in fact, become a very valuable one. In due course, Selkirk would be given the confirmation that Winchester was likely in with the Russians, but for now, believing him to be busy under the Gibraltar waters, the admiral kept it to himself.

When Selkirk did finally hear of the admiral's meeting with Winchester, both men agreed it was time for him to join the others in Santorini. Dekker would stay and lead the Gibraltar team, which was likely to be successful any time soon. Santorini would probably become a major focus point, and Selkirk wanted to be there with his second team. He would leave early next morning.

With the Russians on Santorini and clearly aware of the search team's presence, Selkirk felt he needed to support them more. The admiral agreed and promised he would call Dekker on Gibraltar regularly for updates, and also to provide him support from Whitehall.

Selkirk would arrive on the tiny Greek island the next morning by hitching a lift on a Royal Navy vessel en route to Cyprus. It would take Selkirk and some acquired excavation equipment to Santorini before heading onwards to its planned destination. Only De Boer on Santorini had been notified of Selkirk's pending arrival so the wider team would not get distracted.

◆◈◆

None of De Boer's team would see the setting sun's fire dance on the caldera's water that night. The only inhabited caldera of enclosed volcanic water was deemed a safe place for its residents despite the still-active volcanic centrepiece. However, on this day, with Russians out to inflict massive damage, the island had become a dangerous place to reside.

They all refuelled from a second and more tiresome day under the Aegean water. They had eliminated three further locations, and only three more potential targets remained.

The team felt positive but fatigued.

Biddiss and Peterson agreed to meet at the bar inside the

Officers' Mess and share stories over beers. Lamberti and De Boer decided on a walk to the restaurant just outside the confines of the base, and both would carry pistols this time after the experience of the night before with the Russians. Isabelle agreed she would stay inside the base and turn in early after calling her mother and Nathen. De Boer insisted that if her plans changed, she must contact him first.

It wasn't long before Isabelle did indeed decide to do something else.

She left the safety of the base to explore the main town of this famous volcanic island. Isabelle had texted De Boer her intentions, unaware that Biddiss had had the confrontation the previous night.

He had requested that she always inform him of her whereabouts when she left her room and, believing that she had done so, she walked past the sentries at the gate and out into the hustle and bustle of Thira, as Biddiss had done the night before.

When De Boer came out of the shower, he immediately noticed the flash from his mobile on the table signalling that he had been contacted. He picked it up and opened the text.

It read 'Off into town. Won't be long. Just checking in as you asked me. Isabelle'. It had been delivered six minutes earlier.

"You stupid girl, you stupid, stupid girl," he said through clenched teeth as he searched for his clothing thrown in a pile in the corner.

Thumping violently on the wall, he tried to get dressed; his door was forced open. "Trouble, Hog?" said Lamberti, gun in hand.

"She's left the base and gone into town."

Not waiting for further words, Lamberti turned and left

De Boer's room as fast as he had entered, door still open and the inhabitant still naked inside.

As Lamberti ran across the yard and out towards the gate, he shouted to Peterson, who he knew was close by.

Minutes later, both men were walking the parallel streets of Thira, armed and expecting a firefight while also searching for a woman likely looking in shop windows or drinking wine in a bar.

They peered into each and every bar as they passed them and ran up and back down the adjoining streets and stairs, still hoping that Isabelle was close.

De Boer called her mobile twice and each time it diverted straight to voicemail. Not wanting to reveal their connection should she already be captured by the Russians, he left no message.

At the best of times Thira is a maze of narrow, poorly-lit cobbled streets, but at night it is much worse. With several cruise liners docked close by, the streets become awash with tourists all looking for that volcanic memento, or some Minoan gold jewellery.

Both men walked fast down and along the narrow streets, looking into every shop and bar that they passed, making snap decisions as to whether or not to go in and investigate further. On this night, the tourists would not find the two men courteous or patient but rapid and forceful when they needed to move in a specific direction.

Isabelle hadn't been told about the previous night's encounter, but her time spent with the team did have its educating benefits. She was much more conscious of her surroundings. This was to prove life-preserving when the first man entered her eye line. He was dressed oddly. Even she could tell that he didn't fit in with the group of American tourists marching at pace behind the guide holding up a flag for the group to follow.

Instinct took over and she turned sharply into a noisy and busy bar, striding straight through and out the other side onto a parallel street. She didn't know if he had seen her do it, but as her heart pounded faster, she turned back up the hill and towards the base that she decided she was foolish to have left.

Her body was full of adrenalin and this told her to run as best she could up and along the ancient cobbled streets. Reaching a small, open square, she momentarily stopped to get her bearings. Then, looking back and down from where she had come, she could see the strange man dressed in black amongst all the other heads.

Reassured that, for now, he was not behind her, she looked around the square. It seemed to be just tourists and locals, until suddenly a small gathering of them moved on as instructed by their guide, revealing a second man, one not aligned to any sightseeing group, on his mobile. This second man was also out of character to the place, and as she decided to move on, he turned towards her, still talking to someone on his phone. For a split second they gazed at each other. Then, instantly, he seemed to talk more urgently into his phone as she turned towards the road back to the base and safety.

Now convinced that she had two men after her, she started to panic much more and her emotions flew into overdrive. As she ran, tears of anxiety streamed down her face. Then, as she came to a sharp bend, she was grabbed hard and firm and thrust towards the wall. A second hand was put over her mouth and she was turned to see her captor.

"Isabelle, don't talk." It was Peterson, and he too had

seen the second stranger, making much the same deduction about him as she had done.

He released her and a hand went into his jacket, clasping the weapon concealed inside.

Lamberti entered the square, as yet unaware that Peterson had temporarily retrieved their target.

"There are two of them," she barked, out of breath and in a panic.

"Two? Where's the other?" he asked.

"I think coming up from there," and she pointed towards the street from where she'd entered the square.

Deciding it best to join up with the searching Lamberti, he grabbed her hand and moved out into the square, into visibility and towards his colleague.

As they stepped back into the square, he saw both his colleague and one of the two men who had pursued Isabelle. Peterson pointed towards the stranger, and Lamberti turned and saw him. Now all together, the man dressed in black stood motionless, just watching the three. Occasionally, the direct line of sight would be interrupted by people walking past.

The second man joined his friend and, for one surreal moment, all five simply stared at each other.

Whether it was the certainty of the death of innocents or indeed the appearance of Peterson and Lamberti themselves that made the men turn and disappear back into the mass of crowds, Peterson could not be sure, but he was relieved that a firefight had not kicked off.

They, too, turned, senses still heightened, and fast walked back to the base with Isabelle.

─●◆●◆●●─

Selkirk called his team together early next morning and was keen to tie up loose ends and avoid any repeat of ill-discipline. He met them away from prying eyes and ears, out near the caldera edge but still inside the protective fencing of the Santorini military base. After reading the riot act to Anniken in front of the others for her private and risky trip to Israel, he brought the emotion back down to a professional level and did what Selkirk did best, lead.

After only a short while, they had their assignments and were walking back away from the cliff edge, and a three hundred metre drop, towards the accommodation block. The sun was now rising fast over the still water, the heat from it more evident on the slightly tanned group of faces.

Selkirk had stayed a little way behind them to call the admiral in private.

"Good work on the undersecretary, sir," he opened the conversation.

"Yes, Tom, it's as we suspected. We can't trust him, but we do need to work with him," was the admiral's response. "So where are we now?" he added.

"I am confident Deks will get a sighting today, or latest by end of tomorrow, so if you could keep in touch with him, sir, that would help me," replied Selkirk.

"Yes, of course. Are you diving?"

"We will all be at some point, yes, but we also need to be aware of our Russian visitors, sir," he said back to the admiral.

"Right, Tom, I get it, best not to ask, then. OK, so where are we with the search of the island waters?"

"We're down to three locations now, and I hope to reduce that further today. But these caldera waters are not like Gib waters, sir. Here the seabed falls sharply and the underwater currents are strong. Then there are the bloody tourist boats. We can't sanction the area like we have in Gib," he explained.

"Very well, I will stay on top of Dekker to allow you breathing space. Remember, Tom, and I mean this, what happened before is over. You have my full support and you won't be, well, you know, left ..." came through the phone in a calmer, mellower tone.

"I know, sir, thank you, over," and with that, both men walked their respective paths back to colleagues in silence, but many hundreds of miles apart.

<hr />

Selkirk had joined the Santorini team on their first few dives that morning, and seeing their level of fatigue rise quickly, battling the strong, deep-water caldera currents, he decided to cut short that day's operation. One further location had been taken off the search list and he felt confident they too would find their 'prize' the next day, as had now been done in Gibraltar.

He instructed De Boer to take them all to the small local fishing port of Ammoudi, in Oia, on the eastern tip of the island, where they would rest and recuperate for the remainder of the afternoon. That night they were to meet up to review the progress to date.

The boat was moored up a short distance from three water's-edge restaurants, and one by one, they stepped onto the shore. Selkirk and the team walked over to an empty table and sat awaiting service. Being neither locals nor tourists, everyone had stopped their conversations and watched them arrive and reorganise the furniture so they could all sit together. Their equipment was safely stored on the boat, which was in view a few yards away, bobbing up and down gently on the waves.

They ordered beers and investigated the menus.

The beers arrived and their orders were taken, and they relaxed into their chairs and the falling rays of the pending sunset. It was rare for the unit to get together in this manner and chat normally, but they did and it was refreshing and enjoyable.

"Are you lot here regarding the scientists?" came from the table close by in broken but understandable English.

It was occupied by three weathered old locals that had clearly spent more time on the water than the land.

"Scientists?" said Peterson.

"Those same ones that went missing here a short while back; are you the team they sent to find them?" the same old man asked again.

Selkirk turned to face the three, and having looked around the other tables first, replied, "Well, we are a search crew of a sort. What else do you know?"

The same man spoke a third time, "I know you're looking in the wrong place for them, that's what I know." Not waiting for a reply, he went on, "I've been fishing these waters all my life, and I told them that their diving vessel was too small and fragile for the depths. Seems I was right: they never came back up that day."

While they were talking, Biddiss had googled the scientists, and reading the news article about their disappearance, he came to a short paragraph that caught his attention. "The scientists, it claims here, were looking for Atlantis or something. Tom, the scientists ..." he said, interrupting his conversation with the three locals.

Selkirk knew Biddiss must have good reason for

interrupting. "So, Atlantis? People have been searching here for decades, what's different?"

"They were searching around the start of the Hellenic Trench, a fault line intersection on the seabed, much like what we are looking for. And now they have disappeared, with the Spetz on the island. Coincidence?"

Turning back to the fishermen's table, Selkirk spoke to them all, "Can you show us where they were last seen diving?"

"I'll be waiting for you over there, sun up, at five," the first man said to Selkirk, as he pointed to his fishing boat moored a little out into the bay.

"Don't be late, boy; I have a busy day ahead of me," and with that, the three men rose and spoke in their local dialect to the restaurant owner before retiring for the night.

The group watched the three old men wander off slowly along the water's edge, not exactly sure what had happened.

Selkirk took over again, "Bert, you and Petes find out who these scientists were and what they were diving for … as much detail about them as possible. Remember who one of them was …" referring to Isabelle's father. "Let's meet in two hours at the base. I suspect our plans for tomorrow have now changed."

Chapter 9
Sinking City

Isabelle was struggling to cope with the news of her father's disappearance. Anniken had left Nathen and her at the airport only days ago, with just a fleeting comment that their father was missing, and quite likely dead. Isabelle had not been particularly close to him for years – the victim of his career that had taken him away from home too often. He remained, however, her father; she was struggling. She tried to balance her internal stress by reminding herself that, while he was searching the Bermuda Triangle, he had failed to appear for her graduation. Now it seemed she would never get the chance to say goodbye, wherever he might be and whatever awful fate may have befallen him.

Nathen was also suffering, torn apart inside with similar mixed feelings. But his love for his father had triggered a need to help the team, to find him, to save his dad, whatever the cost may be. Only events in Gibraltar could distract him enough to stop him racing towards his father's last known location in Santorini. He kept his feelings much more private, and would let himself be distracted by the adventure he seemed to be having in Gibraltar.

Tom Selkirk could see that Isabelle was suffering. Losing her father and witnessing a friend's violent demise could have sent her over the edge. Selkirk remembered his first taste of similar emotion in the jungles of Indonesia. He wanted to steer her away from that abyss and save her the inevitable bitterness that he endured for so many years after that incident in the Barents Sea.

Selkirk called Dekker from Santorini.

"Deks, how is the boy holding up?" he said as it was answered.

"He's fine, Tom. We're keeping him busy, and Kirk's been taking him to the camp's firing range, so he seems to have let off all the steam he needs to about his father," came Dekker's reply.

"Can he stay with you? I think I'm sending the girl back to her mother for a day or two."

"Yup, leave him with us and if you need his support, I can always send him over to Santorini. We're almost done here, I think."

"OK, good work, Deks, keep in touch," said Selkirk ending the short conversation.

———————

When she left the base the next morning heading to the airport, Isabelle had been fully briefed on security and the need to stay under the radar. If the Russians were still on the island, they would be watching. She had become a short-haired brunette in her room the previous night, a vast change from her natural long blonde hair. Together with her casually dressed colleagues, she would leave to fly out to join her friends and mother in a couple of hours and start the recovery process back in Cambridge. Nathen wanted to stay with the team and had asked to go to Santorini and join Selkirk's crew when they were finished in Gibraltar. He would be allowed to do so, after that final day and the recovery of the bomb. Now it was for Nathen to take over the lead position on seabed properties, vacated by his older sister.

Isabelle's plane landed without incident, and she was met in the usual manner by her minder and whisked through security into the waiting car to be driven back to her mother. Selkirk had asked that a firearms police officer stay with her until she returned to them. She was assigned one and together with the driver, set off onto the motorway and the relative tranquility of home.

Whilst a tearful Isabelle was reunited with her mother at their suburban house in Cambridge, Nathen had already been out on the Mediterranean waters for over four hours and was cold and tired but happily distracted. The two women sat and chatted about her work over in Santorini for nearly an hour before the subject of Isabelle's father was finally raised.

"Your father knew Santorini very well, Izzy," her mother started. Then, turning her gaze away from her daughter to the fields visible outside the window, she carried on, "He was there recently. He was there only a few weeks ago in fact, and now ..." she stopped speaking and, as tears started to well up, she grasped Isabelle's hand tighter. They would open up to each other much more over the next few hours before they turned in for the night.

<hr />

The designated recovery area for the bomb was filled with vessels of all types. All encircled the dive area from a pre-arranged distance. The massive support vessel, *Goliath*, carried a ten-ton crane that would be used to lift the bomb up from the seabed with a steel dome placed over it for fear of any possible detonation. While this made the users feel more secure, none actually believed it would be good enough in reality. Then, once inspected and evidenced that it was a decoy warhead as they had started to suspect, it would be taken out to deeper water, where a controlled explosion would render it harmless.

Dekker had spent many hours under the waves photographing the device and surrounding area, and even his Navy SEAL background had not prepared him for the amount of time he would spend in the cold and murky waters off the Gibraltarian coastline. But when he surfaced for the last time, he had all the clarification he needed.

The device was a fake and was not built to cause huge damage. The team had agreed that it had been placed to keep Selkirk's team off the scent in Santorini. The fake device had done its job well. They had suspected it for a few days, but only on this final day of diving did they have the evidence they needed to confirm it. The Russians had wanted to keep Selkirk's team on Gibraltar, but why? Could it be to make them weaker on Santorini, or just to keep them off their trail? More questions than answers arose from the discovery of this fake device.

Dekker had suggested that he and Kirk stay to bring it up top and investigate it for any clues in the daylight, and Selkirk had agreed. They would have twenty-four hours to do so before they, with Nathen, would make their way to join the rest of the team in Santorini. It was late on a Friday but there would be no respite for anyone.

Dekker's mobile rang. It was the admiral and he knew he should take the call. Moving as far from the noise of the crane winch as he could, he pressed the secured encryption answer button.

"Good evening, Admiral, I am pleased you called me," he started.

"Lieutenant Commander, Selkirk tells me you have the device and it's a decoy," was the admiral's reply.

"Correct, Admiral, it's on its way up as we speak and should be on board within the hour. We will check it out and then the support crew will dismantle it best they can here, and it will then be taken out into deeper water to get rid," he explained.

"Good work, can you let me and Tom know if it throws up any clues, then get straight over to Santorini with the others," he replied.

"Yup, will do, sir, got to go now as it's going to get noisy," and with that the two mobiles in Gibraltar and London fell silent.

As he walked the short distance back to Kirk and the rising crane, two Spanish jets screamed low overhead. The Spanish Air Force was again on manoeuvres and making their presence felt over the disputed territory. Dekker looked up and scowled. *Boys and their toys*, he thought, before recovering his focus towards the device rising up out of the water.

The two team members carried on together with their work and the recovery of the fake bomb. It was incredibly realistic looking.

"Why would someone take the time and effort to build this, just to dump it in the water without a warhead, Deks? Makes no sense to me," claimed Kirk.

"Hmm, yes it is weird but deliberate, and that's what's scary about the whole of this," came Dekker's reply.

———◆◆✕◆◆———

In Santorini, De Boer, Biddiss and Lamberti were following dutifully and painfully slowly behind the fishing boat of the locals from the night before in the restaurant. They made slow forward progress out from the harbour and to the edge of the island's enclosed caldera waters. Their objective was the point where the three scientists had been last seen diving.

Selkirk needed them to establish if the location held any meaningful significance, and indeed if it would reveal some possible mooring for a Russian stealth boat. Recent events meant the three men were heavily armed and a little on edge. Progress towards this point was very slow and the tension rose gradually, especially between Biddiss and Lamberti, now stuck together on a small patrol boat for what felt like an unbearable length of time.

Selkirk remained on the island, with Peterson and Neeman. He encouraged the two men to leave the base and look for any signs of their Russian visitors. Like the others, they, too, were heavily armed. Selkirk knew there were greater powers at work somewhere on the island. No one could be fully trusted; not even the admiral to some extent. Too much time away from the front line pushing papers across a desk in Whitehall can leave a person exposed to the politics and less focused on the reality.

Selkirk's most immediate problem, however, was to try and commandeer a manned submersible, and quickly. This was not going to be easy. The admiral would be the first logical contact, but something held him back from going down the usual chain of command. What Selkirk had learned, perhaps more than anything else in his long special forces career, was that familiarity was a disease, the enemy of surprise and, more worryingly, it presented opportunities to be infiltrated and outmanoeuvred.

The update call to the admiral was a short and unfruitful one, but he suspected this to be the case anyway. Selkirk suspected the admiral may be under surveillance, so chose to feed him disinformation. Selkirk knew that the admiral would soon understand why.

"We are getting nothing from the caldera, sir," he stated. "We have no sign of boats or activities so we've decided to go towards the smaller islands to the east and the shallower waters," Selkirk followed on.

"Are you sure that there is nothing where you are? Have you exhausted every possibility?" the Admiral asked.

"Yes, sir, I would put money on it," came Selkirk's reply.

"OK, Tom, keep me informed," both men ended the fake conversation.

Selkirk could not convince himself that any uninvited listener would fall for what was said, but then he had to believe they would.

In a different office in a different corridor in Whitehall, a different plot was unfolding. Someone who had eavesdropped on Selkirk's conversation suddenly had a surge of adrenaline. Perhaps the plan could move forward quicker, with the admiral's team way off the scent? He put his suit jacket on and left the office for the night. Only the security guard saw him go, and as they exchanged pleasantries the guard thought it strange that this man had stayed so late.

A moment after he ended the call to London, Selkirk's phone rang again. It was Dekker.

"Morning, Deks, do you have the device yet?" Selkirk asked.

"Yes, boss, it's on board and the guys are checking it over for any markings, but currently nothing," he replied. "I don't get it really; why would they go to that trouble and expense just to place a dummy device? And then there's

Harry; why would they risk the chase and the firefight? I just don't get it, Tom."

"Hmmm, yes, I did wonder but the only conclusion I came up with was that they wanted us in Gib while they did something much bigger over here in Santorini. I mean, it was a real gamble to crank up an operation in Gib and show their presence, but I guess that sort of confirms to me that here is where we should be and that they are powerful," Selkirk paused for a moment, "and clearly ruthless."

Dekker acknowledged and then spoke, "So what's the plan now?"

"Trying to find a bloody minisub from somewhere, and fast. I can't ask the admiral for help – Intel is leaking like a sieve over there – and we can't get down to where the missing scientists got to without one: it's just too deep to dive." Selkirk sounded increasingly frustrated.

There was a moment's silence. "We may be in luck ..." was Dekker's surprising, almost smug, reply.

Selkirk didn't initially take the bait. Instead he looked at his phone, a little surprised with the response. Dekker was often the joker of his team, but even he would know the severity of the requirement.

"Tom," he blurted out, "I can get you a minisub," knowing his first comment was probably not helpful and wasted precious time.

"Talk, Deks," said Selkirk, now slightly more upbeat.

"Well, I know my SEAL buddies are over in Syria doing their thing, and they always arrive from under the water, deployed from a larger sub just off shore, if you get my drift. I could make a call and get you one for a short time, perhaps even get it to Cyprus so you don't have to get involved in the Middle East stuff. What you think?"

"Deks, I am ending this call," Selkirk said back.

Confused, Dekker replied, "Why?"

"Because, my very useful American friend, you have an important call to make to your friends – just tell me when it will get to Cyprus. Well done, Deks, bloody well done," and Selkirk did indeed end the call. When Selkirk rang off, he paused and smiled to himself, completely reassured that he had the most capable and professional team he had ever been involved with in his military career.

The smile was short lived, for there was work to be done. He needed the whole team to get together on comms, as he would bend them to his will, raising the tempo of the operation. They needed to get inside the enemy's decision cycle and gain the initiative.

All the time knowing he was acting in the correct and only manner available, something nagged at him in the back of his mind. Something seemed wrong. He had experienced the very same emotion in the Barents Sea: raw fear and a sense that not all was as it seemed. He could feel the rot at the very core of the apple, but this time, he would resist the feelings of guilt and submission. He would not succumb to the depression, but instead he would stand and fight back. They would all stand and fight back at this unseen enemy.

That night, as Selkirk lay on his bed and stared at the ceiling, unable to sleep again, a short distance away an American hunter-killer submarine slowly and carefully deployed its minisub with two Navy SEALs on board. Dekker had played one of his trump cards, but Selkirk suspected they had very few left.

———•◆◈◆•———

In a small cottage on the outskirts of Cambridge, the minder thanked Isabelle's mother for the coffee and returned outside to walk the grounds, leaving mother and daughter to try to come to terms with a missing husband and father, who, according to the only information provided to them, was believed to be dead somewhere in the Ionian Sea.

They spoke in earnest, for what seemed to be hours, trying desperately to piece together the events of the last few weeks. Neither of them could believe the reports, and neither would accept his demise without a detailed analysis. They only paused briefly when interrupted by Isabelle's minder, Mason, who would knock the door as he entered.

Isabelle's mother could not hide her anxiety every time she saw her daughter's bodyguard and would wonder to herself why her little girl needed such a fierce-looking protector. After all, what could she have done? Isabelle deliberately only told her mother part of the story of the last couple of weeks, trying to avert a greater level of stress. She suggested that Mason's presence was merely to monitor her health after her ordeal on Bouvet Island.

"Your father really loved you, Izzy," her mother said as she entered from the kitchen carrying two cups of tea. "He was so proud when you, and your brother, decided to follow in his career steps. He was convinced that one day you would make some world-changing discovery."

"Yes, Mum, I know he did, and despite his absences, I always tried my best." Isabelle continued, "Even Nathen will do great stuff one day," she said with a smile, trying to lighten the dark mood.

"He had a special treasure trove of photos and memorabilia for you, you know," said her mother. "I was to give it to you if anything ever happened to him and, well … well, you know," she said, her voice beginning to break with emotion.

"It's hard not to think like that, but he's just missing currently, which means he could still turn up," she replied with conviction in her voice. "I know my father and what he's like."

Standing up again, Isabelle's mother went towards the stairs that led up to the attic. "Do you want to come and see?" she asked.

As they reached the top of the stairs and pulled the attic ladder down, Mason appeared, "Everything OK, ladies?"

"Yes thanks, we're fine. Just searching for my dad's old pictures and stuff," replied Isabelle and, reassured, he turned away to make a private call.

The attic was typical of most: full of boxes and junk that at one moment in time was valuable, but somehow many years and much dust later was just an impediment.

Isabelle's mother seemed to know exactly what she was looking for and where to search amongst the mess. Pulling away a couple of boxes, she reached down and grabbed an old shoe box and brought it out into the light. It was secured shut with tape, and Isabelle thought to herself that the contents had probably not seen daylight in many years.

The two sat on a rug in the attic and, like giggling school children, looked forward to the floods of pleasant memories that this magical shoe box could hold within it. Isabelle took over from her mother and pulled the tape apart. She opened it and discarded the lid.

At first disappointed, both looked into the box and saw only worn-out folded maps and small lumps of rock and stone. They had seen these many times before and so it was not the surprising magical discovery they had hoped for.

"Never mind," said Isabelle, slightly cursing her father

for the disappointment. "I have maps and lumps of rock hidden away myself," she went on.

"Keep looking, Izzy, your father was a brilliant man. There will be something, I promise, but only you will know what it could be when you see it. He really wanted you to have this box one day," she replied to her daughter. "There will be a reason why."

For the next few minutes they explored the folded maps, all with annotations on them. They held the small rock samples, wondering where they were taken, and looked long and hard at each of the numerous photographs of her father and many others, some known to them, some not, before reaching the bottom of the box and a small black notebook.

Picking it up, Isabelle flicked through it quickly, glancing over the sketched pictures and maps and her dad's occasional notes. She recognised his handwriting and this made her smile openly. Then she popped everything back into the box and, so as not to disappoint her mother, promised to study everything closely the next morning.

Back in the comfort of the downstairs sofas, the two women sat and drank cocoa for a while, listening to the sound of Mason pacing around like some menacing Captain Ahab. Fatigue had set in and both realised they should try to get some sleep. When they did at last go to their rooms, Isabelle already knew she would be unable to sleep. She knew that the box held some clue and that she was missing something. She had to figure it out; it could be a clue to solving the puzzle of her father's disappearance.

On a military base far from his mother and sister, Nathen had already packed his stuff, ready to join Kirk and Dekker, who were still trying to decipher the enigma that was Gibraltar, and who were soon to join the others in Santorini. Nathen felt a surge of both excitement and fear at the thought of the team being at full strength. Especially now that he was part of it. However, when he did finally make it to bed, he, too, could not sleep, instead tossing and turning over the perfectly ironed military linen. He would eventually get up and pace the small room, knowing all the time that without sleep he would be joining the others tired and unprepared. He, like his sister many miles away and connected only in time, felt the anxiety of their missing loved one and also, like her, wondered about how he could contribute to finding and returning his father.

<hr />

She didn't know how late it was but when Isabelle sat upright from a very shallow snooze, she almost fell out of bed as she reached over to the table. She had brought the shoe box to her bedroom. Something inside it seemed to be calling her and stopping her from proper deep sleep, which her body needed. Conscious of not waking her mother, she switched on the bedside lamp and took the lid off the box.

Something resonated in her memory. An image had stuck out through a quick glance. An image from the notepad, one she had seen before. Thinking about exactly what she had seen in the attic earlier with her mother, she fingered the pages looking for it again.

As she scanned the pages of her father's old notebook, a part of her brain went back in time to when she had first seen it, meticulously completed and annotated. It had meant little to the teenage girl but now was to prove a talisman for herself and her newly-adopted colleagues.

She quickly found what she was looking for – a sketch of the famous basilica on St Mark's Square in Venice. Then, on the next page, what she saw made her stomach churn as the pieces of the puzzle began to fall into place. It invoked a deep shock, but also feelings of unexpected pride. In that very moment, she dared not believe what she saw as the realisation of her full understanding struck her. She had figured it out. Her eyes fixed upon the maze of drawings of tunnels. At the top of the page there were three words pencilled in bold. It read 'Hellenic Trench – Atlantis'.

In her excitement she let out a cry she tried to stifle with her hand but, falling off balance, she thumped down onto the wooden floor. She immediately heard Mason stir downstairs, and as she scrolled through her mobile to the phone camera, she saw a light appear in the crack beneath her door. Her mother burst into her room with a deeply worried look on her face.

"Izzy, what happened, are you OK?" she asked.

Without looking up she continued to photograph the two pages of the notebook.

"Mum, it's fine, I just fell out of bed," then in a manner that further alarmed her mother, "oh, I am leaving tomorrow; I have to go somewhere urgently." Her mind was working overtime, wondering how best to get the new discovery to Selkirk and the others.

Isabelle's mother couldn't take in what she had just heard, having been woken up from a deep sleep. She repeated her question, "Izzy, are you OK, I mean, what's happening, love?"

Mason entered the room soon after hearing the thump and the subsequent voices. "Everything OK here?" he asked with a firm tone.

"Yes, all good. I just fell out of bed, nothing more," she replied to him. Look, can you help me? I urgently need to leave for Venice tomorrow. I have important information that I must get to Tom Selkirk," she asked of Mason, hoping that he would reply positively.

After a short moment and seeing the determination showing on her face, Mason acknowledged before leaving the room, reaching for his mobile to make the necessary travel requirements.

Isabelle went back to scrolling the menu on her phone, looking for the multimedia function and attaching the picture of the tunnel network to send to Nathen. Only on its delivery confirmation did she look directly at her mother.

"Mum, listen, I simply must leave tomorrow. I am not in trouble, but I am leaving to help my friends out. They need me urgently," she said in a calm and reassuring voice.

"That book, your father's book, was it that?" her mother asked, almost afraid to hear the reply.

"Dad was right, Mum, he was so right, all those years ago. He knew then, and no one believed him except us." Then, looking back towards her phone, she ended the conversation. "Mum, go to bed, we will chat some in the morning. For now, I have to make a call."

Reluctantly, still confused and even more tearful now, her mother turned and left the room, wondering what sort of person would be up this late to take a call.

Isabelle pressed the call button and within a few seconds it rang the international dial tone.

"Isabelle, what's wrong?" came the voice upon answering.

"Tom, I know where they are and I know where the bomb is. I know!" she said loudly, in an emphatic tone. Her voice was full of excitement and determination and this resonated with Selkirk.

After a short pause, he responded, "OK, what's happened?"

"Too much to say, but trust me, Tom, you need to get to Venice. I will meet you there. Mason is sorting the travel now, so please agree things with him." Selkirk had never seen this side of Isabelle; a strong, leader-like quality, but he liked what he heard. Hairs on the back of his neck stood tall. He knew not if it was from speaking to Isabelle or from the news that she delivered.

"OK, Isabelle, I trust your instincts. See you tomorrow," and Selkirk hung up so he could call Mason.

When the conversation ended several minutes later, a plan had been drawn up. Isabelle went back to bed, wide awake, to wait for the morning instead of trying to sleep. As immediately as she lay down, she rose again, went down the hall, and got into her mother's bed to comfort her. She knew that her mum was sad that another family member was leaving in the morning. The two slept well for the rest of the night.

Chapter 10

Convergence

A few thousand miles away, Selkirk started to move his assets from Gibraltar to Santorini. The team was given instructions and as they received their next tasking, they felt they were getting closer to their target and the end game.

For the first time, Selkirk felt that he had actually got the jump on the Russians. They would not expect his team to have figured out their plan so soon and would certainly not be expecting to encounter Selkirk and the others before they could progress their plan further towards their objective.

Dekker was bringing information about the decoy bomb that could assist them with their pending search. The casing had been made to a specific tension and one that, if copied, with a real warhead included, could be placed deep under the water and survive the pressure. In fact, the casing had revealed that any real bomb made to the exact same specification could survive the pressure of water at depths in excess of two hundred metres. This clue was the Russians' first mistake, but for now, they would not know that a mistake had been made, or that Selkirk's team had discovered it.

Selkirk would join Isabelle with Biddiss, Lamberti and Peterson in Venice, while De Boer would pair up with Neeman and Kirk, taking Nathen along most of the way. They would travel to the Greek mainland and on to a small town called Lefkada. Then the three would carry onwards to its hydroelectric plant, identified by Nathen as directly above a main trench passageway, where his father had suggested an entrance into the tunnel had once existed. The hydro plant had been funded by Russian oligarch money, and this was too coincidental not to investigate.

As for Anniken and Dekker, they would be tasked with diving the caldera in the soon-to-arrive Navy SEAL minisub and follow the more direct path of the three scientists still presumed missing somewhere under the water.

If the two youngest and newest members of Selkirk's team were correct, and some massive network of air-filled tunnels did exist under the seabed, then they would soon be searching them, likely entering from different locations.

Selkirk felt, for the first time, the pendulum may just be swinging back his way. As he walked with airport security past the public check-in areas, he called the admiral to bring him up to date and to get assurance that the minisub was indeed being moved quickly to Dekker. He chose his words carefully, suspecting their conversation was being shared.

So Selkirk's team was to be separated, yet again, across the Mediterranean, but this time heads were up and confidence was high. They had the edge and were determined to exploit it.

It was a full moon in Santorini and its reflection on the calm waters failed to pick up the stealth ship, now configured back to its invisible state, as it slipped out of the caldera and onto its next role in the plan.

———◆✕◆———

Mason handed Isabelle over to security at London City Airport and went back to the car. He had promised to get her tearful mother back home before stepping down. At each point along the team's path, things were beginning to move fast.

Dekker and Anniken ran the island along the cliff edge three hundred metres above the caldera, waiting for their special delivery later the same day. Both stopped only when Anniken signalled that she had received a text message and perhaps it was the arrival of their equipment. Opening the text, she saw it was from her dear friend Eyal. It read 'Barak gave us nothing so now he can't do anyone harm anymore. E'.

"That bastard's dead at last, Deks. Harrison can finally sleep," she said. Then, putting her phone away, both started running again, waiting for their minisub to arrive.

Selkirk and his team boarded the Hercules bound for Aviano Air Force Base close to Venice. De Boer and his three team members would be island hopping towards Lefkada on the Greek mainland, arriving early the next day.

Selkirk was to be proven correct.

His enemies didn't know that his team was closing in; the Russians continued their work, mostly in the darkness, in an inhospitable environment. Each hour that they drilled and moved dirt and dust became just like the previous one. Nothing separated the last hour from the next hour to come, but they all knew the sands of time were falling quickly and that Kharkov expected nothing less than success. Their lives and their country's future could depend on their efforts.

They took shifts drilling and moving dirt in teams of four, while two would stand guard in the darkness, watching through night vision visors for something out of the ordinary. Nothing appeared, yet.

———◆◆◆◆◆———

It was an exceptionally hot morning when Isabelle made her way from Marco Polo Airport to the agreed meeting point in St Mark's Square. She would sit and wait and drink coffee while she did so. Her monitor had sorted her belongings and checked in at a nearby hotel. For now, she stared at the basilica in front of her and wondered where, within its grand structure, her father had once found the ancient entrance down into the fabled Hellenic Trench, if indeed he had. While she waited, she started to doubt herself.

For a few minutes, however, Isabelle sat and drank coffee and waited for Selkirk and the others, occasionally flipping the pages of her father's journal and practising her opening gambit for when she had company.

It was around an hour, and several reviews of the journal chapter entitled 'Sinking City' later, when, almost simultaneously, four chairs were moved to her table. The team had arrived, and sitting so quickly next to her surprised Isabelle a little. It was a harsh interruption of her tranquil reflection.

"Isabelle. So, what have you got for us?"

"Hello to you also, Bidd," she replied, "and the rest of you." She was determined not to be intimidated by these four 'musketeers' and eager to get them to believe her discovery. She remained strong and focused in front of her slightly intimidating table party.

Lamberti caught the waiter's attention and gestured that he bring them all coffee.

"Sorry, Isabelle. Manners, boys," Selkirk replied with a smile on his face.

"Fuck, its hot here, and it's still early," Peterson said, pulling at his shirt collar as if to let out trapped steam.

"Petes, language, there's a lady present," again from Selkirk, maintaining his smile, aware that Isabelle was feeling a little under pressure from what could be a daunting group sitting with her.

"Isabelle, what you got, why have you dragged us here?"

Selkirk asked.

For the next two hours, the small gathering sat and chatted privately, occasionally each would take turns to look towards the basilica towering above them, wondering what secrets it held for them to discover.

———◆◆×◆◆———

Meanwhile, on the water and a distance away from Venice, De Boer paced the vessel, impatient at his slow progress towards his pre-arranged area of interest. Nathen sat and enjoyed the sun's rays while he could. Neeman and Kirk stood by the captain and quietly watched their progress on the ship's GPS.

———◆◆×◆◆———

Over in Santorini, the calm of the caldera would be disrupted soon enough with the arrival of the deep submersible. It had surfaced to communicate to Dekker, and once decrypted, it proved to be time for the two of them to make their way out to the designated switch area. The two Navy SEALs would return to shore in the fast rib boat and have a day off, taking in the sun while Dekker and Anniken took control of their equipment. The securing point found, the two returned to the harbour and shared an hour catch up with Dekker's former colleagues before going their separate ways again, back to their respective operations. It had proven a pleasant, relaxing moment for both parties, but this was over now.

Back at their temporary base, Dekker and Anniken had been planning their next day for a while now – both were beginning to get tired.

In Venice, the conversation regarding the entrance to the fabled tunnels had reached a suitable end and Isabelle stood and took the lead, as requested to do. The others moved their chairs and also rose, Biddiss handed the bill to Lamberti to pay before setting off after the fast-pacing Isabelle. The group walked quickly towards the main entrance to the basilica, with Lamberti running to catch up, scattering the pigeons and a few tourists in the process.

Now at the main steps, they entered the building, and as their eyes adjusted to the subdued lighting and flickering candles, Selkirk looked over at Isabelle, "We're in your hands, Isabelle. Where to?"

"Well, as we said, the sketch in the book shows narrow, unlit stairs, eleven of them, leading up to the four bronze horses stolen by the Venetians on the fall of Constantinople. Then there is the winged lion on one of their shoulders, so I guess it's this way," she replied, moving towards a staircase up to the magnificent bronze horses. The group followed after her, with Biddiss glancing over his shoulder at the tourists mingling through the cathedral. He was a little uneasy but didn't know exactly why.

When she found the steps, Isabelle led the way with great earnest and ran up two at a time, quickly reaching the statue. The others followed and gazed into the gloom, searching for the famous Venice winged lion. It eluded them and like all teams caught in the moment, they floundered for a second.

"Spread out," whispered Selkirk, wondering why he had automatically lowered his voice. After all, despite the need for secrecy, he was in the House of God, searching for a biblical weapon of sorts. Ironic, he thought to himself.

Several minutes passed as these special tourists moved around and through the elaborate basilica amongst the bronze horses, and scoured the surrounding walls looking for the lion.

"It's not here, it's just not here, Tom," she said.

"OK, listen, Isabelle, are you sure you have got the right location? Could your father's book be wrong and you have missed some detail?" he asked. She thought for the briefest of moments then looked Selkirk squarely in the eye. "No, my father was always right," she responded. "He must be right!"

"Fine, then stop and think," he said, disarming the tense situation and walking closer into her personal space. "Think, Isabelle, what obvious clue are you missing? Take your time."

She did as he suggested and the others watched her, almost unable to breath, they could practically hear her thinking.

Biddiss received a text and for a tiny moment his movement to read it distracted her as she looked over to where the phone noise had come. She snapped at Biddiss for the rude interruption, then returned to her thoughts again and her father's book.

Biddiss gestured to Selkirk, "Tom, the package has arrived with Deks," before walking back to where he had a typical sniper's vantage point over the rest of the basilica. Something about the place bothered him.

Isabelle paced the candle-lit corridor for inspiration, while looking hopefully at her father's annotated sketch.

Speaking to herself, she spoke the notes out loud, "Eleven steps, over the shoulder of one, follow the stare of the winged lion," and then stopped dead in her tracks. Looking to her right, she stared intensely down the stairs, which she ran up minutes earlier. She walked fast over to them. Counting to herself this time, she walked down the stairs. Reaching the bottom she turned around and smiled up at Selkirk, who suspected she was on to something.

"Twelve," she said to him. "There's twelve steps here, not eleven, we're on the wrong stairs!" still smiling at her apparent revelation.

"Right, we're looking for a set of eleven stairs. Obvious but well done, Isabelle," said Peterson.

"This place is huge, so let's split up," replied Selkirk. Without further comment, Peterson, Biddiss and Lamberti set off in different directions, searching for the elusive stairway.

"Isabelle, would you come with me?" said Selkirk. He felt a sense of regret that she had been dragged into the most lethal of scenarios and a need to protect her that was more than just his duty.

As they temporarily went their own ways inside the huge basilica, a choir in full ceremonial dress took up position, and it wasn't long before the cathedral was filled with the deafening chorus of Italian Mass.

The team, now separated, could not see each other easily and all felt a bit isolated in the basilica's enormity, just wanting to get the job done and get out unnoticed.

Meanwhile, Isabelle walked just behind Selkirk, occasionally speaking out loud to herself in an act of reassurance, hoping that her father was indeed right, "Eleven steps and then the horse will reveal the winged lion," she muttered repeatedly.

It felt like an eternity for Isabelle, but in reality, it was actually only several minutes more when Biddiss' mobile vibrated in his pocket. It was Lamberti. A look of confusion came over his face.

The text simply read, 'Bidd, southwest corner, near the emergency exit, look what I've found'.

Still confused as to why Lamberti had texted him, not Selkirk, he made his way quickly over to the southwest corner of the building and saw Lamberti standing at the top of a staircase.

"She said eleven stairs, but she didn't say they had to go up," he said to his arriving colleague.

"So there's eleven, yes?" questioned Biddiss.

"Si, undici scale," he replied.

Biddiss looked down the dark passageway.

"And the lion?"

Lamberti smiled and pointed down the stairs.

Biddiss walked down, counting to himself, and peered out of the only point where light seemed to enter the odd, random staircase having no purpose or features apart from one tiny window.

"My God, look, Bert," momentarily forgetting he didn't like Lamberti, "over that horse's shoulder, a winged lion up on the far wall."

"Yup, a winged lion hidden from view from all but here. The girl was right, let's tell the others," he replied.

When the team had gathered, each took it in turn to look through the tiny aperture at the eleventh stair and the winged lion that was positioned so it could not be seen easily from any other location in the basilica

"Right, how do we get to that thing, especially with these people here?" asked Biddiss.

"Tonight," came the sharp and instant reply from Selkirk. "Tonight, when this place is closed. For now, let's get back to the hotel and check-in on the others."

Nathen called his sister from the hotel in Lefkada.

They had arrived and were preparing for their entrance into the hydroelectric plant and, more specifically, the water-surge pool. Nathen's research had indicated that it was not man-made, but was in fact a natural phenomenon sinkhole and where his father had drawn a second possible entry point into the trench.

This massive sinkhole was used twice a day by the power plant to generate huge amounts of electricity through releasing tons of water down it, before pumping this same water back out and up to repeat again.

The timing of De Boer, Kirk and Neeman's entry into the hole was critical; any mistake at this point would mean certain death for all three. It would have to be meticulously planned and timed to avoid the huge surge of water, and even then, they needed to be far enough into the trench – if it existed – to be out of harm's way. As divers, all three were well aware of the dangers, yet with no knowledge of the trench, it would prove very difficult to develop a full-proof plan.

In Santorini, under a falling sun, Dekker took the lead in the deep submersible. The water in the caldera was calm and the swell from large tourist liners had ended for the day, so the initial descent would be easy for the former Navy SEAL. Immediately behind him sat Anniken. Her expression was a mix of impatience and anger, and she would spend some time fighting these emotions that called out for revenge for Harrison's death. She was ready for the operation, perhaps more than any of the others, but her heart and soul were feeling the strain of the last few weeks. She told herself that payback was coming and that she would smile as she killed the last of Harrison's assassins.

Meanwhile in London, in a white-walled room overlooking Whitehall, the admiral stood and looked out over the road, watching the black cabs and red buses pass merrily by. His thoughts were with his three small teams entering the unknown to chase a mysterious foe in an environment untested. *Like all special forces operations, what could possibly go wrong?* He thought to himself, grimly.

When Selkirk had informed him earlier that they were searching further east, he had realised straight away that it was a false lead and that they were acquiring a minisub and moving towards Santorini and likely Venice. He understood Selkirk's lie and he carried it on with the suits in Whitehall when asked. Tom Selkirk had learned his lesson. He had learnt a long time ago that you keep your enemies close, and, as long as it doesn't encroach on the operation's success, you keep your superiors guessing.

The admiral stood and watched and waited. There was nothing more for him to do now. It was out of his control. His bag was packed and his most feared and most trusted of special operators stood on the edge, waiting to go into hell and happy to do so.

Night had fallen in Venice, although the scurrying of tourists between restaurants and bars would continue for a while. Selkirk and the others moved out of the dark and across the east side of the square towards the side entrance of the basilica.

----•◦×◦•----

In Lefkada, Nathen would return to the relative safety of the hotel with the three men's unwanted equipment once they jumped into the darkness, while Isabelle would do similar, having insisted that she attend the gathering in the square to witness Selkirk's experts disappear like ghosts into the gloom. She reluctantly returned to her hotel room, aware that this was likely to be a long and very anxious wait ahead of her. The two family members were not to contact each other now but to await further communication from Selkirk on his return. Should this not happen within forty-eight hours, both were to make their way as far as possible from their current location, as quickly as they could, and then contact the admiral.

The darkness was intense as the four-man team disappeared into the side entrance of the basilica and onwards towards a winged lion and the unknown. Simultaneously, Dekker navigated the minisub down and through the portal. It would take him around two hours to reach the point of the last known transmission from the scientists and from where the GPS signalling-positioning balloon had been picked up by their support team just prior to them entering the tunnel system themselves,

In three separate locations, darkness engulfed the whole team, but what focused the minds of the three men in Lefkada was a sheer precipice and a base jump into hell. De Boer looked straight down into his destiny while Kirk re-checked his gear. Neeman turned to Nathen and with a slight smile, spoke to him.

"Nathen, remember, eyes and ears, stay low and take care of yourself. You have done a great job, but now your involvement is over." He continued, "Get back to London and your sister. If you don't hear back from us soon, the admiral will protect you." Then, turning to face the darkness below, he touched De Boer on the shoulder and smiled again. The three men then, without hesitation, walked forward and jumped into the dark hole below.

Nathen stood and stared in disbelief at what had just happened. His friends had jumped into the abyss and were now gone. They had disappeared for perhaps the last ever time but had been concerned for his wellbeing. Confused and sad, with his heart pumping madly, he picked up the unwanted gear and made his way to the hotel. He pondered what would happen next and the vulnerability of his new friends. On three separate fronts they were making their way towards an unknown end game in an attempt to avert a catastrophe of such a scale that should they fail, the existing world order would never be the same again.

It had started, yet no one could know how it would play out.

<hr>

A few candles still flickering would quiver more violently as the four in Venice passed by and disturbed the air. Then, reaching the given wall, Peterson flashed his torchlight in the direction of Lamberti. He was waiting and within seconds had positioned his night vision goggles and was searching the wall for the winged lion.

Lamberti could hear his breathing as he scanned the wall until he saw it. A winged lion built into the upper wall and just below a massive gold-leaf painting of Saint Mark. He reached into his pocket and took out the laser pen. Pointing it directly at the lion, the green beam dissected the basilica through the darkness. From below, Peterson started the ascent towards where it struck the wall and the winged lion. Having already secured a rope around a granite outcrop above the target area, it was relatively easy for Peterson to ascend.

Biddiss took up a position watching for any activity in the church, while Selkirk kept a watchful eye on Peterson as he scaled higher and higher. He was around ten metres above the others now and rested for a few seconds.

Then, reaching the symbol, Peterson lifted his arm to signal to Lamberti, and the beam was cut. The lion was visible to him now. Lamberti left the stairs and returned to the others.

Desperately trying to keep his balance, Peterson reached out to touch the lion in the wall. Not sure what to actually do, he pushed it and then hit it with his fist. He reached further up right and ran a finger around the perimeter of it, trying unsuccessfully to figure out its significance.

He looked down at Selkirk through the darkness. There was a silent acknowledgement that this was not as straight-forward as it looked. Lamberti made his way over to the others, sensing as he did, that there was tension.

"No joy, Tom?" Lamberti asked quietly.

"No, not yet, but she's right, I know she is, but nothing yet," he replied.

Looking back up towards Peterson, they stood together, unable to help him.

He looked at the winged lion chiselled into the basilica wall and started to breathe more slowly, "Come on mate, what are you missing?" he mumbled to himself.

Then, staring at the symbol, he reached up above it to grab the frame of a painting to help stabilise him, as fatigue was starting to enter his legs. The picture moved slightly as he did so.

"Christ, I didn't expect that to happen," he said a little too loud so that the others and any mice that scurried around could hear.

"Careful, mate, watch what you're doing up there, we have time," spoke the reassuring voice of Biddiss, who now stood with his colleagues in a tight group, conscious of the ever-increasing need to find something significant. Every minute dragged like an eternity.

"Come on, Petes, do your stuff," Selkirk said to himself, willing his friend on.

'Up there', resonated with Peterson. Staring straight at the symbol, he now saw the connection. The lion was roaring upwards. It was almost speaking to the painting above it, which he was currently hanging on to with his fingertips.

"Could it be?" he said out loud.

Shifting his attention and pressure away from the carved lion to the hanging painting, his mood changed in an instant.

As he moved the painting aside just a few inches, he saw something that blew his mind, something from the old world. An apparent tunnel. Whatever it actually was, it was something they all sorely needed.

"I can see some sort of entrance behind this painting," Peterson panted.

"Well done, Petes," said Selkirk, "can you get in or do we take the thing down?" he asked, knowing that the latter would reveal that they had been there, unless they could pull it back up behind them.

"Negative," said Peterson. "We can get in at the edge,

as I can hold this painting to one side and jam it. Find me a length of wood or similar about three foot long. I will then go in and secure a rope so you can attach all the gear and follow me in."

"OK, Petes," and with that, the four men sprang into silent action, with Biddiss lifting a prayer stool conveniently shaped to use as a prop for their new door into the unknown.

The four operators moved quickly but made no noise as they lifted gear and weapons up and then into a black hole in the high wall.

Then, as the fourth and final member of the elite team entered the dark tunnel, adjusting the painting back to its correct, upright position from behind it, the basilica returned to its watchful mood, waiting for daylight and the murmur of prayer to begin.

As night vision goggles powered up, the mood was completely different in the tunnel. Each knew his role, but an acute sense of trepidation suddenly overtook the team as they marched through the darkness and down the roughly made stairs. Then, this emotion intensified further as the stairs got steeper and steeper, until they suddenly ended and there was nothing but a void beneath them. Selkirk suddenly tasted fear and confusion, for they were trapped with nowhere to go.

———————

Back at their respective hotels, both Isabelle and Nathen sat on their beds, alone and scared. Neither of them was used to waiting for events to happen. They were proactive individuals, just like their father. In her heart, Isabelle knew they would find the tunnel.

Under the deep water of the Santorini caldera, the currents were being kind to Dekker and Anniken, allowing their descent to be a relatively easy and quick one. For now, the minisub followed its preprogrammed route to the very place where three scientists had made the journey of their lives some weeks before and had entered a part of the fabled trench.

"Annie, I think we are very close, the instruments show forty metres to the seabed, but it feels wrong. I'm powering-up the main beams. I just don't trust technology as I do my own eyes."

Then, just as it had done when the three missing men arrived at the entry point and switched on their lights, the underwater world lit up and was visible to anything and everything around. However, just like the scientists had found before, there was no sign of life at this depth. The inhospitable environment gave nothing away except that Dekker was right: they were deeper than some instruments had indicated.

"So, easy bit done, Annie, we just need to find the bloody entrance now. We're looking for the so-called 'breathing water' that was in Isabelle's dad's book," said Dekker.

They strained their eyes looking into the endless night of the deep Mediterranean Sea, and would do so for a while longer.

Meanwhile, hundreds of metres under the Greek mainland, Neeman, Kirk and De Boer had landed successfully, but not without a few bruises, and were already starting their long march into and along the tunnel.

Parachuting into near darkness had taken its toll on De Boer, who had landed on rocks and turned his ankle. He took painkillers and bound the foot and, for a while, would become dulled to any further pain or injury. They wasted no time checking they had all their gear with them and that none had been lost in the jump. Setting their compasses, they quickly started moving northwest towards Selkirk's team and anyone else they might encounter on the way.

———◆◈◈◆●———

Selkirk was dumfounded as they gathered on the edge of the abyss. How could this be so? He frantically started searching all his pockets for the photocopied notes that Isabelle had handed him from her father's book. Peterson could not see anything from the small platform but bare rock walls and no bottom. The steps had ended abruptly, as if to provide protection from whatever might come up from below, or to stop anybody going further down, none of which made any sense whatsoever. Selkirk peered at the pages in the dark.

"According to this, the stairs run down unbroken for around two kilometres, with only a small step to over-come," he read in a monotone voice as if praying for some inspiration.

Peterson broke the silence further, "Right, all of you get the fuck off this platform. I need to lie down and look under-neath. They made their way begrudgingly back up the tiny stairs, allowing their colleague to get into position to look under the ledge. He startled them all by saying, "Bingo!"

So often they would look for the complex while the simple was staring them in the face. "The steps go backwards under this ledge, but it looks tricky to gain access," Peterson informed.

Selkirk took back control. "Let's get on with this, but be careful, for God's sake," he spoke earnestly, worried about not just their necks but the time. They had taken three hours to go the square root of nowhere. "I will lower you, Petes, and we can make a fixed line," instructed Selkirk.

No one in the group felt easy about swinging above the chasm on a rope that was too thin, and with too much heavy kit.

"This is why we get paid extra," mused Biddiss sarcastically, he, too, having a healthy respect for heights.

It would take a further twenty minutes to get the four men and their gear safely back on track and downwards again, further into the tunnels.

In the minisub, Dekker started to feel movement that was irregular, even for strong currents down on the seabed and without hesitation let the minisub move along the mass of swirling, breathing water unguided. As their predecessors had done, he took his hands off the controls. The current moved them at speed, seemingly down into a confusion of bubbles and currents before slowly ascending and coming to a stop, floating on the surface of an underground lake. It appeared to be some form of subsea aquifer and most likely their pathway to the mystery of the giant Hellenic Trench and volcanic tunnels. Both of the submariners gasped – it was not dark, but instead the alien space was illuminated by a ghostly, forgotten light shimmering across the now calm waters.

"It's beautiful," remarked Anniken.

"It's deadly," replied Dekker, surprised by his friend's sentiment, being much less enamoured of their situation.

⬥◆×◆◆⬥

As all the teams converged, time almost stood still except for the digital readout on a bomb. A bomb so big it would generate a series of deadly tsunami waves that would wipe Venice from the face of the earth and continue miles inland.

All nine wanted to close with their enemy. They wanted to stop the pending carnage.

They would not have to wait long.

Chapter 11

Confronting Bears

Isabelle and Nathen both disobeyed the very specific orders given to them by Tom Selkirk and Neeman respectively. Like all siblings, there was a powerful draw to be together and compare notes, especially during a crisis. It may have been naïve of Selkirk's team to think they would just sit still and do nothing, but they were in danger and Selkirk hoped that this fact alone would make them go to ground and stay quiet.

As soon as she could, Isabelle broke the order from Selkirk and called her brother to let off steam. He had underestimated the bond between the brother and sister, strengthened through the recent traumatic experiences. She was not to know that it would have far-reaching implications for Neeman and the others. After all, why would she? As soon as the number dialled through, Nathen answered and started talking excitedly. "Izzy, where are you, what's happened? I am so worried about the team in Venice; where the fuck are they?" he said in one continuous breath.

"Nats, they've gone. They went into the basilica and have found Dad's tunnel. Into Dad's tunnel, so I guess they are way out under the sea somewhere. It's completely unbelievable, but, you know, he was right, he was bloody right. There is an enormous tunnel under the Med and he knew it was there all the time," she said in an excited tone.

Then, after a moment's reflection, she was interrupted by Nathen, which took her back a little, "Izzy, we must not talk, they all said 'sit still and wait' and there must have been a reason."

"Yes, I know, and we will be in the shit if we are not careful, but I had to talk to you," said the over-excited Isabelle.

"Listen, there must be a reason why they said that," and as he spoke, he figured it out, "perhaps people are listening to our calls; perhaps it's those men you encountered in Santorini?" This time he was interrupted.

"Shit, yes, but I needed to tell someone. OK, sorry, remember what Tom said about what to do if and when, little brother?" she went on.

"Izzy, quiet! Now you've said his bloody name, quiet now. Bye, take care," he hissed, ringing off. Neither Isabelle nor Nathen noticed the third click on the line, confirming Nathen's suspicions that they were being listened to. In a small room inside the high walls of the Kremlin a signal intelligence officer picked up his internal phone and rang a number.

Nathen had spent long periods of time with members of Selkirk's team, and with that came a level of understanding and some experience of their world. Certainly enough to know he had to make the short journey into town and purchase a new, cheap mobile phone.

An hour later, his sister's mobile vibrated with the receipt of a text message from an unknown number. He felt more in control and a little safer now.

The message simply read, 'Buy new mobile, text this number when done, N'.

———◆◆❈◆●————

Dekker and Anniken's arrival at the tunnel would not have gone unnoticed, but multiple approaches were part of Selkirk's plan, and he hoped somehow to wrong-foot his enemy. As they started off along the main tunnel, their progress was limited due to the weaponry they carried. While they knew their journey was possibly being tracked, they also knew they had to get to a supportive position as soon as possible.

Dekker knew they had drawn a bit of a short straw and, as such, were considered the least likely to reach the objective first. No one really knew how long it would take them to find and enter the tunnel using the minisub, so Selkirk had positioned them in the plan to bring forward a weapon that could turn the tide of the battle if need be.

Selkirk also realised that the weapon could spell all their deaths, because if he ordered its use, it would take out the ceiling, and in seconds they would all be buried or drowned. A last resort, but an option Selkirk knew he had. As they marched the dark tunnels, a little faster than expected, Dekker turned to Anniken.

"This is heavy," he said, "and I am worried about the noise and, frankly, the lack of any sort of presence, even a trip wire. Nothing, no laid traps, despite probably knowing we're coming. It does not make sense."

"Well I am not surprised, Deks," replied Anniken. "Why waste your resources miles away from the target. We got here by luck. Let's build on that and not look for what is not there."

None of the three converging mini-teams expected any contact for a while. They had many dangerous and unknown kilometres to travel before they would reach the location of the weapon. So for now, they travelled as fast and as quietly as they could, but the noise of their boots reverberating off the prehistoric walls was likely giving advance warning of their approach.

De Boer and his two colleagues knew they had used the fastest, boldest, and definitely the most dangerous entry method into the target. They knew they had done so for good reason: they needed 'eyes on' as soon as possible to find out as much as they could while waiting for the rest of the assault force under Selkirk to arrive. De Boer knew how critical his part of the mission was. He had learnt from bitter experience not to commit to an assault until they had gained as many facts as possible.

Despite De Boer's injury from a bad landing, they made fast, but cautious, progress along the uncharted tunnels miles under sea level. Their ammunition and weaponry was heavy and they had little room for much else than some precious water. Experience told them that they must arrive ready to operate, and each also knew they must make sure that whatever they did supported the mission. Selkirk's orders had been very specific, urging them to observe the target as soon as possible and not to engage the enemy until he got there. Selkirk's main concerns were the number of guards they might have deployed and the surveillance devices in use. Their approach had almost been too easy, without a bullet being fired.

The two main teams were able to work more closely together than they could with Dekker and Anniken. They knew their backup carried a heavy and tiring force multiplier – a plasma automatic machine gun, a lethal and devastating weapon that could make all the difference if the battle with the advance force did not go well.

De Boer's team, and that of Selkirk, periodically dropped

encrypted signal boosters as they moved through the tunnels, allowing communication between them, when required, by sending a signal along the boosters and out to a land-top transmitter.

Selkirk and De Boer's small teams knew they could not rely on their other two team members. Dekker and Anniken were un-contactable, so they had to plan for any confrontation as if the duo were not going to be present.

<hr>

Selkirk slowed from the front and stopped. The others did the same and waited for him to explain his action.

As he shone a tiny torch onto his watch, he spoke.

"OK, we are to speak to Hog in six minutes. I suggest we take this time to have a rest and eat some food." Seeing the other three start to take their heavy backpacks off, he continued, "Let's eat up and check ourselves over. We can't be taking on injuries or fatigue, so use the time wisely."

"Chief," came quietly back at him.

Both assault teams had stopped and were benefitting from the rest. Selkirk would call De Boer, and the two teams would then calculate their relative positions to the probable target and from each other, and re-figure the plan if need be. For now, they all ate and drank water. The dust from the tunnels had invaded their throats and no doubt reached their lungs by now.

<hr>

It was rest time for most of Selkirk's complement, but not for their adversaries. They worked on, still unaware that there were others in their tunnel under the sea hell bent on reversing their hard work.

Then the call came from Selkirk, "Hog, you all OK?"

"All good, Tom, we're good, how are you?" came De Boer's reply.

"Let's keep this short. They said these comms may not be totally safe. So, are you at recon point one yet?" Selkirk asked.

"We have passed R1 by five clicks, despite having one bad fall," he replied, keeping the conversation sharp and direct.

Selkirk knew what the simple code meant.

"Do you remain good to go?"

"Good," came straight back.

"We are at our designated point and fuelling up for P2. Let's end, time check for next chat still good?" asked Selkirk.

"Yes, over," and with that the conversation between close friends in different parts of an uncharted trench under the Adriatic Sea ended. The silence and darkness enveloped them once again now the light from the phone went dead. The dust was a constant companion, however.

<hr />

Many miles away, standing on the balcony of his hotel room, Nathen contemplated all that had happened to him in the last few days. How could he explain to his friends back home, and what should he do now as a result of his sister's call?

Likewise, many more miles away inside the walls of the Kremlin, two intercept operators re-ran the short conversation they had just heard and began to narrow down the origin of the call. When they did so, it would show two locations underwater, not on land.

Nathen texted his sister: 'Going back, contacting the Ad', suggest you do the same'.

He was much more aware of the environment in which he had been thrust and, as a result, had taken security very seriously.

He went back inside his room and started flicking through the foreign television channels, hoping to find something that could occupy his mind for a while.

When she replied, Nathen was disappointed but not surprised.

'Staying, waiting for Dad. Let me know when you see Mum'.

Now he was confused. Was his sister starting to understand the need for subtle and sharp contact, or was it just text language? Either way, he thought, he knew she would do her own thing and that he must now do likewise.

Moving across the room to a drawer by his bed, he picked up his original mobile. Within seconds he had found the admiral's private number and had sent the text as agreed.

'Leaving now. Can you sort the travel plans. N'.

Nathen was now out of the equation and probably for the better, Isabelle thought. Within twenty-four hours he would be back in Cambridge with their mother, trying to explain why his sister was not there with him.

She sat on the edge of her bed, and while she was happy that her little brother was heading to safety under the wing of the admiral, she was also very scared as she now felt very much alone.

"Wine, yes, wine helps," she said out loud, as if hoping for a reply from a nearby friend. She stood and exited the hotel room, en route to the small licensed café bar across the road from her hotel.

———◆→◆←◆———

As the team's two main elements worked their respective ways along the tunnels under the sea, their activities were being monitored on top of the water. The Russian stealth boat had been instructed to move position and get closer north by leaving the Ionian Sea and entering the Adriatic waters, all the time unseen but getting closer to the target.

The next morning seemed to arrive quicker than usual, and sitting high above the very same stretch of water, Nathen sat quietly by himself on a Royal Air Force Hercules. He would be back home soon and 'out of it' as he said to himself, all the time wishing that Isabelle had joined him.

The admiral had sent one of his trusted subordinates to collect Nathen from the small private airfield just outside Cambridge and glean as much additional detail on the team's activities as possible, before delivering him to his family home under the protection of a second guard. In the meantime, he paced his large, echoing office in Whitehall, hoping for the best, yet expecting the worst. He took comfort in the fact that he had sent his best man in to do a job that only he could do.

Likewise, but for a different reason, Kharkov was in a bad mood and paced his own private office. He had received news of the intercepted telephone calls and also seen records of the departure of a British military plane out of the Greek mainland close to his hydroelectric power plant. He correctly feared that his operation could have been compromised.

He called Barishnikov.

"Talk to me now, my friend," he said, in a tone that was not friendly.

"They may know, Mr President. The British. We have been monitoring, and it seems the team may have unwanted company any time soon ..." Before he could explain what steps had been taken, he was interrupted.

"Sort it with immediate effect, my friend, or I will get involved directly and you don't want that!" barked the president at his long-serving friend and trusted confidant.

"Yes, Mr President, I am already taking appropriate action and you will not be disappointed." Barishnikov wanted to get off the line quickly. "I will keep you ..." but as the last word came from his mouth – "informed" – it fell on deaf ears. Kharkov had ended the call and returned to pacing his office. His mood was not any softer despite the conversation he had just had.

———◆◆◆◆———

The activity above the water, even wider afield, was much more chaotic and uncontrolled than the sinister developments way under it. Meanwhile, the Spetsnaz would continue to drill their deadly weapons into the very foundation of the sea, currently unaffected by their unwanted guests, but aware that they may be arriving soon.

One of Selkirk's main adversaries took a break from supporting his colleagues and walked over to their hostage.

"Scientist, are you hungry yet?" said Falco with a smile on his face. "It is really important that you are not in any discomfort down here when we leave you alone with the device," he went on, now searching a bag for rations to give him. "When it ends for you it will be as quick as it was for your two colleagues. That, my British scientist, I promise," but this guarantee came from a face with no smile on it.

"I'm a fuckin' geologist and a bloody good one, you idiot," but he was stopped from speaking further by the barrel of Kel-Tec KSG assault rifle forced into his mouth.

"Foul-mouthed fool, you will be dead soon enough. Do not speed the process up." As Falco walked away, deciding not to provide his captive his own rations to eat, he spoke again.

"There will be no rescue. We know they are coming, and when we deal with them, we will travel to your home town of Cambridge and deal with the leftovers. Cambridge is a pretty city, I hear. Your whole existence will be wiped out, courtesy of the Spetsnaz, no?" And with that he turned his back on Isabelle's father and rejoined his colleagues, leaving Spencer Braving bound and hungry, chained to a bomb so destructive that a whole major European city would feel its wrath soon enough.

Over in London, it was that time of day again and the admiral was called to the office of the permanent undersecretary.

He would have to be on good form to tell the traitor only what he needed to know without giving away any key information.

The regular morning briefing had a different atmosphere to it this time, thought the admiral. His boss was much more formal than usual, perhaps even a little anxious.

"Something bothering you, sir? Shall I call back later?" were his opening words, wondering if the undersecretary was feeling the strain from his Russian paymasters.

"Sit," was the abrupt reply.

The permanent undersecretary was a civilian working in a military world and only he could get away with such insolence towards a high-ranking officer. The admiral sat as instructed.

"Where is Selkirk, and why did our American friends give

his team a bloody minisub?" Carrying on in an ever aggressive tone, he let slip yet again. "If they have found something, or someone, to go after, Admiral, you had better tell me now. I have to report all covert activity to the PM, you know!"

"Who do you think Selkirk is after, Undersecretary?" asked the admiral, trying to draw him out.

"I ask the questions here and you answer them, promptly!"

He stood up, placing both hands on his large, leather-clad desk and leaned over at the admiral. "I repeat, who have they found and where? And why the sub?"

The admiral sat and contemplated an answer but refused to let his boss affect his own confident mood.

"Permanent Undersecretary, as you know, these teams work on initiative – beyond the law when need be. I would hazard a guess that Dekker has called in a favour from his past life and went to help the Greeks search for the three missing UK nationals. I'm sure you would call that proper use of resources this time, wouldn't you?" challenged the admiral.

"Listen, you, like me, know that's bull ..."

"Well, it's all I have, sir," interrupted the admiral, not letting his boss finish his retort, in an attempt to get him angrier and perhaps let his guard down further.

"And Selkirk and the others? Do you even know why they went to Venice? They have disappeared off the radar!"

"Sir, when did they go to Venice, and how could you know that?" The admiral was somewhat excited; this could be his moment.

"I said, I ask the questions here!" but yet again the undersecretary was interrupted and undermined by a rallying admiral.

"Sir, with all due respect, you can ask all you want, but you have just divulged information about Her Majesty's special operations units that you had no opportunity to glean from this side." He pressed the attack, taking the undersecretary by surprise, "And when I say 'this side', I mean the British and any of the other *five eyes*. So now, sir, I repeat my question to you, how do you know Selkirk was in Venice?" demanded the admiral, standing up as his sentence ended. The undersecretary sat back down in his chair.

"Your briefing told me that Selkirk was in Venice, have you forgotten?"

"Undersecretary, I never told you he was in Venice. I deliberately kept it from you," the admiral said with an examining stare.

In what was clearly an act of self-preservation, the undersecretary spoke firmly, albeit with an air of defeat, "Listen, I am the superior here, so you had better stop this insubordination and get back to your morning briefing."

"Sir, in matters of national security and matters against Her Majesty's forces, who could be in harm's way and in danger, rank is absolved according to the Covenant. Do I need to quote you the page, Undersecretary?" The admiral was not for giving up. "Let us lower our tone and act like the highly-paid officials we are. I will ask you for the last time, sir, how did you know he was in Venice?" The admiral changed tack and sat back down, appearing less menacing to his soon-to-be former boss. He could wait as long as needed for an answer.

The men stared at each other for an uncomfortably long time before the undersecretary conceded, turning his chair to face out onto a busy Whitehall. He gazed at the multitude of red London buses and the famous black cabs for another minute.

Then, the silence was broken.

"He was seen at the airport by one of our own spooks on a different tasking," came from the undersecretary without turning to face the admiral. He waited to see if he had any reprieve from the admiral's challenge.

"Right, OK, that would be ... forgive me, Undersecretary, I can't remember the name of all the airports in Europe ..." and he was interrupted as the undersecretary started to think he may have an out from a believing admiral.

"Marco Polo Airport," and again, he waited for the admiral to reply.

"OK, I understand better now. That would have been on Tuesday, then, at Marco Polo?"

"Precisely, Admiral, Tuesday," and now turning to face the admiral again, the undersecretary's face dropped when he saw the expression on his questioning colleague.

"Time to tell me what you have done, Charles. It's game over for you, I'm afraid," and, carrying on before the undersecretary told more lies, "they landed Monday, and at Aviano Air Base, undercover and without proper regs, so no one but the very top brass, and I mean 'top brass', would know."

The admiral continued for a while. "The PM is already aware, Undersecretary. I informed his office of Selkirk's movements and of my suspicions. It seems you've been receiving calls from our Russian friend Kharkov, and the PM is keen to understand why. So, I recommend you tell me everything, and I will see if I can save your pension rights for your lovely wife and family while you enjoy a long visit in a certain establishment, courtesy of your former head and patron, HRM."

The admiral had won.

It was game over, and as he started to record the undersecretary's admission of his betrayal and blackmail, his relations with the Russians and the unauthorised intercept of Isabelle's mobile, the admiral wondered if it was too late to get a message to Selkirk. Could he warn them that they no longer had the edge and were against the clock? They were very likely marching into a trap. *Selkirk would know it; he would assume it's an ambush…* he continued to ponder as he watched the tourists bustling along the pavements outside.

As is customary in these situations, a third man was summoned and sat in silence to act as witness should the now former undersecretary change his evidence at a later date. An hour later, the undersecretary had resigned office, and his belongings and mobile phones were confiscated. They would be quickly transferred by motorbike to GCHQ, where they would be analysed for evidence and traces of other double agents lurking, perhaps now trembling, in the power corridors of Whitehall.

The admiral remained for a short while in the same room as the others escorted his former boss away. He was mentally fatigued but at the same time, elated. He pulled out his secure mobile phone and scrolled the call logs. It was not long before a series on 'Tom S' appeared. He pressed the green call button but it did not ring out. Quickly reverting to text message, he simply wrote and sent 'Extra vigilance needed. They know about you'. This would not reach its desired destination in time, but strangely it made Selkirk's old friend and master slightly more reassured that he had at least tried to help.

———◆◆◆◆◆———

Many miles away from the recent activity in that room overlooking Whitehall, Dekker and Anniken continued their speed march towards an uncertain battle zone and faceless enemy. They had made huge gains, eating up the miles as they both remained focused and determined to be a part of the pending battle and not a late arrival. Still unaware of where the others were and whether or not they had even initiated contact already, they marched the dark and dusty underwater tunnels, carrying heavy equipment but never slowing or stopping. After all, their friend and colleague Selkirk had given them an order, and they would see this through or die trying.

Still many hours fast march from where Dekker led Anniken, the Russian targets had started to finish up their task and prepared to leave their inhospitable home of the past six days. Of course, without natural sunlight or any stars, some had forgotten exactly what day it was, but it didn't really matter at this stage.

Nearer to their target than they knew, Neeman, Kirk and De Boer continued the trek through their part of the tunnel. All three men knew that they would reach the Russians first, but didn't know just how close they were. They had base-jumped into the tunnels less than forty kilometres from where the enemy worked and had made good progress. They would be on top of the Russians and terribly outnumbered, if they continued their pace, within the next two hours.

There were no accurate GPS or map-reading capabilities to tell them when and where they were in conjunction with the target zone. They would have to do it the old-fashioned way and use instinct and common sense. All three of them had both qualities in abundance.

Then there was Selkirk's small team. They had chosen not to stop as originally agreed, but keep marching and refuelling with water and rations as they did so. This had gained them thirty minutes and that would prove invaluable.

They were now so far into the tunnels and so deep under water that their trail of signal boosters was no longer a viable communication option. Instead, all nine of the admiral's special team would have to rely upon experience, training and luck.

———◆▸◈◂◆———

"Commander, we need perhaps three more hours, maybe four, and we will be ready to up and go," came from one soldier, who had seen that his leader, Falco, had stopped and rested for a moment.

"Yes, my friend, thank you. I wonder how long we have before our followers are upon us. We must believe it to be sooner rather than later. Please carry on and remind the others," he said, before standing again and walking over to the hostage bound tight to the explosive device.

Falco sat close to Isabelle's father and this time broke off a piece of chocolate and offered it to his captive.

"You know, if you promised to behave I would make you more comfortable and untie you. Look around and you will see my impressive team in the shadows. They are all heavily armed and happy to put a bullet in your head at any time."

Falco broke off more chocolate, "So, what is it to be, a dignified end, or an uncomfortable one?"

"Please, yes, I would like that," he said, raising his bound hands as high as the ties would allow.

"Alexis," shouted Falco, "I am undoing his ropes; let the others know," and he started the quick process. Whether symbolic or as a warning gesture, he did so with an eight-inch serrated knife that seemed to appear from nowhere. The ropes were deftly slashed without cutting the hands or feet, and he was again able to move freely.

"May I stand and stretch?"

"Of course, and when you have done that, I have water here for you," Falco replied in a tone that echoed the relationship of teacher and student. However, there was never any doubt which of the two men held which role.

They sat together and shared water and rations.

"What is your name, my friend?" asked Falco as a conversation opener, despite the fact he already knew.

"Em, Braving, Spencer Braving, and yours?"

"Call me Falco. That's all you need to know, Spencer," Falco replied, still in a friendly manner.

"OK, so you found these tunnels, or, well, we did, but you wrote of them many years ago, didn't you?" Again, Falco already knew the answer.

"Yes, I established their existence a while back and it took me this time to get the equipment and sponsors together to get here," there was a pause and a smile came across Braving's face before continuing, "and, well, look where it's got me."

"Humour, in your current position, that's good, my friend. We all need to laugh sometimes." Then, changing direction, "Do you know him, Thomas Selkirk? Like your daughter does?" Falco asked, leaving Braving confused as to how his daughter was now in the conversation.

"Who is Thomas Selkirk?" was Spencer Braving's reply. He wanted to extend the conversation and continue the bonding that he felt was occurring.

"He was my friend, Spencer, and now he comes through these tunnels to kill me," he responded.

"Mr Falco, I guess this Selkirk, well, you must have pissed him off big time for him to come here, down here, after you?"

"Yes, well, Spencer Braving, people change and things that once didn't matter sometimes come back to, as you say in the West, bite you in the arse," replied Falco. He was enjoying the conversation. "Anyway, he was a friend once – he even saved my life – but as I said, despite fond memories, the past is the past and now he comes to kill me."

"So, when you discovered the tunnels, did you know my organisation was already looking?"

"We watched you all those years back, in the conference room on the Greek island. We had people there, and we were the only ones that believed you. I understand you were laughed off the stage, together with your young daughter. Isabelle, isn't it?" asked Falco.

Spencer Braving went cold and numb. "You know Izzy? Christ, Falco, leave her out of this, please – she's just a girl," he said, trying hard to remain calm and as if friends with the assassin sitting next to him.

"Seems we know everyone, Spencer. But be still. Neither you nor I will determine what happens to her." Seeing that his prisoner was confused, he carried on and explained. "Some men are coming to kill us," said Falco, looking at Braving directly, "but we are going to kill them first. And if that becomes the reality, then you too will be dead and unaware of pretty Isabelle's fate.

"You can't help her, but hey, Spencer," he said as he rose to his feet, "she followed us here, so she's resourceful. So who knows? She's following in her father's footsteps." As Falco walked away towards the others, he said to himself out loud, chuckling, "Now it is me with humour."

The admiral called his own war cabinet together. He was free from prying eyes and ears and now had only his trusted colleagues around him.

"The op is going down here, here and here," he said, pointing to a satellite map of the Hellenic Trench. Some of those present looked at him in amazement. The admiral had pointed to sea positions, but the earlier pre-briefing had led them to understand that their assistance was required for a land-based assault support operation.

The admiral, anticipating their reaction, said, "Yes, I know where I have just pointed," as he looked in the eyes of each and every one of the four men and two women he had summoned to his office.

"They are in a trench under the seabed, and look, it's not that far-fetched. We have the bloody channel tunnels don't we?" He waited for their acknowledgement, which came quickly.

"Good, so eyes back down. I want you to explore options for where the target could be. Why have the Russians gone to this extent and what is their end goal? I need likely places, people, events and facilities all explored and then explored again," he said, banging his hand down on the table. "We cannot get this wrong. Something is going down and if Selkirk's lot can't stop it, then we have to, understand?"

Within seconds the team had taken the maps and communication records and left the admiral to his thoughts and his fears, alone and wondering how his friend Tom Selkirk was coping.

◆━━◆◆◆◆◆◆◆━━◆

Isabelle worried for her father and, strangely, for Selkirk. She had tried to deny any emotion towards him, but alone in the café by her hotel, she felt her heart beat a little faster when she thought of him.

Spencer Braving also worried, not because of his own predicament, but more for his family.

Advancing along the tunnels, Neeman raised his hand. The other two stopped and waited for further instruction from their point man colleague.

Instinct had brought them safely to the edge of danger.

The three men had reached their observation point, less than three hundred metres from where they had identified the moving shapes of around six men. Their night vision goggles had struggled in the dank environment and the storage batteries from the sun, and then moonlight, were reaching their end.

They secured their vantage position and waited. They waited for something to happen, but none knew if it would be instigated by themselves, by Selkirk's team, or by their Russian enemy. They just waited in the dust and dark of the trench, deep down under the Adriatic waters.

So it was, as Neeman had moved forward on his own and now crouched behind rocks less than one hundred metres from where they worked, he could almost hear them chat amongst themselves. Kirk and De Boer hid a short distance further back and they readied themselves, their weapons and their minds for pending activity, all understanding the gravity of any action.

Selkirk and his team marched on; Dekker and Anniken resumed their speed march after a short rest; the admiral paced back and forth; Isabelle wandered anxiously back to her hotel room; Nathen and his mother hugged tightly; Spencer Braving sat in obedient silence and thought. All the time, the Russians continued to work, stopping only for the occasional glance down the tunnels, waiting and listening.

———◆◆◆◆◆———

Yet another hour passed in the dusty trench, with little obvious activity.

When it happened, it happened so fast that it took everyone by surprise, even the Russians, who knew that they were coming.

As Dekker ran full throttle into the lit area occupied by the Russians, followed closely by Anniken, both full guns blazing, it began. The team had initiated contact with the 'Russian Bears' and it could not be retracted now.

Both Dekker and Anniken had assumed the relative silence meant that the others had been killed, and they were now on a revengeful suicide mission, whereas the truth was very different. The two strongest had marched the furthest and had arrived in the killing zone quicker than any could have anticipated. They would have even surprised themselves if they had time to see the distance they'd travelled.

Deep under the water, and closer to purgatory than most land-dwellers could ever imagine, all hell was about to let loose.

When Dekker let rip with his machine gun, Neeman knew straight away that he needed to make himself seen and known to them to avoid the possibility of cross-fire injury. As Neeman stood, the two behind him needed no further hand signals in the dark. Now five of Selkirk's team found themselves in a direct firefight with their Russian Spetsnaz enemy. Dekker stumbled and fell, still discharging his weapon, such was the strength of his entry into the contact zone. This saved his life as bullets whizzed over and above where he had been a fraction of a second earlier. Anniken's glance was momentarily distracted from the target and directed towards Neeman and two other colleagues now running down towards them from her left. She knew in an instant that Dekker had crashed the party and that a new, currently unwritten, plan had to be acted out, and fast.

When he heard the gunfight a short distance back down in the tunnel, Selkirk dropped his backpack, as did the others, instinctively allowing them to speed up their run, weapons armed, towards what they assumed was a premature battle with their Russian counterparts. They were right and yet were still two minutes away from evening-up the odds.

Anniken shouted above the noise of a new, third shooter firing back at her.

"Stay down, Neems, stay down," she shouted as she started laying down covering fire, allowing Dekker a few precious seconds to roll to cover behind a large rock. When he lifted his gun and head to look past it, he saw Kirk, and now Neeman, crouching behind cover, shooting back at two more Spetsnaz soldiers. In that second he, too, realised that they had arrived early, not too late.

The tunnel lit up with the combustion of gunpowder and explosions, allowing both sets of friendly elements momentary glimpses of the enemy and, importantly, their faces, as masks and night vision equipment were hastily torn off. Ricochets echoed and moved around the tunnel network. It proved to be a miracle that in the over-ambitious moment when Dekker and Anniken piled in, firing rapidly, no real damage had been done.

As quick as the noise had started, a surreal silence suddenly descended as both sets of opponents took stock of the situation and considered their next move. This allowed De Boer time to replace his night vision goggles and look around. He instantly saw a man cowering behind a strange-looking metal container. He took this to be a hostage, one of the missing scientists and possibly Isabelle's father.

<hr/>

The silence allowed Selkirk and the others seconds more to get closer, but it also confused them: why had the noise and firefight stopped so soon?

Could it be over? Could his team have killed their entire enemy so quickly? Could they have done the same to his team? Whatever it was, they continued their run in the dark towards an uncertain destiny. Soon enough they would also be confronting these 'bears', but they didn't know this just yet.

<hr/>

Dekker felt uneasy.

He ran at speed towards Anniken, who was in cover behind a second rock. Reaching her position without being shot at further confused him.

"What the fuck's going on, Annie?" he whispered.

"Hmm, fucking weird, I agree. The others are here, did you see Neeman? He's there," as she pointed to his approximate location.

"Yup, that means Hog and Kirk are around somewhere. Have you counted them, do you know how many?" he asked.

"No, it's too hard, but the more we wait this out, the more time we give to Tom and the others," she replied.

"We can't work on that assumption, Annie, they may be dead for all we know. We have to go in and get them, end this," he encouraged, but before he could make the next move, it was done for him.

A series of bullets rained down on their position in a manner suggesting suppressive fire and that the Russians were on the move.

Neeman let off a series of short bursts from his machine gun and was immediately accompanied by De Boer, crouching a metre behind him.

When the first Russian fell it was hard to tell exactly how many bullets hit him, but if they were able to stop and count, it was well into two digits. Instead, the firefight rose its head up again violently.

Both sides flexed their muscle and let off round after round, in hope more than in purpose. The Russians were moving to new positions and the team was simply responding, trying to slow their advance, if indeed they were advancing and not retreating.

The tunnel lit up with sparks and small weapon explosions, the noise was deafening and the empty metal bullet cases danced merrily along the dirt, bumping into the walls and rock that littered the area.

There was so much lead flying around, the risk of injury from a ricochet off the stone walls was as great as any direct hit. This prompted a second and even more confusing silence. The Russians had moved position and then suddenly stopped their assault. It was becoming clear to the team that the distance between them and the enemy was increasing. They were in fact moving towards a specific location in the tunnel. Dekker was last to stop firing back. He was pumped up and focused on one specific Russian, less than thirty feet away, however, like the others, he did stop and take stock of the situation.

Still to discharge his weapon, Kirk walked the edge of the darkest wall and around a few metres to a clear vantage point. From where they crouched, both Anniken and the others could see him signal separately to each of them in turn.

Anniken whispered to Dekker, "Kirk sees five more. I think we wait to see what he signals next." The same hand gesture was delivered to Neeman, who repeated the action to De Boer. If there were indeed only five, then the arrival of Selkirk and the others would surely prove decisive enough to initiate their own assault.

All eyes were on Kirk. Both Dekker and De Boer had moved so they could see him directly. De Boer was now positioned well enough to also see the shadows of his two colleagues several metres away on the other side of the huge tunnel. Together, these two groups at first appeared to have the upper hand strategically, cutting off any escape route, and able to pin their enemy down from two positions.

Kirk again gestured to Neeman. His left arm appeared to suggest to Neeman that he was planning to go in amongst the Russians. Dekker and Anniken, however, interpreted it differently from their direction of view.

"Did you see that, Deks?" she asked in a quiet voice. "Is he suggesting we go in?" They took their attention off Kirk and looked at each other, instinctively trying to determine what the second gesture meant, but in doing so, both Anniken and Dekker missed Kirk's third and last signal, this time using both hands. The first gesture they missed was an instruction to halt, to do nothing because he had seen something new. His final gesture in the dark and cold tunnel was that there actually appeared to be eight Russians, reducing their advantage considerably.

Dekker rose upright and with misinterpreted trust in his colleague, moved towards the Russian position. Anniken followed close behind; both were primed and certain of an imminent hell firefight.

Kirk saw them move forward and his face turned to fear. They were walking into a firefight that would prove to be their last. The Russians had assembled in a tight diamond shape, waiting the attack. They were in a highly protective formation, using the natural environment and their transport boxes. It was as if they had been expecting the team to arrive and had rehearsed their defence.

Kirk knew he had time to do only one thing before his colleagues made contact with their enemies. He chose to go in to support them, rather than turn and communicate the pending firefight to De Boer or Neeman. He expected them to follow him in. They did so when they saw him raise his gun and move forward.

The five trusted and loyal friends of Tom Selkirk moved towards the fortress diamond defensive position of eight highly trained and waiting Russian special forces soldiers. Selkirk did not know this, of course – he and his team were still seconds away, running as fast as the dark and shadows would allow, still wondering why there was a second firefight and a second eerie silence quickly after.

Those few seconds felt like an eternity to Selkirk, Biddiss, Lamberti and Peterson. Lots of bad things could happen in mere moments when highly trained soldiers faced off together.

Dekker started to ready himself and the shoulder cannon, when Anniken intervened and stopped him. Selkirk raised a hand to likewise stop him from using the end-game cannon

– his team had arrived. So it began for a third time, but this firefight had a different tone. Both sides knew that letting off rounds so close together in a walled environment with machine guns would mean no one would likely get out alive. The bouncing of bullets off the walls would make sure of that. Instead, instinct and training took over on both sides. Like some mad but fatal synchronised dance, both sides entered the fray with semi-automatic handgun in one hand and lethal knife in the other.

Dekker was first to be seen. He was also first to take a bullet and, luckily for him, it grazed his left shoulder, puncturing his armoured suit, continuing out and into the darkness behind. He moved to his side and groaned, but it was in shock rather than pain. The adrenaline was such that he would feel no pain, not even when the second bullet grazed his hip and passed on.

As the second bullet did its damage, Dekker had released three rounds of his own into the face of the closest Russian, who had, to his fatal detriment, focused his aim upon the advancing Anniken.

Neeman was next to make contact. Taking aim at the only enemy he could clearly see when he turned into the killing zone, he raised his handgun. As his finger squeezed the trigger, a knife blade was pushed hard into the side of his neck.

Neeman's target had turned out not to be the closest Russian. One hid nearer and waited for him to come into lunging range.

As Neeman fell, seconds to live, the Russian tumbled with him and put a second deadly knife blow into his neck.

When he saw Neeman fall, Selkirk found a burst of energy, and at a fast run, fired his machine gun towards the assassin, in anger. Seeing that his weapon was not accurate on the move, he threw it down and reached for his pistol. Still running, and with handgun out in front of him, Selkirk fired three quick shots. The mini explosions as the bullets streaked out towards their target temporarily lit up Selkirk's face. To anyone that could see it, they would have glimpsed years of pent-up anger, but also the determination of a soldier who had seen friend after friend fall before his eyes while he remained alive, returning from operations and fated to watch them enter the ground, six feet down.

The first bullet struck its target in the chest as he was rising up to his feet. The impact of it knocked him back down to the dirt and dust. A second left the barrel, this time puncturing the Russian's ear and through to his brain, before exiting out the back of his head, along with flesh and skull bone. Now three yards away, the third and final bullet struck the Russian mid face, destroying what little remained of his appearance.

Selkirk jumped both dead bodies, one being his friend Neeman, with whom he'd shared several tours and many close-death experiences.

What remained of Selkirk's team complement entered the Russian Bear's lair and were amazed at what happened next. No amount of training could have prepared Selkirk and his squad for what he saw, or his friends for what they were to experience.

They seemed to simply fall down into the ground in one simultaneous movement. Three dead Russians lay nearby, but the others just fell down into the ground and out of sight all at the same time. They released a mechanism unseen by any of Selkirk's team, and simply dropped down out of sight. All, that was, except one, who seemed to wait for Selkirk's astonishment.

Selkirk froze when their eyes met. Anniken took her hand off the trigger and turned her head to watch her number one. Dekker raised his weapon but was forcibly stopped by a stretched-out arm from Anniken.

Biddiss spoke, "Tom, I have a clear shot," but before he could question whether to fire or not, Selkirk lifted his hand. This signalled the others to stand down.

Several seconds passed, and the two former friends, now enemies, were metres apart.

"Falco."

"Hello, Tom."

Nether wanted a conversation. They weren't really prepared for one either.

Confident that Biddiss and Selkirk had the situation in hand, Anniken turned to Dekker and started to address his wounds. De Boer knelt at the dead Neeman and in foolish hope, lifted his wrist, looking for a pulse. There was none.

"Fuck, I thought you were …" Selkirk started.

"Dead?" Falco interrupted.

Now it was Selkirk's turn to question back, "I saw the Osprey blow."

"Yup, but hey, people like us seem to live forever. Last rat standing and all that. I have to leave you again. My boys will be far enough away by now," and just as Selkirk raised his handgun, Falco, like the others, seemed to fall down through the floor of the tunnel.

As he did, Biddiss noticed him release a hand grenade, pin out.

"Grenade!" he shouted, and each and every one turned and hit the dirt, making themselves as small as possible, with boots facing the pending explosion.

When it exploded, it echoed down the tunnels for many

miles. Falco ran the new passage and smiled as he did. Selkirk and the others looked up from the ground, now disorientated.

"Anyone hit," shouted Selkirk.

The others signalled back they were good. All except De Boer. He had taken a shrapnel wound to his neck and quickly covering it with his hand, tried to nod to Selkirk that it was nothing. As the others started to focus on their whereabouts, De Boer suddenly made a decision. He wandered off a short distance and addressed his wound with his first aid kit. Anniken watched him for a few seconds. De Boer being silent after a firefight was not something she was used to. Her intuition told her something was wrong.

Recovering their focus and checking their bodies for any further injuries as well as the existing ammunition, the team was together for the first time in a few days. Together, that was, except for Neeman, who lay in the dark and dust and would inevitably remain there, unable to receive a dignified burial on home soil. Selkirk knew he would not have cared and would understand.

"Hog, Kirk, secure the holes, check for booby traps, and let me know how the fuck they just fell through the floor," barked Selkirk.

"Deks, you good?" came second, and was received with a nod from both Anniken and Dekker.

He continued, "Bidd, what we going to do with Neems? We can't leave him," but as he said the words, Selkirk already knew the procedure and the answer pending from Biddiss.

"Done over, Tom. Let's cover him from the rats and say goodbye; we can't stay here," and as Biddiss spoke, Kirk shouted loudly.

"Tom, over here, I've fucking found it, and the man! And

this time, its fucking ticking, mate!"

Selkirk looked over to De Boer and then Dekker, "Stay here please, and watch those fucking escape holes – if they can go down, I guess they can come up," he said. Patting Biddiss and Lamberti on the shoulder, they walked over to Kirk.

Peterson was about to follow the others but he turned to Dekker in request, "Good here, Petes, off you go," Dekker said.

"It's a nuke; it's big, Tom, and it's ticking. It's fucking ticking, mate!" yelled Kirk as his colleagues approached, eyes transfixed on the metal device strangely drilled down into the dirt and more oddly, vertical in position.

"It's firing down in a controlled detonation," said Selkirk. "We must be on or near a plate, like Isabelle said. Christ, that's it, they did Bouvet and they want to do it again here. Knowing Falco, this is not a random location."

"Tom, look," Kirk pointed to a mangled and dying body lying close to the bomb. "It's her dad, he's all cut up." Unable to speak and with blood running from several wounds, Isabelle's father had seconds to live. He knew this from what he felt and what he managed to hear.

"Do we take him?" asked Kirk.

"We can't take him, he is going to die and he would only slow us up. We'll get him when we come back for Neems," replied Selkirk.

"Well, grenades and bullets will do that, mate. Not our concern," said Biddiss as if to reinforce Selkirk's decision. "Tom, what do we do? We may be able to stop this, but we can't go after them as well. It's one or the other, I say."

"We sort this fucker, then get out of these bloody tunnels," was the swift decision.

"Roger that," and Biddiss went to inform Anniken that she had a more important task to attend to than dress Dekker's flesh wound.

"Dignify Neeman and the father, check for traps and evidence, kick those fuckers out the way," ordered Selkirk, pointing to the closest dead Russian. "Then report on our ammo and rations. We need to follow them down the holes, so please do it now. There may be a second bomb, or worse, they may have a detonation trigger with them," he forcefully instructed.

"Annie, no pressure, but this little beauty is a bit naughtier than those you dealt with back in Palestine. Can you handle something this big?" Biddiss asked with a smile, trying to relax her before she started her deadly task.

"Big things are right up my street, Bidd. Stand back," she replied smiling.

Overhearing, Dekker said, "As expected," and for a moment the team's spirits were raised as they forgot that they were under an ocean, in the dark, and about to dismantle a nuclear weapon.

Chapter 12

Finding Falco

She had worked on the device for around two hours and had made some progress. She was to disengage the timer from the warhead, and in doing so, they could leave it and go after Falco. Most of the others had left and were in pursuit of the Russians, but that didn't worry Anniken. She had the company of Dekker and Lamberti to keep her motivated, not that she needed to be.

So it was, Selkirk's team was yet again split and weakened, covering too many bases. The five men paced the newly discovered lower tunnels at reduced speed; they expected both ambush and traps. De Boer tried to keep up with the others but his neck injury, the extent of which he hid from his friends, was now becoming an issue. He feared he would slow them down and they would lose touch with the enemy. Somewhere up ahead, and probably having explored the tunnels prior, were their Russian adversaries, the remaining five targets and Falco. It was always Falco; he never seemed to die despite the odds being stacked against him. Selkirk would never stop going after him until hell was his home, but for now they walked the dark tunnels in anticipation of an ambush at any moment.

They walked in one long line, one behind the other, through the tunnels and through the darkness. The lower tunnels were wet and damp as water ran down the walls, reminding the five men that they were under water in a place designed for the movies, only this was no film set. They were chasing adversaries with an hour lead in a place unimaginable to most.

———◆❖◆———

"I'm getting bored with this, Annie, can you move your arse, nice and perfectly formed though it is, can you get a move on?" said Dekker.

"Yes, fucking yes, Deks! It's just a nuke and I haven't quite found the 'off' button, but yes, you just keep looking at my perfect arse," she replied without taking her attention off the device, her head almost inside the bomb casing, always focused.

"You two just need to do it and get this thing over with," came from Lamberti, "get a hotel room and stop talking like a frustrated couple," he continued.

"Bert, Dekker doesn't do girls," was the muffled retort from Anniken.

Refusing to let it go, Dekker replied back, "I only do women and there's none down here in this shit-hole place." Dekker's last comment ended the bored chat, and the three soldiers seemed to return to their roles of supporting Anniken and securing the location from surprise attack. The three sat with an operational mindset and were, in the scheme of things, comfortable and enjoying each other's company.

———◆❖◆———

Isabelle left her hotel and walked the tourist-filled streets of Venice. She walked over numerous bridges and alongside the gondolas, all the time thinking of what may be happening with her friends. Her feelings towards Selkirk were strong. Stronger than she expected, or even knew. They had crept up on her over the period and now she didn't know if he was still alive. Would she see him again and would he even be interested in her?

Isabelle walked and never looked over her shoulder. She walked without a care in the world as her friends marched the deadly tunnels many miles away – they weren't thinking of her.

Then she received a text message, as her phone in her pocket vibrated.

Opening the message it simply read 'Back home, you should be also, N'.

She smiled briefly as she knew her little brother was safe and home, then she went back to her imagination and thoughts of Tom Selkirk as she walked the cobbled tourist-filled streets of Venice.

———◆◆◆◆———

Back in London the admiral was called to the Cabinet Office and to his surprise, the audience included the prime minister.

"Prime Minister," he said.

"Admiral, nice to see you again, news of your team? Do you have a target?"

The others in the room remained silent and stared at the admiral.

"Am I free, sir, you know, to talk?" was his reply.

"Yes, all good, what is going down in Venice," the prime minister said as if to reassure the admiral that he could speak freely.

"Sir, right, OK, lots to say," and as they sat attentively, the admiral spoke to the occupants in the room, most of whom he had never met. Around an hour later they all knew what he knew.

Selkirk and his team were very likely under the Adriatic Sea, in air-filled tunnels, chasing Russian Spetsnaz while others tried to defuse a nuclear bomb designed to initiate a tsunami through tectonic plate movement and destroy a target yet unknown.

The unknown contingent in the room simply wrote notes on pads as if this was a routine occurrence, which it certainly was not.

It's as if this happens every day, the admiral thought to himself. *They accept this weird shit like its normal,* but then he felt rising emotion and the need to speak out. "This doesn't happen every day, you know. This is simply exceptional, and if our boys can't stop this, something very bad will happen. Prime Minister, sorry for this short outburst, but something very dire is happening and I felt some in the room just needed to know that."

"Admiral, your men have my admiration and support. I, for one, never take our special forces for granted," he said, landing a gentle hand on the admiral's shoulder.

He made his apology and left the room, with only the prime minister acknowledging his efforts with a special and warm handshake. "Oh, and on that other matter, Admiral, your intuition was right and your country owes you. We should have known he was a mole much earlier." Those words, however, didn't warm the admiral as they should have done. He had ended the life and career of a former boss and in doing so had irretrievably halted the happiness of a family.

————◆◈◆————

Selkirk led. They let him. They knew he had to be in front and technically closest to Falco in the chase. He didn't speak, but when he stopped, the others did, too. He was their leader and their inspiration. This once 'fallen angel', as Anniken had called him, was back and was stronger than they had seen him in a long time, both in mind and in body. Selkirk had been through too much. He had endured more than others could have coped with, and now he was back. He had risen up out of the fire and became the soldier again that they knew and needed.

───◆◆◆◆───

A distance back, in the upper tunnels, Anniken had worked tirelessly and now she found help from her own 'angel'. She stood up and stretched, having been in an uncomfortable stress position for a while. "Right, we are down to three coloured wire choices and very little time," she said as she once again positioned her head and right shoulder in the cavity of the device.

"Deks, red, blue or green?" she asked out loud.

"Christ, Annie, I have no bloody idea," he replied.

"Choose!" she barked back at him.

"Red, it's always bloody red!"

Anniken moved her tool and snipped the blue wire. As she did, a timer device jumped into life.

"Boys, it wasn't the blue wire, then; and we seem to have a countdown clock," she said from inside the housing. She carried on. "Bert, green or red?"

"Fuck, Annie, stop this, cut the bloody red as Deks said!" he shouted back at her.

She smiled to herself and moved the cutters towards the green wire. Then she cut it. The clock stopped counting down.

As she stood up and dusted herself down a little, Dekker spoke, "You just needed to listen to me, woman!" But as she moved off a little, she pointed into the deactivated bomb.

Both men peered in and saw that the red wire remained intact.

"Yup, she had us, Deks," Lamberti said under his breath.

"Right, boys, we off to help Tom, are we?" she said, and, without questioning her comment but simply assuming that the device had been made safe, they likewise stood and prepared to leave.

"Set a GPS point, Deks. We will need to retrieve this bomb when this is all over," said Lamberti.

"Yup, done already," was his friend's reply.

"Anyone want to say farewell to Neems?" asked Dekker.

Anniken replied sharply, "He's only staying here temporarily; we'll say goodbye when he's up top with us again, so now, let's go."

The three soldiers then systematically lowered themselves and their remaining kit down into the lower tunnels and, moments later, were moving at a fast pace after their colleagues.

It was time for De Boer to make a decision. He suspected he needed to from the moment he felt the grenade shrapnel rip into his neck.

"Tom, guys, I need to rest," he said. "Seems this fuckin' cut is draining all my energy. I will wait here for the others and evac out with them, fully rested. Kirk, give me your torch and I will be fine here for hours, waiting."

Kirk did as he was asked. Selkirk looked straight into the eyes and soul of his injured friend. Then he turned and walked on, "Hog, extra training for you when we get back to base; you're not fit enough," he said over his shoulder.

Anniken and the others were free from traps and ambushes, knowing that Selkirk's squad had already cleared the tunnels, so they set off, at speed, to unify the team again.

It wouldn't be long before Lamberti found the first deliberate leave-behind from the team in front. A small torch was rammed above the running water into the tunnel wall. The battery had a three-hour lifetime and the beam remained very strong.

"I would say they passed by here less than an hour ago," Lamberti concluded.

"Yes, agree, we're catching them up, let's crack on," Dekker replied. They moved on, leaving the mini torch in the wall to run out of battery life and return the tunnel to darkness. They continued onwards and slowly upwards, as the past few kilometres had seen a gradually steepening incline.

When the door opened to the admiral's office, he was deep in thought. The sudden movement startled him, but when he saw who it was he came quickly together and spoke, "Good, you have the list then?" he asked. "I hope it's short."

"We have three, sir, three highly likely targets for this bomb – to which the wave could hit," said his senior team leader, Russell Jenkins.

"Good," but before the admiral could continue, he was cut short.

"No, sir, not good, all bad, let me show you," and then the two men went eyes-down to the map and the trusted colleague's conclusion.

"So the first problem we have is that we don't know the size or magnitude of the bomb and its precise location," said Jenkins. He went on, "This is crucial – it could tell us the direction of any likely tsunami and make target prediction and evacuation easier."

"Yes, I get that, but we do know the tectonic plate lines. Can't that help?" questioned the admiral.

"Not really, sir, because if it's a shaped charge it could split the seabed in one specific direction, thus focusing the resultant wave toward a target. Then the location, if it's South Adriatic, the wave could be less destructive, as its journey to land is longer and its power will be partly dissipated." He looked up at the admiral to gauge his understanding, then carried on. "If it's north side, then it's a completely different ball game. The wave could reach eighty to a hundred feet high and, well, goodbye Northern Italy, for example."

"Right, I understand. So the unknowns are its location, magnitude, if it's directional, if Selkirk's lot are alive and whether or not it's been stopped. Christ, that's not helpful for planning," the admiral was speaking to himself out loud.

"So we have to hope Selkirk has found and stopped it, end of," he concluded, this time looking directly at Jenkins, who nodded.

"OK, so your three likely targets are what then?"

"You know my team spent all night on this, and their three most likely targets are, firstly, the annual boat show in Split Croatia. It's about sales of super yachts, and all of President Kharkov's oligarch rivals will be in attendance. The Intel suggests that his power and influence would increase massively inside the Kremlin without rivals swaying the balance in the corridors of power."

"OK, I get that, but it's a bit extreme. But let's keep in on the table and set up a planning team specifically for Split and an evac," said the admiral. "What else?"

"San Marino, but this one needs more work. The heads of

every major global charity are gathering there to discuss the migrant crisis currently raging through Europe and North Africa. Now, we don't yet have an angle on the why, but it could be about that: by taking out the management structure of leading charities, governments would temporarily lose a handle on where they are arriving from and numbers."

"Yes, I can see that, but why does it benefit Russia?" asked the admiral.

"Well, it is currently distracting the world powers away from what is happening in the Ukraine and Russia's latest expansionist purge into Belarus. They are piling tanks and men into its eastern border, and they could land grab with nothing more than strong words from the UN."

"Now that I get; it is a bloody mess with the migrants. OK, and thirdly?"

"Well ..." Jenkins hesitated for a second, making the admiral raise his eyes from the map in front of him. "Venice."

The admiral repeated the conclusion, "Venice, right, why?"

"The European Union Treasury officials are meeting there from tomorrow. They are rewriting the member countries' contributions and rebates. The thinking on this, sir, is that wiping them out would bring immediate European instability to the London and Paris stock markets, and this in turn will then spread to New York. The run on key stocks and shares could bankrupt some smaller countries, which in turn would then have to be bailed out by richer countries, pushing them close to economic ruin too." He looked at the admiral, who was now looking out his office window, deep in thought.

"You know, sir, if both Europe and America struggle economically, then along comes ..." and then Jenkins was interrupted.

"Along comes Kharkov and his billions to the rescue us all, but at extortionate rates and terms. Jenkins, focus on this option, put everything into this target. Selkirk went in at Venice, it must be that."

"Yes, sir, right away," and with this, the admiral was again back to his solitary thoughts and hopes relating to his best option – Tom Selkirk.

<hr />

They were all struggling against deeper water as they made their way up the dark, lower tunnel. Their wet clothing became heavy, a burden, and slowed their pace a little.

Up ahead, Anniken could hear a flow of water that didn't sound natural. They continued on, and occasionally the three could hear voices but were just too far away to determine to whom they belonged. They pushed on hard, battling fatigue and the steep incline, which was clearly leading them all back to sun and wind and daylight once again. At around one hundred and fifty yards away they stopped and listened. The water was reaching knee-high now, but as it originated from the walls and not some current, their location would not likely be compromised by the noise of boots through water.

Lamberti whispered to the others, "It's Selkirk, it must be, we should conduct the challenge."

"Can you clearly see it's our lot, Bert?" replied Dekker.

"Yes, I am sure, us Italians, we can see in the dark, you know."

"Whatever, you're also the most full of bull. If you're sure, do the challenge," said Dekker and as Anniken nodded her agreement, he shouted out.

"You fucks going to wait up or what?"

There was a pause and the three could see the shapes up ahead had frozen, the silhouettes of their weapons raised and ready for use.

Then came the response, "That's not the fucking challenge, Italian!"

The stress on Lamberti had become apparent and he had decided to disregard pleasantries and procedure and simply ask.

It was indeed Selkirk's team, and they likewise knew the three now moving towards them were friend, not foe. The challenge was so ludicrous in their current predicament that it was the perfect test, and this was not wasted on the others, who now had no worry of any surprise in the gloom being Russian.

"Where is Hog?" asked Dekker. "He left with you lot."

"Fuck, you never met him back there? He was hiding an injury from the grenade, but assured us he was fine. He said he would wait for you guys – he didn't want to slow us and he needed the rest," and in a continued and rushed voice Biddiss looked back down into the darkness and summed up what they all now suspected. "Guess that fuck was in a bad way after all and thought we were better off without him as a distraction. Brave fuck."

Selkirk took over. "If he is alive we will get him when we recover Neems' body. Now, we go on!"

They turned and carried on towards the perceived exit. Anniken's heart felt heaviest. She had seen him wander off alone back in the tunnel, after the grenade, and had not gone to his aid.

They were again united, but it would not be the last time that one would disappear. For now, Selkirk acknowledged each of his returned colleagues and spoke first, "Exit just five hundred yards ahead. Petes has been up to recce and confirms nothing sinister up top. It's a steep and unstable climb, so keep your game face on until you're properly safe. Our friends have exited and won't yet know if we've stopped the bomb. Annie, you did stop it, didn't you?"

"Well, Tom, it will need to be retrieved and made secure, but yes, it won't go boom anytime soon," she said.

"Good job, let's go and get out of this shithole," and then, minutes later, the seven were back into the daylight, exiting upward into clean air, but not yet exactly aware where they were.

For the six Russians now making their way rapidly down the hillside to the shoreline less than a kilometre away, they all knew exactly where they had exited the trench and where they were going. The stealth ship rested hidden and prepared for its next journey, should it be asked.

It hid amongst the hundreds of tiny islands close to the fishing village of Zadar on the Croatian coast. It would rest and wait until the deadline had passed. They would then know whether to sit out the surge of a giant tsunami, or whether their work was not yet finished. If not, they would be called on again to power the nuclear reactor on board into the walls of the famous Doge's Palace in Venice, where thirty-four senior government treasury officials from across Europe, together with their closest aides, would be sitting and planning the well-being of millions of other Europeans.

In the Kremlin, many others simply waited. They waited for the deadline to pass and the sea to rise and break open in anger and destruction. Kharkov especially waited.

The Russian foes also waited, on the stealth ship, and while they did so, they refuelled their stomachs, arsenal and minds.

The admiral was becoming inpatient, but he was to have the shortest wait of all. His phone rang. The caller ID said 'Tom S'.

The admiral banged the table with his fist, "Yes, thank Christ!" and with the commotion, his private secretary burst into the room.

"Sir?"

"It's fine, Max, it is Selkirk calling," he said, answering the call, waving him off.

Max left as quickly as he had entered and closed the big, heavy, leather-clad door behind him.

"Tom, bloody Tom, talk to me," the admiral's relief was palpable as he spoke to his ace for the first time in over six days.

"Well, I never fuckin' thought I would be so happy to see the sun and breathe fresh air again as I am right now, with respect, sir," was his reply.

"So you're out and everyone's good?"

"Most of us, Admiral, Neeman will need to be brought out later."

"Bugger. Sorry, Tom, I know he was also a friend."

"Yup, but when this crap's done we will get him out and sorted properly, won't we, sir?"

"Yes, bloody yes, Tom. So, speak to me," as the admiral changed to listening mode.

"Right, we are seven and we believe that with three downed Spetz, they are six. We just don't know where they have gone," and as Selkirk went on, the admiral sat back down.

"Annie's stopped the bomb, firstly, but it will need to be collected and secured when this ends, when you get Neems back," and as he spoke to the admiral, Lamberti offered Selkirk his water bottle. The admiral didn't know why there was a longer pause than normal as Selkirk drank, but sat quietly. The dust washed away, Selkirk carried on.

"Peterson is grabbing the coordinates now as to where we have come out, so stay with me," and not stopping to await confirmation, he carried on at speed. "So, we stopped their main game, but they will have a backup. We don't know where they are, but they knew the tunnels and their escape route well, so they will have transport ready. I suggest you keep looking for a target, as these guys don't give up," and as he took another drink of water, the admiral took the opportunity to talk.

"We have a target, Tom."

Selkirk looked at the phone and then the others around him. Biddiss was closest and he also heard the admiral's claim.

Selkirk raised the phone back to his ear as he heard Biddiss tell the others, "They know the target."

"Venice, where you went in. It's finance and the EU; they want to fuck up the economies and the markets," the admiral said tersely. Selkirk didn't need to know specifics – his team just needed to know where they were off to next and who they were protecting. They already knew who they were safeguarding the targets from.

Peterson interrupted the call with a hand gesture to Selkirk.

"Standby, Admiral," said Selkirk.

"Tom, we are at some fishing village called Zadar in Croatia," and he carried on, "Bidd, says the target is Venice, so we are around one hundred and ten kilometres away, without transport," and with those words, Peterson walked back to the others, allowing Selkirk to talk again.

"I heard that, Tom," said the admiral. "Do we know anything about the Russians and what they could be thinking when the deadline passes?"

"Well, sir, we do know that something entered the Med a couple of weeks back, which even the NSA couldn't see, and we now believe it to be up top, not under the water." He stopped to think for a second.

The others could see that Selkirk's brain was working overtime. The admiral couldn't, but knew something was happening, so he waited, quietly sitting in his office, unable to help directly.

"Right, what method of propulsion is hardest to see from space?" Selkirk never waited for anyone to answer, "Yes, there will be power trails, but much later and smaller, like in Gibraltar."

Anniken spoke first, "The fucking mystery vessel is nuke powered! Of fucking course, fail with one nuke, then there's the plan B nuke!" and as everyone, including a listening admiral, realised the danger had not passed, Selkirk addressed them.

"OK, target Venice, and it's just got harder. The next fucking bomb is mobile!"

"Christ, get transport onto the water, head for Venice.

I will get you air-lifted soon, but for now, get anything you can and get going!" the admiral demanded.

"Yes, Admiral, on it," and the line went dead. The seven picked up their gear. They didn't need instruction and walked fast down the slope towards the fishing village of Zadar to requisition transport.

The admiral was busy. He liked being busy; it made him feel that he was at last truly helping the team.

In minutes, he had passed the Intel over to his colleagues in GCHQ and they would likewise do so to the Americans. Next was his command team in the navy, who were to contact the Italian fleet while also determining whether any allied forces were currently patrolling the waters close to Venice. For now, Number Ten would have to wait.

"Sir," as his number one came back into his office several minutes later. The admiral swung round in his chair and ended the call he was on to his Royal Air Force equal. "Sir, Marina Militare has the vessel *Comandante Bettica* in the Adriatic right now," said Stephen Peters, a young but quickly rising officer.

"Yes, good, and is it carrying?" was the admiral's response.

"Yes, it's got a Lynx on board, sir, and it could take all of Selkirk's team, now there are only seven."

"Get me a direct line to the ship's commander, now!" bellowed the admiral, but Peters had already suspected the request and handed the admiral the lengthy call sign and encryption codes for contacting the control room of the *Bettica*.

The admiral wasn't surprised and sat down, picking up the telephone again.

Thirty minutes had passed since Selkirk had relayed the news to London, and now his whole team was at the harbour edge, pacing the line of fishing vessels but hoping for something faster.

Anniken was the best linguist in the group, and she went off to the harbour master's office. Her broken Greek language would prove fruitful.

Selkirk turned around and looked through the line of old and dilapidated fishing boats, all in need of repainting, when a couple of minutes later he heard the approaching noise of a powerful outboard motor.

"Found this, boys!" she shouted as she came into view of her colleagues. She moored up alongside them in the twin-engine inflatable rib. Dekker responded.

"What you have to do to get that, Annie?"

"Something you and me will never do, Deks. Get in, *tempus fugit*," she said.

She smiled to herself, but not about her sarcastic comment to Dekker, more that she was imagining the faces of those who would walk in on a tied-up harbour master, who was now one fast boat down.

"Petes, get me a rough bearing and speed for the admiral, as I suspect we have a date with a helicopter," instructed Selkirk as they took their positions inside the boat, their remaining gear and weapons by their side.

As she manoeuvred the vessel away from the harbour edge, now a much heavier and more sinister-looking boat, Selkirk glimpsed a woman walking on the deck of one ship nearby.

"Hey," he called out, and as he did so, a look of bewilderment came across his face. He didn't know why he had shouted – she could not possibly have been there.

"Tom?" enquired Kirk.

"Oh, eh, nothing. I thought it was someone I, well, never mind," and he turned forward, viewing the horizon in front of him, still confused why a vision of Isabelle had popped into his mind.

For her part, she was many miles away in Venice, thinking of Selkirk and all the time not knowing that he had started the journey back into her life.

As the rib accelerated up to fifty knots, the occupants were showered with sea water, but no one cared. They sat and looked out across the water. None spoke, not even when Selkirk relayed the text message around that he had received from the admiral.

'Lynx in the air, monitoring your position, uplift in twenty'.

They simply looked down at their watches, then back up to the water as it sped past.

It had been four-and-a-half hours since Anniken had made safe the device in the tunnel. No one in London, in a hotel room in Venice, or moving at speed northwest through the Adriatic Sea, knew that they had thirty more minutes before the deadline would pass and the Kremlin would initiate a secondary plan involving the stealth ship.

———◆◆◆◆———

When Kirk spotted the speck in the distance moving towards them and pointed it out to the others, a much more sinister motion was underway, with a planned setting and target of Venice. The Russians on both the stealth ship and behind the high walls of the Kremlin knew that their tsunami bomb had likely failed, and for those on the boat, they now knew they were on a suicide mission.

Anniken cut the rib's twin engines and the boat quickly slowed and then succumbed to the mercy of the waves and currents, no longer able to fight against both.

As the Lynx hovered directly above them, the downdraught from the helicopter's rotors made dropping the rope close to the rib hard, but both pilot and recipients below had done this many times before and contact was quickly made. Dekker and Peterson held the line firm while the others climbed upwards through the downdraught and into the helicopter. Dekker went up, leaving Peterson in the rib alone. Their gear, now tied secure, would be attached to the rope by Peterson, who would then be winched up with it. As the helicopter turned and accelerated upwards and towards the stealth ship, Peterson rode the rope as he got ever closer to the Lynx.

Now down below him, the rib was left to float where the currents took it, no doubt causing confusion for the finder as to the whereabouts of its owner.

The Lynx crew needed instruction, so when Lamberti returned back to the others after talking to the pilot, he let them know what was to happen.

As he shouted above the noise of the helicopter engines, he gave them the news that they had been expecting.

"Seems the deadline has passed. The Russian ship's on the move; they've spotted it now it's moving in such enclosed waters." The others knew not to respond, for there was more coming.

"The ship's to be taken out at any cost, and we are to expect that our Russian friends will know that their only escape is to be blown up with it. Pilot expects to be on top of it in under forty minutes, so best we prepare ourselves."

"So you are useful after all, Lamberti," commented an unforgiving Biddiss while the others simply looked at their gear, making individual decisions on what to start preparing first.

———◆◆◆◆◆———

As he walked the short distance to the headquarters of the Russian secret service at the Lubyanka, Barishnikov sent a message to Falco on the boat, and this was quickly circulated to his soldiers.

'You are being watched. You must now prepare to end days for the Mother Land. Your country will live with you. Do not fail. B'.

As Falco instructed his team on their tasks, each one of the crew took a private minute to gather their thoughts and accept that their time on this world was coming to an end, an end initiated by Tom Selkirk, as they headed towards a sinking Italian city. They knew that their current lead over their rivals was being crushed as their pursuers travelled towards them at two hundred kilometres per hour low above the water.

———◆◆◆◆◆———

Back in London, the admiral received a call from the head of the fleet of the Italian Navy.

He would have a hard time for the next hour as he tried to persuade the fleet admiral not to evacuate the finance ministers, or indeed send out a military welcome to the advancing Russian vessel, but to keep activity constant so they would not know that they were being countered.

The admiral would fail in this task – very soon, three

heavily armed naval vessels and two attack helicopters were powering-up their engines in preparation for imminent contact. The admiral's concern was tangible. If Selkirk didn't get to the vessel first and stop it quickly, he and his team might be destroyed along with it.

When the pilot turned to face Lamberti and lifted his headphones off one ear so he could hear himself speak, the others knew that he had received significant news.

"Sir, please," and as Lamberti leaned forward towards him in an instinctive gesture to hear him better over the engine noise, the pilot told his team the news that would complicate matters much more.

"The Marina Militare, they have launched three fast-intercept vessels and could be in contact with them in around forty minutes. They will likely have helies in the air also," he said, turning back in his seat to the controls.

"Bert, how long until we hit the target?" questioned Selkirk.

"Fifteen, Tom, should we hold back and watch or ..." but before he could finish, the answer came.

"We go in and do this," Selkirk's response was firm and slightly more aggressive than moments earlier.

"Seems someone wants payback on Falco," smiled Anniken as she stared at Selkirk. He clearly heard the comment but chose to ignore it. She went on, as was her provocative manner. "Best none of us pop Falco or we may have Tom to watch out for," and with that, the others went back to their thoughts and their gear, knowing both would be utilised very soon now the command had been given.

In Venice, in the convention centre, the officials, ministers and aides carried on with their important work. They were shaping the continent's economic future, and with it, were influencing the entire globe. They were unaware that a black, former stealth vessel, manned by six Russian special forces soldiers and nuclear powered, was heading towards their position on the water's edge.

The Russian finance minister received a text message on his secure phone. He took his attention away from the speaker and read it.

Then, as the German finance minister was ending his speech to the delegates, the Russian contingent stood in unison, collected their papers and walked quickly out of the auditorium and towards a waiting car whose engine roared to life as the driver saw their approach.

The remaining delegates, while temporarily bewildered by the rudeness of the Russians, carried on with their attentive listening. The German minister sat down and closed his papers, as his job was done. The conference continued as per the agenda.

Isabelle flipped through the channels on the TV in her Venice hotel room, looking for something interesting to take her thoughts away from Selkirk. It didn't work as she hoped. Reaching the Sky News channel, her eye was caught by the breaking news ticker-tape running along the bottom of the screen. It read 'Italian Navy deploys warships to intercept unknown vessel not responding to maritime command'.

She knew – she just knew – that Selkirk was involved somehow. She smiled as she realised that he was still alive, but this soon turned to anxiety. He may still be alive, but he was likely chasing, or on, a fast moving vessel that could be blown out the water at any time.

She turned the TV off and left her room, hoping again to take her mind off the man she could not stop thinking about. Yet again, she was to fail. As soon as she exited the hotel, she stopped and turned back. She returned to her room. Switching on the TV again, she would sit on her bed, eyes fixed to the news channel.

Over in London it was all starting to get frantic.

With the demise of the permanent undersecretary, the admiral now reported back directly to the prime minister's office until such time as a replacement could be appointed as the emergency unfolded, but this would not be for a while.

The secure phone rang and lit up on the admiral's desk. *Like some antiquated James Bond gadget*, he thought to himself as he answered the call. It was the PM's office.

"Admiral, something is happening in the Adriatic, what do you know?" was the voice on the other end. The unknown voice had to be treated with the greatest respect, as only the PM and his closest staff could use the secure line whose receiver was now firmly pressed against the admiral's ear.

"Sir, it's the Russians, they are on the move, being tracked, and now the Marina Militare is planning to blow it out the water," was his opening gambit.

"And we care why?"

"Sir, we have Tom Selkirk and his team en route and imminently in contact. They must be given the chance, sir," and he paused to think, "to resolve this, sir. Can you support this?"

The admiral looked down at the blinking phone.

"How imminent, Admiral?"

"I believe they are less than five minutes from contact, sir," was his now more desperate reply.

Then it was the turn of the unidentified man on the other end of the line to pause and reflect.

"The PM will call the Italians. We will get you fifteen minutes, no more," and with that the line went dead and the red glow from the telephone on the admiral's desk disappeared.

As he wiped his brow, the admiral knew that, yet again, his friend and number-one operator had been put in an extremely difficult position. And, while Selkirk thrived on 'difficult', it was obvious to the admiral that, once more, he could be let down by so-called friendlies whom he risked his own life to protect.

"There, over there, sir," came across the helicopter speaker aimed at Lamberti, but heard by all of Selkirk's team. Hearts would now beast faster and hairs would rise in anticipation as they all knew what the helicopter pilot had spotted.

Selkirk rose to his feet, as did Lamberti, and both men moved through the others and their gear towards the cockpit. In the distance was a fast-moving black boat leaving a long and noticeable wake as its engines thrashed against the water in an angry churn – stealth was no longer a concern.

When Selkirk saw it, he suddenly felt an ache in his heart, a pulling of his stomach and a rush of blood around his body that didn't come often.

"I smell Falco," he said out loud but meant for himself. "I'm coming, and I am ending it this time." Lamberti looked across at his friend but knew no response was requested or merited.

Three further minutes had passed beyond the fifteen the admiral had secured. The Italian naval command would take back control of the pending situation and make decisions based on their own national interest. Selkirk didn't know this, nor would it have influenced his decision to send his team into harm's way if he had.

"Annie, you're last to drop. Keep your eyes wide and your sights filled with Russians as we board," instructed Selkirk.

He knew she would want to be first into contact, but she was the best sniper and most likely to keep them relatively safe as they fast-roped down to the boat. The Russians on board would also know this trick, and they would be in the sniper's crosshairs if they showed themselves too openly or stayed still for too long. They would have to choose their targets and their movements well.

"Bert, tell the pilot I want two sweeps all around. They know we're here so there's no surprise, just keep a safe distance. Let's take a good look at what they have on board before we drop," said Selkirk as he climbed over gear and legs back to the others and his own weapons, which were quickly assembled and strapped on.

By now, the rest of his team was waiting. They were armed and silent. They had done this many times before, but no amount of training could ever reassure them fully against the noise and wind of a live bullet whizzing past an ear, designed to kill you. No amount of training could ever prepare them for meeting their maker without saying goodbye to their friends and family but, again, they waited for the command to drop.

The second sweep now done, the pilot positioned the helicopter directly behind and slightly off-centre from the Russian vessel. There was no obvious on-board static-weapon, but he decided to stay a little off-centre, just in case he had missed something. In doing so, he also facilitated a more rapid escape.

Anniken positioned and secured the rifle to counter the movement of the boat and the helicopter, keeping her focus and her aim at all times on the deck and bridge of the enemy vessel.

"Going in twenty, Annie, keep it tight," said Biddiss as he leaned towards her and pressed a friendly and reassuring hand on her shoulder.

"Yup, don't get killed, Bidd," she replied, "remember, you owe me money from cards, loser," she replied, as was her style. Biddiss expected nothing less, and with a smirk, lifted himself up and threw the rope out of the open side door.

As the downdraft of the helicopter blades swung the rope violently back and forth, they assembled, one behind the other, armed and primed, and waited while the pilot mirrored the speed and direction of the boat. By now the Russians would be preparing a 'welcome party' for them, but, as was the nature of their business, they would go in anyway.

Dekker grabbed the rope and prepared to drop.

Dekker always volunteered to go first in these situations, and Selkirk knew better than to challenge his superstition or his confident arrogance.

"Annie, missing you already," he shouted as he fast-roped down, disappearing from the others' sight for a fraction of a second.

Still no, Deks, I want men, not boys, flashed across her mind as Selkirk exited and Biddiss, likewise, disappeared downwards, all three hanging precariously from a rope, from a moving helicopter, hoping to land on a fast-moving boat, knowing Russian special forces were on board and wanted them dead.

Then, as she scanned the deck for trouble, with the telescopic sights on full magnification, she saw movement, and right after, the glint of metal against sunlight.

Gun! Fuck, gun! she thought and trained her weapon on the movement, just as Lamberti and Peterson dropped out the side of the helicopter.

Kirk saw her adjustment and took out his pistol to give the others cover should it be needed.

Then, as the bullet left Anniken's gun, the boat veered sharp left and threw off her aim.

She didn't see the slug hit Dekker, but Anniken instantly knew something had gone wrong, and she felt responsible. She retaliated with her own trigger finger, and one Russian was dead, his head pulped, open to the elements, against the glass and wall the behind him.

Dekker's grip on the rope weakened and he fell.

Selkirk saw him drop, but even as he did, he returned to the task at hand, just as Dekker splashed into the water. Selkirk held on and waited, vulnerable, a target, waiting for the pilot to get back over the boat, which seemed to take an eternity. The reality was something much faster.

Down they went as fast as they were able. Biddiss let the rope go from ten feet and landed with a thump next to Selkirk. Both men fired randomly at the front of the boat, allowing Lamberti and Peterson some element of cover and a safer landing.

Kirk grabbed the rope, "Annie, you're staying here, we got this, stay focused, we can do this, but we need your eyes in the sky," he said, disappearing out of her sight and soon dropping onto the deck of the Russian vessel.

"Get back to one hundred and give me side view," Anniken demanded of the pilot. The helicopter turned aggressively left and then right, repositioning at one hundred metres, parallel, alongside the boat as her five colleagues began direct contact with the five remaining Russians, one of whom was a former team player and friend.

As the boat sped on towards Venice and a likely confrontation with the Italian Navy, Dekker's body disappeared under the waves, now over a kilometre away from the others.

Anniken glanced over her shoulder, back towards where Dekker had fallen into the water, but she saw nothing. *Can't happen now, Deks*, she thought before turning back towards the ship. She saw movement from the control room. Two targets were moving towards Peterson, isolated on the wrong side of the deck after his descent, and, from where he sat, they would be on him in seconds. He could not see their approach from his position, nor could the others.

She didn't have a shot at either of them, but she had to do something to warn her colleague.

Frantically thinking, she did the only thing she could do. She shot at her colleague.

When the bullet whizzed past, he looked up and over at the helicopter and saw an anxious Anniken giving the danger signal. She had saved his life for sure with the advanced notice, but for how long? He was also a little shocked that his friend had shot at him.

Peterson drew his seven-inch blade from its sheath as he crouched behind a crate, and just as he saw the shadow of the first attacker less than two feet away, getting closer, he thrust it fully into the nearest knee. The blade went straight through the patella and severed the anterior cruciate ligament. Blood exploded in a sickly spray as Peterson wrenched the knife free – the Spetz fell to the deck in traumatic pain. Without being able to see the second Russian, he fired three bullets in rapid succession, guessing where his opponent was.

Two bullets hit the Russian square in the face, with the third missing and disappearing out over the water. The third bullet didn't matter. The first two had done their job: his face seemed to explode backwards – blood, brain and bone flying violently out to sea.

However, as Peterson attempted to rise to his feet and reposition his aim at the first fallen Russian, he felt the thump of a bullet. No amount of armour could prevent it entering and then exiting through his body. The first Russian, while in excruciating pain, had taken aim and fired at close range. As Peterson fell, a second and then third bullet hit him, and Selkirk's team was down one further member. Peterson was dead.

Anniken saw his death unfolding in front of her, but was made powerless to prevent it by turbulence a hundred metres away. She was not, however, helpless – he would be avenged. As the helicopter settled, she fired two fourteen millimetre rounds from her sniper rifle into the chest of the prone, kneecapped Russian. He would feel no more pain from his badly mangled limb, nor from the entry points of two more armour-piercing rounds.

The spray of the sea water had already started to dilute the blood from the three dead men, now running like a small river along the deck, back and forth, as the ship bounced off waves at high speed. There was a lot of blood and some would make its way to the other side of the deck and the remaining members of Selkirk's team.

<hr />

The admiral's fifteen-minute moratorium had elapsed, and he feared the three Italian naval ships would be given clearance to blow up the Russian vessel, and with it, Selkirk's team.

He tried to call the lead ship direct, again using the codes he had been given earlier, but they had changed. He knew it was procedure to encrypt communications and rotate codes during live operations. He knew this because he had introduced the scheme into the Royal Navy three decades earlier, and now his system, adopted by the world's other navies, was to possibly stop him from saving his friend for a second time.

Then, as he pondered his next move, he remembered that he had been connected by proxy to the helicopter pilot that had delivered Selkirk's team to the target.

"Peters, in here now!" he screamed loud enough to be heard in the next room, through the sound-proof leather doors.

He instructed Peters to contact the pilot via the NATO central command and control secure line, which opened up during times of national security. A nuclear-powered Russian stealth ship hell bent on sinking Venice was one such moment of necessity.

As Peters started the process of initiating contact, the admiral rang the PM to try to persuade him to speak with the Italian high command.

The contacts were made almost simultaneously.

"Prime Minister, I need your help," said the admiral, while keeping an eye and an ear on the call his number one was making.

"*Questo e l'alto commando Britannico,*" Peters said in his best halting Italian to the helicopter pilot as the line went live from Whitehall to the Aegean Sea. But before he could scramble more poor Italian to his lips, he heard words that surprised him.

"Yes, you want to speak with your team, yes? I have one still on board, sir."

"Em, yes, please," he replied, still a little confused as to why one team member was not yet engaging the Russians, and marvelling at the efficiency of the NATO communication system.

There was a short pause during which Peters gestured towards the admiral.

"Prime Minister, I have something, please hold, sir," he said, interpreting the gesture correctly.

Peters put the call on speaker.

"Hello, yes, am kind of busy here ..." came over the speaker in a female voice, partly muffled by the noise of helicopter blades.

"Anniken, it's the admiral, I don't have much time, report please," and remembering his audience, he spoke again, "oh, and we have the prime minister on the other line."

"Admiral, I'm fucking busy trying to secure the team against the Russians, from a moving helicopter. I don't have much time," and a short pause followed, "sir."

"Yes, of course, sorry, report please."

"We are two down, but they've lost three as far as I can make out. We have four on board and I am up top riding shotgun," she yelled. She then noticed the pilot looking at her in his rear view mirror. A live operation and she was taking a call from London.

"Annie, we don't have much time. They have sent

warships to end this, so can you do it first?" he questioned.

"Admiral, we're winning, we're fuckin' winning, so you do your bit, cos we are doing ours. Now, I'm fuckin' busy!" she shouted, ending the call.

The admiral looked down at the secure phone to Number Ten.

He started to speak, "Em, sir, I ..." but was instantly interrupted.

"Admiral, I heard all that, she has a tongue doesn't she? I will get you fifteen more, but that's it, final," the PM said over the secure line, ending the call. The admiral's office went quiet. He suddenly felt alone again.

Peters and the admiral stood and looked at each other in the safety and quiet of their office on Whitehall with the fresh realisation that as they did so, live bullets were being exchanged somewhere in the Adriatic on a boat now much closer to Venice and the waiting Italian Navy.

———◆◈◆———

Selkirk knew he was one further soldier down. He hadn't seen Peterson's demise but something deep inside him had been cut. He just knew he had lost yet another friend. But duty called, and while his current predicament was both violent and unsafe, and he would follow his lost friend to hell at any time, he knew he had to carry on regardless and put those thoughts to the back of his mind.

When the three men moved slowly and deliberately forward, one behind the other, they were all well aware that their colleague, Lamberti, was now isolated on the other side of the boat. Still, they had to go forward, irrespective. He knew the risks and could look after himself.

Selkirk led the final assault. Behind him was Kirk, and

Biddiss brought up the rear. As they moved closer to the final contact with the three remaining Spetsnaz soldiers, Anniken watched from her moving platform.

"Get closer, I want to be able to take shots at close range!" she barked above the noise of the helicopter turbines.

"It's too dangerous, lady," came back from the pilot.

"What's fuckin' dangerous, my Italian friend, is not doing what I ask!" and with her penetrating stare fixed on him, the pilot turned back to the controls and the helicopter suddenly veered right and closer to the moving ship.

Biddiss stood up, looking over the other two to get a clearer view of the control room. He did so just as the 'eye in the sky' was repositioning – his brash movements were not yet covered. He had become vulnerable.

As Biddiss focused his eyes and looked into the control room for signs of movement and numbers, the window burst under gunfire, shattering into a million shards of cutting glass. He saw one Russian inside taking aim and promptly flattened himself back to the deck, bullets pinging around him.

Selkirk, Biddiss and Kirk glanced at the helicopter and Anniken. Had she taken out the threat in the wheelhouse? They realised very quickly that she had not. Instead, the bird was still repositioning and she was unable to cover their imminent assault.

Biddiss raised his head and looked over to his right. He saw a smiling Lamberti take aim through the window and drill the Russian. He mouthed, 'you're welcome, Bidd'.

Biddiss returned the gesture, raising one middle finger from his left hand, but he also smiled and nodded to his colleague.

Then, as if the stars had aligned, all four men rushed the control room at once.

A flashbang grenade entered first through the shattered window, followed by a second from Lamberti.

They went in. In towards their fate and the Russians. Selkirk went first. Without Dekker, he always went first.

The Russians knew they were coming. They knew the stun grenades were coming and they were ready for it. Lamberti's shot through the control-room window had injured one of the three remaining Russians in the shoulder, just enough for him to drop his gun. Scrambling backwards, he'd taken out a serrated eight-inch knife instead. He had decided that the end would be up close and personnel.

They waited in the corners, shielding their eyes and ears from the debilitating effects of the stun grenades. They had practiced ship assaults like these many times before. With British assets passing through the Suez Canal daily, pirates had become the real enemy of that region. These foes, however, were no sandal-wearing pirates with AK47 assault rifles.

Selkirk fired through the door as he entered the control room at speed, hitting a rising Russian in the throat. It was dark, very dark, apart from the red and green flashing lights of the consoles. The boat was now unmanned and set on a fixed course at top speed, allowing the 'crew' to focus on the intruders.

Kirk went left as Selkirk had gone right into the room. Biddiss fired his weapon straight in front and between his two colleagues at perceived movement in the far corner. However, as he entered the control room proper, Biddiss was struck in the face with the butt of a rifle as one assailant revealed himself from hiding. Reaching for his knife in the dark and a little disorientated, Biddiss lashed out wildly before coming to his senses and narrowing the target to the shadowy shape in front of him.

Lamberti shouted from the other side of the room, having entered from a different door to the others.

"Bidd, drop, drop now!" and without waiting for his reply, Lamberti released two rapid-fire shots from his handgun straight at his colleague. Selkirk had anticipated the call and kicked a leg out, striking Biddiss on the back of his right knee, forcing his friend to drop, still in a daze from the strike and now falling, freeing up a clear line of sight for Lamberti.

The first bullet struck the Russian firmly through his right shoulder, splintering his clavicle before ending its fury in the wooden cabinet secured to the wall behind him. The second piled into the wall and disappeared.

As the Russian started to fall, Selkirk raised his knife and thrust it viciously into his stomach. Turning the knife back and forth, the serrated blade tore a gruesome wound before he pulled it out and let his foe drop like lead to the floor. He fired a round into the body of the Russian, just to make sure, while all the time looking around the room for his true target, but the wheelhouse was otherwise empty. Selkirk had not seen Falco, who had been down below rigging the boat to blow up, and yet it appeared only one Russian remained. He knew it must be him and he took control, once again, of the chaotic situation.

Selkirk's left arm was covered with the dead Russian's blood, but he didn't notice, nor did he care.

"Kirk, find a way to contact the admiral. Tell him to get the Italians to step down. We have this," he commanded. There was a strange lack of friendship and camaraderie in his voice. Then came the second instruction. "Biddiss, get Anniken to prepare for our evac back onto the heli. Lamberti, you're with me, outside. We're going after Falco, but listen up," and as he looked back at his Scottish commander and close confident, Lamberti saw an evil side of Selkirk that made him shudder, "he is mine. No matter what, he is mine, and you will not engage. Do you understand?"

Lamberti looked at the others. Biddiss nodded. Lamberti turned to Selkirk and nodded his acceptance.

"Oh, and Kirk, when you are done with the admiral, I want you and him," pointing to Biddiss, who was now attending to his minor bleeding wounds, "to stop this fuckin' boat. Do you understand?"

Both men understood and didn't feel the need to confirm their acceptance back to Selkirk – now that the action was over, their commander was incandescent with rage at the loss of his men.

As Lamberti walked out with his handgun poised, he heard the thump of bullets into bodies once again. He knew Selkirk was ready for Falco. He had wasted four more rounds, firing two into each of the felled Russians. As he held the door open waiting for his commander, Lamberti heard, "I hope your mum has dental records, you fucker," and knew that Selkirk had targeted their heads.

Lamberti released the door, walking carefully out onto the deck as it closed slowly, leaving the commander to his personal moment of hate. Selkirk was reloading and ready.

He joined Lamberti outside. They looked over to the helicopter and gestured at Anniken, asking Falco's location. She replied in the negative, dropping the rifle from her face and accepting that most of the battle had been won.

Selkirk returned to the control room.

Lamberti stood guard, and as Kirk put the receiver down on the secure phone, he nodded to Selkirk 'done', and they knew that the Marina Militare would step down. They could disable the boat without fear of fifty-millimetre shells smashing amongst them, one after the other.

Two tasks remained: stop the boat and find and kill Falco. Selkirk, for his part, didn't prioritise the order, but instead picked up the intercom and spoke with purpose into it.

"Falco, I am coming for you. The others are all dead. Get ready," and Selkirk threw the microphone down, leaving no one in any doubt as to what was about to follow. It hit the side of the console and swung on its wire.

Anniken had signalled to Lamberti that the helicopter had around thirty minutes fuel remaining, and they both knew that land was a distance away. They may need one final favour from their Italian counterparts and a warship landing deck. Lamberti gestured for Anniken to leave. With a heavy heart she smiled back at him and then turned to the pilot to give him the instruction.

Then, when the relative silence returned and the helicopter engine noise dwindled into the distance, Selkirk saw him.

Falco climbed the steel ladder up onto the main deck. Lamberti raised his handgun to take aim, but seeing this in his peripheral vision, Selkirk raised a hand high into the air. Lamberti questioned his judgment.

"Thomas, my friend, let's just get this done, end it!" Falco pleaded.

"If you do, then it never ends for me." Selkirk walked past Lamberti and towards Falco, thirty yards in front of him, arms outstretched, exposing his vulnerability – he held no gun. He did, however, make no attempt to hide the long and deadly blade of the knife he carried.

Falco spoke. His accent and tone burned a hole through Selkirk's soul. Selkirk knew he hated the man standing in front of him, but he had forgotten just how much. That time, that betrayal all those years ago on operation in Columbia, where he traded Selkirk for his own safe passage out, leaving his former friend to months of ill treatment and torture before he himself managed to escape. The damage had been done, however … Now, the news that Falco had visited his wife when he was missing in action, presumed dead, after the Bearing Straits incident, had only intensified his vitriol. Yes, he hated this former friend and needed to end the relationship on his terms. It seemed they both needed to.

The control-room door opened and Kirk joined Lamberti on deck, standing just behind Selkirk, who faced the man he had spoken of with poison and venom for as long as they had remembered.

Lamberti turned to Kirk. "Is this thing stopping?" he asked.

"Biddiss is on it," he replied.

"Christ, let's hope it still floats after."

The four men on deck seemed to simply stare. Two waiting for something to happen and two knowing what was about to.

They had hoped that Biddiss would take the easy option and figure out the controls, but the sound of rapid machine-gun fire in the engine room, and the resultant smoke and smell, could never be taken for granted.

Seconds later, everyone repositioned their stances as the ship lost momentum, the wake thrown up in front and the wash returning to hit the side of the vessel a few times, making it more difficult to stand. Biddiss soon joined his colleagues out on the deck.

"Listen up, this is my fight, not yours," Selkirk said.

"Gentlemen, we have never formally met, my friends. A pleasure. Thomas has your best interest at heart. You should back off," Falco said, tauntingly.

"Look, you fucker, you don't get to tell me what I should and should not do," but as Kirk puffed out his chest and adrenalin filled his veins, Selkirk took command.

Selkirk always took command.

"Boys, stand down," he said. "We have won. He knows it and you know it."

"Listen to him, 'boys'. Like you listened to him in Hereford and then in Ireland, Columbia and all the others, and as you do on every operation we watch," challenged Falco. "Like you listened to him throughout your soldiering careers, putting your lives on the edge just because he asks. Think of all the friends he's killed," he continued.

"Tom, do this fucker! If you don't, I'm next in line," and Kirk stepped back, but staying near enough to interject should he feel the need to. Selkirk's small team held their handguns.

Biddiss looked directly at Kirk, then started towards Falco. Kirk became a little anxious, edging forward. Biddiss had attended to the dead Peterson after he had blown the ship's engines, and for a moment, he wanted to give his former friend some overdue satisfaction.

He walked determinedly towards Falco but made a point of dropping his handgun to the deck before walking past Selkirk.

The team watched, temporarily surprised at Biddiss' temerity.

"Bidd?" questioned Selkirk.

He ignored the polite challenge from his commander and walked towards Falco, who knew that he was being provoked, but not attacked, and stood his ground. Falco had trained with Biddiss many times and had served the British

Commonwealth together all over Africa. He knew that the grim-faced and imposing soldier walking towards him did so with purpose but understood the end game was not his to have.

"Nice to see you again," Falco said as Biddiss entered his personal space. Without reply, Biddiss struck a clenched fist into Falco's solar plexus in a lightning-quick move. He fell to his knees, gasping for air.

For a second, Biddiss towered over his foe, fists clenched. "Tom, your game now," he said as he looked over to Peterson lying still and dead in a pool of blood. Then, looking back towards the wake of the ship's passage and to his missing friend, Dekker, then the others.

"So, Tom, what took you so long to find me, old friend?" Falco wheezed as he stood, regaining his composure.

Selkirk edged forward. He was so close to his enemy now, he could smell the sweat and odour coming from him. He stared and watched Falco, analysing his body language but chose not to reply. Two helicopters were making their way in from the east.

"Cat got your tongue, Tom?"

Falco continued his verbal attack, adrenaline now pumping around his body. With more heavily armed foes against him, he suspected that it may not do so for much longer, so he chose not to bother with niceties.

"It was me who comforted your wife when you vanished in the Arctic, and Hereford pronounced you MIA. And the same me who held her close when they put your name on the wall in the Officers' Mess. And now you don't say thanks, Tom? Instead, you come here to kill me, don't you?"

"You turned, Falco. You left Her Service and that makes you my enemy. It's ending here, now," Selkirk had to shout

– the helicopters were hovering above the boat. One was an attack helicopter from the Italian Navy. The other was a news helicopter from Canale Italia, trying for the scoop after realising something was amiss when three heavily armed naval ships left harbour at pace, unscheduled.

"Seems we are to be on television, Tom," said Falco, but as quick as they had arrived, the news helicopter was shepherded away by the military chopper. There was no doubt that the navy crew had reported the fast-moving Russian ship was no longer mobile, and that the British-led team dropped on board were in full control.

"You need not worry about celebrity status, Falco. If I was you, I would worry about what the fish will do to your dead body as it sinks," replied Selkirk.

"Tom, oh Tom, I have always expected this moment. Indeed, I have prayed for it. I knew that Alexandra and my boys would not see me again when I left Sevastopol naval yard weeks back, but I also knew that their new home in Russia would take care of them."

Falco stopped and looked away at the retreating news helicopter, then spoke as he watched it disappear, "Can you say the same, my old friend, of your family back in the United Kingdom? I hear a soldier's pension is barely enough to live on, never mind support a family."

Kirk interrupted. "Tom, don't bother with this crap, just put one in his head," and raised his handgun as if to show Falco how easy it would be to end his life.

"No!" shouted Biddiss. "He does it his way and it ends here, and now."

Kirk looked over at Selkirk, a little bemused that Biddiss had bellowed out the refusal.

"What he said," affirmed Selkirk as he smiled and turned

back to Falco.

The two men raised their knives, both serrated, and both with deadly, razor-sharp blades.

"Ladies first," said Falco as he gestured for Selkirk to advance, both hands outstretched in front, teasing, hungry for Selkirk's blood.

Selkirk obliged.

He threw a diversionary right hand towards Falco's face as his knife hand swung forward, then horizontal in front of him. Falco expected this open gambit and stepped marginally back and left before pushing Selkirk's knife hand down towards the deck, then moving fast and forward inside his guard. His own knife plunged downwards towards Selkirk's chest.

The two men swung and counter blocked two more times before first blood.

Falco's superior speed had him counter-parry an outreached block, and the tip of the blade cut through Selkirk's right pectoral, drawing pain and shock as he moved away and back from further danger. On his retreat, Falco's left hand swung round and his fist struck Selkirk across the side of the head, temporarily disorientating him.

Both men stopped, backed off and waited, circling each other like caged beasts. It was honourable to allow the first one cut to make the next move, whether to withdraw or to continue. Falco knew what decision Selkirk would make, but it was customary to wait in these circumstances. Every special forces soldier the world over would honour this unwritten code in these circumstances – one facing certain death while the other wondered if it was coming.

The others looked on; they were ready and willing to step in for their good friend and colleague at a moment's call.

They were prepared to die for the man now lifting his gaze from his bleeding chest and back toward his foe.

Selkirk smiled at Falco, unnerving him a little.

"You only get one strike and now I am batting," he said, and he rushed forward towards Falco, driving a boot into his forward-defending knee. The kneecap would probably be shattered, but Falco had other issues to worry about.

Selkirk grabbed Falco's knife arm, and it was turned one hundred and eighty degrees, exposing his wrist to the sunlight. Selkirk's knife then came down swiftly, like an avenging angel, and was thrust fully through to the other side of his forearm, fatally severing the ulnar artery and limiting the supply of oxygenated blood to the rest of Falco's body.

Falco screamed loudly, but Selkirk was not yet finished. Releasing his free hand from Falco's weapon arm, he jabbed two stiff fingers hard into his throat, crushing the larynx. Falco felt blood bubble into his mouth.

He half fell to the deck, but couldn't, not fully, as Selkirk held his left wrist again after the near-fatal blow to his windpipe. In excruciating pain and struggling to make sense of his injuries – Selkirk's attack was inhumanly fast – Falco turned and looked up at him, unable to speak.

Selkirk showed no pity. His face was thunder and his eyes were redder than that of Falco's life blood now pouring out of his arm and all over the deck he half lay on. Selkirk had the blood of three Russians on him now, but he could not care less.

He held Falco's right arm aloft at ninety degrees as the rest of his body flopped pathetically on the deck. Then, in one final, yet unnecessary, gesture of superiority, Selkirk turned the arm against the natural bend and snapped it over his leg. Falco neither groaned nor screamed. He accepted the pain, which filled his entire body. He was in so much agony from the earlier injuries that this final act of barbarism did not register.

Selkirk released his arm and it fell to join the rest of the dying Falco beneath his feet.

He knelt and spoke to his rapidly dying foe, just inches from his face to make sure he heard.

"Last rat standing, Falco," he said.

Falco tried to speak but by now his lungs were filling with blood, and numbness from his wounds was spreading through his whole body. He was shutting down.

Then, as Selkirk moved to finish what he had started, Falco's head exploded with the impact of a high-calibre sniper-rifle bullet. The Lynx helicopter had been ordered to engage, and on board it, one soldier had completed the action. On the deck of the disabled Russian ship, Selkirk and the others were splattered with blood and brains from the lifeless and unidentifiable Falco.

Selkirk looked over his shoulder at the distant helicopter. He stared at it, trying to establish why his resolution, his right, had been taken, and as anger started to build up inside him, Biddiss took over.

He lifted Selkirk away from the bloodied corpse and signalled to Kirk to deal with the mangled body. "Tom, done, over now," said Biddiss. Selkirk's anger faded as quickly as it had risen up. He nodded and sat down a distance away from the dead Falco.

The fight had ended. It had actually done so a short while earlier, but for Selkirk, it was now finally over. The fight may have taken minutes to complete, but the revenge had taken years to fulfil.

Biddiss then nodded to Kirk, who patted Lamberti on the

back. Both men would clean up.

"The fish won't go hungry today," said Biddiss, and when he heard the splash of the body in the water as it was thrown overboard, Selkirk looked up and cracked a sinister smile. He was happy. For the first time in many years, Selkirk felt a little joy in his heart. He looked at Biddiss, who in turn saw a smiling Selkirk and could not help himself as he smiled back.

Selkirk was free; Biddiss knew his friend was truly back, the fallen angel had risen.

They walked away to sit together and reflect and wait for the launch to arrive from the Italian naval vessel, the *Bettica*, now sitting on the water a short distance away.

———◆◆◆◆———

Anniken's helicopter had been forced to return to the *Bettica*. She would wait for her colleagues there. She would not have to wait long.

The four men would return on the motor launch, back towards where Anniken waited, while their place on board would be swapped with Italian sailors left to clean up the mess.

Selkirk stared into the water. His close friend Biddiss watched him and the waves as they crashed against the small rib. The cold water could not bring Selkirk back from his thoughts as it struck his face.

Lamberti and Kirk sat either side of the body bag of their friend Peterson, while the Italian sailor simply fulfilled orders and transported the special forces soldiers from one ship back to his own vessel.

Anniken saw them pull up alongside. She had been waiting on the deck of the naval vessel, a stand-out character, a weird addition to the crew. None had found the courage to talk to her.

"Annie," he said, acknowledging her as he stepped over the ropes and on board. Then Selkirk looked over to the three Italian sailors watching him, rifles loaded and safeties off.

Suspicion remained, despite being told that this small group of multinational soldiers was actually fighting the same battle that they were.

"Tom, you ok?" she replied.

"Yup, I am now," and with a smirk that lightened her heart, Selkirk walked off towards central control to brief the operations room and hopefully the admiral, if he was allowed to raise London on the comms.

In London, the admiral was waiting for the call, and back in Venice, a solitary female figure stood alone and worried on the balcony of her hotel room overlooking St Mark's Square.

Chapter 13

Rendezvous

The outboard ride from the *Bettica* to the new Italian frigate was a quiet and reflective journey.

It travelled the two kilometres at an annoyingly slow pace for the team who had no choice but to sit and watch the waves hit the side and occasionally cover them with sea spray.

No one wanted to interrupt Selkirk, and he was unwilling to let go of his thoughts.

Anniken's return to the rest of the team would have to wait until after her debriefing and release from voluntary custody of the Italian Navy officials, one of whom sported a black eye from when he had got a little too close to her.

As the rib made its way through the waves to the waiting frigate, Selkirk, Biddiss, Kirk and Lamberti simply sat and immersed themselves in their thoughts of what had happened and of missing friends.

It would be at least seventy-two hours before Neeman's body would be found along with that of De Boer, both dead in a final clasp. They would be brought back to the surface, along with the bomb, which would be safely destroyed. A testament to the work of Anniken much earlier.

Peterson's body would be en route to the UK and he would receive a dignified burial in a private cemetery in Hereford dedicated to those special soldiers who can never be named, or their surviving families identified. The team would visit his last resting place soon enough and say their final goodbyes.

But for now, they were the guests of the Italian Navy a short way away from Venice and the awaiting British Consulate representation. The admiral had flown over from London to be by their side, but it would a busy seventy-two hours for them all. The admiral would have a series of tricky conversations with senior representatives of the Italian military and this would, likewise, keep him busy and away from Selkirk.

They had all lost friends on the operation and each needed to think about them in their own manner and their own time.

Anniken sat in solitary confinement within the Officers' Mess of the *Bettica*, comfortable and well looked after, but alone. She felt even more alone when she thought of Harrison and that fateful day in Gibraltar.

Kirk had operated with De Boer all over the world and could no longer do so, while Biddiss had trained Neeman. Neeman was his protégé, although Neeman would never admit to it. The rivalry was both healthy and precarious, as both men had often taken huge risks on operation to try to outdo the other. And now the teacher had outlasted the student, and that made Biddiss rethink his own mortality somewhat.

Then there was Selkirk. He thought of them all. While Dekker had a special place in his heart and his past, he thought of all of his fallen friends on this operation and the many before it. Selkirk had big shoulders, and they needed to be for the all the survivor's guilt he felt, watching others fall. It weighed great and heavy on his large frame. Even the death of Falco did not ease the burden of his past.

It would be a further twenty-four hours before they would be released from 'debriefing', or 'questioning', as they saw it. Released one at a time so that secrets of their actions and operations could be gleaned for future Italian-forces training rather than to ensure conformity of their stories. They were survivors where other soldiers were not. They were the best of the greatest forces on the planet, and they had secrets, most of which would stay with them all the way to their graves. But for now, they took the long walk out of the naval yard, one at a time, towards an agreed rendezvous point.

Isabelle received a text message.

She'd been waiting on the edge of her seat for some sort of contact for a while now, so when she received a text message from an unregistered number, she got very excited.

'Want to join us?'

The message was both direct and unidentified.

Biddiss had been asked to get the remaining team together, but was unaware that his number was not registered in Isabelle's mobile.

She texted back. 'Yes, where, when?', and as if to make sure the message really was intended for her, she signed it off, 'Thanks, Isabelle'.

She waited a while for a reply. Twenty minutes passed. Perhaps the sender had realised that it was not a message intended for her. Perhaps she had come across too enthusiastic. Isabelle waited.

Then her mobile buzzed again and vibrated on the bedside table. Text message received.

'Café Florian, Piazza San Marco, in the square @2' it read. Seconds later her phone vibrated yet again. Her heart was still beating fast from the first message when she opened the second.

This time it read 'Come alone' followed by a series of

smiling emoticon symbols. Someone was pulling her leg. She didn't care. She was meeting them again. She hoped she was meeting 'him' again. She would soon know. She would be first to get to the rendezvous point. Isabelle left the hotel early and walked towards St Mark's Square ahead of the scheduled meeting time.

She had tried to occupy herself for a while by walking back and forth across the Rialto Bridge, occasionally stopping to watch the gondolas bob up and down on the waters of the Grand Canal. This, however, was not helping. She wanted to go to the rendezvous point. She wanted to see if Selkirk would appear, indeed, if he was still alive.

She had been sitting and holding her coffee – which had turned cold – for a while, before she had her first contact.

"Ciao bella signora posso unirmi a voi," was whispered in her ear. She had not seen Lamberti walk up behind her, but he had seen her. He had watched the square for several minutes before approaching her table. It was habit, but it was also secure practice. He pulled up a chair and gestured to the waiter to come over.

Kirk walked over seconds later, while Isabelle was still taking in Lamberti's arrival. He, too, had been watching the square and the passing tourists, always looking out for potential trouble. When he threw the newspaper down onto the table, Isabelle jumped in her seat. Lamberti had noticed Kirk from a distance and wasn't surprised when the paper landed with a slap.

"Front page, seems someone's pissed," he said, and Lamberti picked up the paper and looked it over.

Ignoring the main headline, he scanned the other stories. The article near the bottom of the page read 'Head of Russian Secret Service Killed in Skiing Accident'.

Lamberti stopped reading; he had seen enough, "Accident, my arse, as you British would say. Kharkov's fingerprints are all over it," he said with a huge smile on his face. "Do you think we would get a visa to attend Barishnikov's funeral?" No one answered. It wasn't necessary to do so.

Lamberti turned to the waiter and ordered fresh coffees all round. It could be a long wait.

Anniken was next to arrive.

She walked the square from the east, deliberately, with the bright sunshine behind her. She would get to within three metres of the table before she was noticed, but, again, not by Isabelle.

When she laid a hand on Isabelle's shoulder, while also moving the chair next to her, she smiled, and Isabelle relaxed from her initial shock. As Anniken sat down, Isabelle started to think this was a game they played.

"Christ, why don't you just say hello, like normal friends?" she said.

"Where's the fun in that, my young girlfriend?" and Anniken moved forward across the table and grabbed the closest arms of her two male team members sitting with her. They were still pondering over the arrival of Tom Selkirk.

"Bert, get me something strong, and I don't mean coffee," she said and he turned to the waiter and ordered a round of drinks in Italian. Anniken would not care what.

A few moments later the waiter arrived and slammed empty spirit glasses down on the table. Then, one by one, they were courteously filled with a yellow liquid and then promptly emptied, firstly by Anniken, as she downed the drink in one quick motion.

"Christ that must be good. I'm having what she's having," Biddiss announced his return back into the fold. He pulled up a chair from a nearby table and sat down with the others.

"Hey, Bidd, what took you?" Anniken said as she stood and gave him a warm hug.

Lamberti took over, ordering another full round of the yellow liqueur, Limoncello, for them all.

"If anyone we know sees us drinking this girls' crap, I will not be happy," said Anniken with a smile on her face. The irony was not missed on the others that the female operative had made the comment.

"It's his drink of choice," replied Biddiss with a widening smile and a stare at Lamberti.

They were growing in number. The team was almost together again. The members that had survived the mission were gathering, but none would ever forget those fallen friends. The relief, however, was there for all to see. They had some down-time after an intense few weeks. They just needed Selkirk.

The sun was beginning to set behind the tower of San Marco Campanile, and for the occupants of the table, the thoughts went to whether Selkirk was going to join them at all. She had resisted asking if he had survived but had established that he had, as they spoke of him in the present tense.

Isabelle had been sitting with her soldier friends for over two hours now and had started to feel the effects of the sun on her neck and the alcohol that she had been plied with. She was happy though. For a few short moments she felt safe, she felt welcome and she forgot the loss of her father. It was a good two hours for the team member that had been with the operation from the start, those many weeks away in Bouvet Island.

Then, a short while, and yet another round of spirits later, chosen by Kirk this time, the square burst into life. The screaming motorbike conducted blood-curdling spins, generating burning smoke circles at the opposite end from where they sat, shattering the late afternoon peace.

Isabelle was understandably surprised, but so were Kirk and Lamberti. Anniken, perhaps feeling safe and comfortable with the company, or perhaps familiar with smoke and daggers, remained in her seat but looked over her shoulder behind her. Biddiss had missed the action, being inside the café, trying to persuade the owner not to expel them, but instead to provide them more drinks.

When he came outside, he stood frozen by whom he saw. His heart started to beat much faster, not a good thing considering the volume of alcohol he had consumed, but he was able to stand still and smile. He acknowledged Selkirk, who was less than a yard behind the table, listening and waiting to be discovered.

The bike seemed to disappear, as if to avoid the oncoming and slightly out of breathe Carabinieri police officers, guns in hand, who were clearly not happy that Venice had been invaded by some disrespectful youth on a motorbike.

Lamberti turned back to the table once the bike had sped off. He saw Biddiss standing at the café entrance, silently mouthing to somebody. Slowly, Lamberti turned, following Biddiss' conversation, and saw him.

Selkirk gestured to Lamberti to be quiet.

Kirk was next. He turned back from watching the motorcycle and the police, picked up his drink and saw Selkirk two yards away.

"Christ, boss, don't do that," he said, wrecking the game. But he stood and grabbed his arm, drawing him closer, then he placed a second hand on his shoulder.

"Come sit, we're drinking ..." but before Kirk could finish, he was interrupted by a sarcastic and firm-sounding Selkirk, his Scottish accent a welcome oddity in the Italian square.

"Yes, I know, Limoncello, really boys? I taught you that badly?" he said, sitting down amongst them, forcing a chair between Anniken and Isabelle.

The shy but overjoyed look on Isabelle's face as she turned away, then down to the ground, was not missed by Anniken, who smiled to herself. It was hard not to admire Tom Selkirk, but the look she interpreted was one of much stronger feelings.

"Bert, get me a proper drink. Don't mess up," said Selkirk with a smile.

Lamberti stood and walked into the café to find his Scottish friend a Bowmore malt whiskey. He knew Selkirk and would not return to the table until he found one.

He had to go to three different restaurants before he returned with his commander's drink.

They all sat together and, for a fleeting moment, there was reflective silence. Then, Lamberti spoke with calm and sincerity in his voice, despite the amount of spirit he had consumed.

"Too many this time, Tom. Four in one gig. Bad day at the office," the Italian said. Biddiss nodded.

"Worst ever," said Kirk and the table went quiet.

Isabelle knew it was not appropriate to speak, so she held back, just turning her glass nervously, waiting for someone to break the ice.

Then, someone did.

"You fuckers need to learn how to count!"

Everyone stood, shocked and dismayed, but alert, preparing for pending violence, chairs scattering.

Even Selkirk stood and reached for his gun inside his jacket.

It was getting dark and the sun was just dipping behind

the buildings, but as Selkirk found the origin of the voice, he quickly relaxed.

They all saw the silhouetted figure. Selkirk was holstering his gun while the others were shielding their eyes against the twilight's glaring edges. Selkirk knew the shape of the man leaning on the alcove wall. He had seen it a million times through night vision goggles on numerous operations.

"Deks, Christ. You just won't die," said his close friend Tom Selkirk, looking for a spare chair for their newest addition to the rendezvous.

"Miss me, Annie?" he said.

She was speechless. She had seen him shot and fall to his death, passing under the waves.

"Deks, you're dead," and while she knew the words were senseless, she said them anyway.

"Thought you would prefer ghosts, Annie," he said in a friendly voice. "Anyway, I promised Tom a few weeks back that I would never abandon him," he said smiling at his old friend.

Anniken moved her chair and walked over to Dekker. When she hugged her colleague, she spoke into his ear so that only he could hear, "You still won't ever sleep with me, American," and left him to be greeted by the others.

"Why didn't you die, Deks? We've already toasted you, mate? We now need to have another drink to welcome you back," said Biddiss, grinning from ear to ear, thinking he had actually said something quite funny.

"Two words, my English brother, Navy SEAL," and Dekker pulled an empty table over to the others and demanded a round of drinks.

Lamberti had spoken with the owners. They had agreed to keep the group happy with drinks now that they knew about the evolving incident of the last few days, viewed live all over Italy and the world, on television. The same incident that had been resolved by the rough, unshaven, swearing group of special forces soldiers drinking whiskey and Limoncello a few yards away outside their family café, on St Mark's Square.

They would spend a while longer on the edge of the square, in the café, drinking alcohol and talking war stories. Selkirk would be happy. He would be the happiest they had ever seen him, and when his arm went around Isabelle as he talked about his escape from the Barents Sea many years prior, it would not just be Anniken that would take notice.

It was now dark. The lights lit up the square and the tourists mingled amongst the tables and restaurants, looking for the best place to have their evening meal.

Selkirk's phone rang.

He took it out from his pocket, taking back his arm from around Isabelle, and looked at the caller.

"Leave it, Tom, do it tomorrow, mate," said Kirk.

"The admiral," he replied, raising the phone so the others could view the display.

"Tom, are you ok?" the admiral asked earnestly.

"Yes, sir, we're all good," came the reply.

"OK, I'm pleased. Listen. Enjoy tonight – tomorrow you are travelling …" and after a short pause, which everyone around the table heard, the admiral continued. "Tomorrow you're off to South Sudan. There's been an incident."

Anniken snarled, "OK, I'll go, but does Deks have to come?" she joked.

They all smiled and carried on with their drinks.